The Story, The legend, That is PANTS

By Derek Pimpkin

Published in 2013 by FeedARead.com Publishing –
Arts Council funded

A CIP catalogue record for this title is available from the British Library.

Bit at the Beginning

As the half full concert hall slowly melted away into a totally empty concert hall and as the cheers, whoops and applause of genuine appreciation seemed to fade into nothing more than seemingly surreal memories, we knew it was time to call it a day.

During the height of our pomp and bombast, top of the range custard in a variety of exotic flavours was a luxury we had both became accustomed to. All supplied in clean dishes on well dressed tables, in ample dressing rooms packed with other niceties such as cheese (strong and mild) neatly cut into bite sized squares along side nibbles, crisps and yoghurt (again in a variety of luxurious and exotic flavours). All this was designed to keep us happy, comfortable and pampered. Alcohol was also in plentiful supply …. And lots of it, at least one eight pack of expensive lager and a half litre of donkey sauce. Those were the days when we called the shots and were the kings of our trade. A trade that was 'rock music' and rock music played at its raw best, no safety net or triple buckle belt here mind, just pure unadulterated rock 'Pants rock' – not even a bass guitar!

However; the cruel fickle hand of fate had called time on our world; well that and rubbish contracts that we failed to read, digest or take any real control over – but a world which was ending none the less.

So as I sat in our altogether more modest dressing room, towel draped round my neck to soak up the sweat after my exertions on the drum kit, I removed my glasses, re-adjusted the gaffer tape and carefully wiped the lenses. Graeme picked fussily at the remaining ready salted crisps and whelks, then cracked open a can of 'Ace' lager. Had it come to this? Ace Lager? - Ready salted crisps? Not even a prawn cocktail; and no custard of any description, as for yoghurt! Those days were well gone.

To be fair it was a good gig and the hardy souls who had turned out were well into us. The hard core 'Pants Army' still believed we were the K9's conkers and loved every minute. Graeme had played a blinder and even got the bloke in the front row to dance uncontrollably, although the fact that he was in a wheelchair probably explained why he didn't stay upright very long and was in fact an appalling dancer. I do regret laughing now as I simply thought he was very drunk. Graeme was unperturbed by this faux par and carried on laughing, well at least he wasn't a midget we agreed, as we had had enough troubles with them curious little fellas most of our career. But despite all this we were both tired of it all. The hits, such as they were, meant nothing to us and I no longer got a buzz from thrashing the crap out of a drum kit or even jaffa cake boxes. Graeme felt the same and this gig, good as it was, was far from sold out and I doubted either of us could take the indignity of being knocked back with our first choice in cheese and custard for the dressing room rider. Dignity! That was one thing we still had a level of control over. WE decided our fate, not Dudley, Howard, Graeme's Gran or any other person who got themselves involved with 'Pants'.

During the time we were together we had experienced many good times, many strange times and wrote some damn good songs. We had memories; memories of times that most people can only dream of having. We had performed at some of the most prestigious venues and events on the planet; we had met other rock stars, supermodels and ate 'Curried Turtle nibblets'. Who else could lay claim to that, well apart from other rich and famous bands. We had done it though and no one could take that away from us. We had our dignity and our pride and the knowledge that we had made our mark in the world of rock music; and I'm not talking about scribbling 'Pants are tight as f**k' on the dressing room wall at the cavern club either. We had lived the dream; even if it was only for a short time and as I gathered the remainder of the ace lager, crisps and supermarket pop into a shopping bag to take home with me, I knew my pride and dignity was one thing know one had control over except me. How it all started? Well that's a story in itself and it goes a little something like this.................................

PANTS
PART 1: A BAND IS BORN

I was born on my birthday in a little known Geordie town called Jarrow, a few miles up the river Tyne from Cosmopolitan Newcastle with all its finery and glamour and a stones throw from a former Whelk farming village known as South Shields - where I now lived. Two years later a certain Graeme Bucket was also born. Graeme was the son of an immigrant cheese sniffer from Romania who had married his childhood sweetheart, a young Spanish woman called Chiquita Clam. Although he was originally destined to be a whelk picker; family circumstances changed all that when his favourite pond dried up and the Bucket's were forced to move to a well to do area just left of a small town called Hebburn, which happened to be my birth town: Jarrow. Now Jarrow was famous for many things but alas, most are forgotten, except however; the world famous march for chips. Back in 1978 over 14 people famously marched from the shopping centre in Jarrow to the top of a large street that ran through the centre of the town in protest of their favourite chip shop turning into a small carpet cleaning shop, (later to be World of Trousers). There was of course another very famous march many years earlier, but very few people can remember what that was all about so it clearly couldn't have been too important. The march unfortunately made little difference as the chip shop no longer exists and is now 'World of Trousers'. This is a young Graeme Bucket's first happy memory, buying his first Pants. However his true destiny was to be a fine guitarist in a famous rock band, so buying guitars were to be more recent happy memories, but that of course, was all to come. .

Meanwhile in sunny South Shields, as I grew painfully slowly out of nappies and into short trousers, I felt that I was destined to be a drummer. There was just something in me that cried, 'HIT THINGS YOU FOOL!' By the age of fourteen I was merrily hitting all manner of objects including sofa's, dart boards and hamster cages, desperately searching for that perfect drum kit sound which neither me nor my parents could afford. During this period I was honing my drum technique, constantly thwacking away all night, much to the annoyance of both my mother and neighbours. In order to deaden the sound of my incessant rim shots, my mother or 'mam' *(as we called them in the north)* insisted that I should at least do something constructive, so she gave me pants to bang on. This worked; as not only was I a lot quieter, but the banging also give a nice crease and helped thwack out the stains which detergents often struggled to handle. Here was an eerie parallel trouser based world; Two Tyneside towns; two young inhabitants who were both destined to be thrown together with pants based backgrounds. Added to this was the fact that I was a drummer and the young Graeme was a guitarist. Fate had played its hand and the potential for a band forming was irresistible.

Many years later I was to meet Graeme, quite by chance outside Jarrow's (or *Jarra's* as we called it), premier cheese shop called 'Jarra Cheese' and from this tenuous link-.a nick name was born, and he became affectionately known by his fans as; Graeme *"cheese"* Bucket, and like so many nicknames forced upon young fragile minds up and down this fair land, cheese stuck and that was that.

My nickname was 'Specky Twat', but I didn't think that was particularly cool, so it was decided to keep mine simple; Deka, (although my dad being the stubborn traditionalist that he was, kept with 'Specky

Twat'). Graeme too had family issues regarding his nickname and his Gran refused to refer to him as anything other than 'that lanky streak of piss', although thankfully these issues were not to affect our bludgeoning career in later years

The seeds had been sewn, a new legendary band was soon to be born and world domination would surely follow. We weren't far wrong either, but that's for another chapter. The White Stripes had apparently cited us as an influence, but not actually named the band - or either of us personally by name in any publicly published interview, but they have; apparently.

In the next exciting chapter; how Pants began to rise and rise.

PART DEUX

PANTS: Rumblings Within.

It was a sad day for the still young Graeme 'cheese' Bucket. His favourite pants shop had closed for refurbishment and to make matters worse, 'Jarra Cheese' Jarrow's premier cheese shop, had closed and became, 'Simply Bun', Jarrow's premier bun shop. Times were changing and Graeme felt ill at ease with fast pace of Jarra life and had no interest whatsoever in buns. Also to make matters worse, the pants shop refurbishment had apparently taken longer than first anticipated, due to a flannel shortage.

Meanwhile; I was still in South Shields thwacking away by myself with no partner to share my vision. Trouser shops were plentiful in the relatively cosmopolitan South Shields and cheese was delivered every Wednesday morning by the Cheese van. However; it wasn't just our love of cheese and a strange trouser based history, but music - and the love of music that brought us two rapscallions together, as mentioned earlier, the ill fated 'Jarra Cheese' had now became

‘Simply Bun’ and a disconsolate Graeme packed his satchel, put on his favourite jerkin and headed towards South Shields in a desperate attempt to fill the void left by lack a of cheese and pants shops.

It was THIS day that we first met properly. Once more I was banished to the shed to thwack on my pants as Graeme happened down the street where I lived looking for kicks in the big town. It was here; at number two Muffin Avenue, that we realised the common threads that bound us together were in fact about to create a musical force, so strong that stars such as Bono, Paul McCartney, Noel Gallagher, David Bowie and Janette krankie all expressed a desire to play with Pants.

I remember the conversation well.

‘Alreet‘, said Graeme.

‘Aye’ I replied.

‘I remember you from outside that cheese shop!’.

‘Aye! It’s called simply bun now… its shit!’ was his plain, mournful response, ‘How long have you been playin' them pants?’ He enquired a little more animatedly.

‘A canny While, I can't afford a proper drum kit and me mam sez they’re too loud, so I've got to play on these pants..... I reckon they sound alright though’.

I remember Graeme agreeing with much enthusiasm, and we ended up talking for hours. The day simply vanished as we plotted and planned, reminisced about ‘World of Trousers’ and the exciting refurbishment possibilities. But more importantly a band was born, a band which was to change our lives forever. That band was to be called ‘PANTS’. It seemed all too obvious. Our trouser based history together had led us to the obvious conclusion that this should be the name of the band. We knew that after a short while ‘Pants’ would stick and would be no stranger than other iconic names such as ‘The Beatles’, The Rolling Stones’, ‘Oasis’, ‘Martha & the Muffins’, Dumpy’s Rusty Nuts and ‘Splodgenessabounds’.

Music was the life blood of every young person round our way and we both had huge record collections which we had built up over the years. Some bought, some stolen, some presents and some that we had simply acquired! One thing that was obvious from the start was that we both shared similar tastes in not only music, but in crisp flavours, cheese varieties, yoghurt and trousers.

In my town trouser shops were the favourite hang out for small groups of kids looking for something to fill the boring days and many a friendship had developed in these small Mecca's of teenage worship. Surly kids as young as eleven or twelve would mix with older teens, all jostling for that prime spot amongst the 'burgundy Stay Press' or 'Birmingham Bags' and I was no different. We would idly flick through the hangers, checking out the labels and cleaning instructions, occasionally we could even try some on, even if we couldn't afford to buy any. Those were great days and a world away from the big superstores and their trouser's section which lacked real soul- nor did they stock rare labels such as 'Duxbury's Crease Crunchers' which only the older, cooler kids wore; Especially the rare Purple ones.

We decided to organise a rehearsal, it was an informal affair, nothing more than sharing ideas and having a bit of a jam. Graeme knew of a rehearsal complex in Jarra called 'Jarrow rehearsal complex - Jarrow's premier rehearsal complex'. It was situated next to the midget farm only a small walk from the

Metro station. I had packed my pants and sticks and made my way there with a heady mixture of nerves and excitement. Graeme was already there and set up, all his guitars were unpacked and a massive amplifier was buzzing, raring to let pants rip. His girlfriend at the time was also there, which surprised me somewhat, but I didn't mind as I was too excited. She was an odd looking but strangely alluring young thing with glasses and blonde hair tied up in a bun. Although quite why she had a piece of bakery product in her hair was a mystery to me, there was little doubt that the vagaries of female fashion had long since eluded me. There was also an oniony type aroma surrounding her which I presumed was cheap perfume. Her name was 'Constance Stains' and her input later was to create some interesting developments.

The first jam was little more than re-hashing old faves but given a unique twist. It was a while before we began to write our own songs and these covers were a good learning curve. Amongst the songs we played were "Public Pants" by *Jonny Lydon.* "Put Your Pants on Me" by *Abba.* "In The Name of Pants" by *U2* and an attempt at Rapping with *Public Enemy's,* "It Takes a Nation of Millions to Hold Our Pants…Up".

We had tremendous fun and we both thought that there was definitely a vibe about the sound we were creating. We had stumbled upon something effortlessly unique and the hours flew by. The owner of the rehearsal complex was also impressed and sensed that this was the beginning of something that could be quite special. His name was "Howard Trowl", and he tentatively suggested we could use his help in getting gigs and even a studio session, as long as we kept on practicing. I remember him saying at the end of the day,

'Boys.....If you want to make it in this business, Pants need to tighten up.' He also suggested we recruit a Bass player to help bind Pants together. We were on our first rung to fame and fortune, *but the bass player idea nearly killed us off before we had even started.*

PART DREI: *(That's German for three)*

A Small Man with Four Strings Enters Pants

Pants were buzzing after our first few rehearsals. We were having a laugh, playing good music and generally enjoying life. It felt right, it felt good and it seemed only a matter of time before "Pants" would be riding high. We had also started writing our own songs, and as much as we enjoyed playing cover songs, such as versions of Adam Ants "Pants Music" and Abba's "Pancing Queen", there was nothing like creating your own song from nothing. I remember Graeme saying to me,

'There's nothing like creating your own song from nothing' and of course he was right. Our first attempts at world domination included a fast paced, bluesy 3 minute little number called 'Squeaky Walk' and a harder edged guitar onslaught called 'Stretch em' Sideways' (*These two songs were to be our first double*

A - sided single). We also penned, 'Inner Thigh Blues' and 'My Exploding Zip' during this period. All these songs were raw, naive, bursting with energy and very loud. Also; I had been playing on a proper drum kit instead of old pants, the sound difference was remarkable. I had bought my drum kit from "Jarra Drums - Jarrow's Premier Drum Shop". Ironically there wasn't a drum shop in relatively cosmopolitan Shields and I had saved up the money by selling second hand socks in Sunderland. People of Tyneside rarely ventured as far south as Sunderland, a strange place on the river Wear, but you were fine as long as you kept to the roads. They had just been connected to the national grid a year earlier and I needed to cash in on their confusion by selling socks. I always made the most money there, especially outside the dole office.

Graeme had already collected a number of guitars over the years, some as presents, some home made, others he nicked from the local charity shop 'Jarra Charity Concern - Jarrow's Premier Charity Shop'. This shop used to direct most of its profit helping blind window cleaners, (for some reason they always had loads of guitars for sale). So that was that. We were up and running.

Earlier, Howard Trowl who had *sort of become our unofficial manager* suggested that we recruit a bassist to help 'fill Pant out'. We decided to hold auditions at the rehearsal complex and a few likely candidates had been lined up. However, unfortunately; only one turned up. His name was Benny Crumpton. Benny was a strange looking lad with thick curly black hair all down his back – not much on his head mind, just down his back. He strutted into the rehearsal complex dripping with attitude, and what looked and smelt like lard. This we learned was because he had just been to the 'chippy' for his dinner (*which had momentarily been kept open after the Jarrow march for chips)* and after guzzling the last dregs from a can of cheap lager he let go an unusually loud belch. I remember that he had his bass low slung, just above his knees and a cocky chin jutting style of playing. Mind you, I have to admit, he was good, very good; he even used more than one string. However; there was something odd about him and as I stared from behind my drum kit it suddenly dawned on me, not only was he covered in chip lard and only about four foot tall....he wearing nothing but a pair of green Y - fronts. Graeme hadn't noticed, but I did. At the end of a very productive audition we said our goodbyes and promised to let him know.

'He's good him', Said Graeme.

'Aye, he is', I had replied.

'Did you not notice that he was only wearing underpants though?'

I remember that Graeme seemed surprised at my attitude. He was dead against judging people by the underwear they wore and the fact that Benny was wearing green Y fronts was of little consequence.

If there was one thing I learned about Graeme over the years was that was he was a deeply principled honest person. His strict up bringing and mixed heritage had instilled an open mindedness towards humankind generally and he had a discipline in him that was so rare, that he was totally focused on what he wanted to achieve in life and very little would sway him away from his goals. I remember being with him once whilst shopping for gravy and he wouldn't waver on his choice of 'super thick onion scented gravy' despite having to search through no less than thirty seven shops to find it. Mind it did help when we narrowed the search down to food shops. He was also single minded in his song writing and constantly strived to improve his technique by practicing day and night - and sometimes he would use his guitar whilst practicing.

Needless to say I didn't want to argue as things were going so well. Also to be fair, he was right, I was being totally judgemental. I probably wouldn't have been as bothered if they were black or yellow underpants. So that night we agreed to let Benny become the bassist in the band. This however was to be our first mistake, and the Midget farm owner wasn't happy either.

PART QUATTRO

SMALL MEN, ***BIG PANTS***

A band bonding night was organised the following Friday. The plan was to go into Newcastle for a big piss up round the many rock bars in the city centre then go clubbing, demolish a sweaty kebab and thoroughly disgrace ourselves. I was really looking forward to it, and it was the night we would really get to know our new bass player - Benny Crumpton. I remember feeling really excited as I got ready to hit the big city, so decided to brush ALL my teeth that evening and not just the front two. I put on my favourite lucky orange underpants which had been freshly washed by my mam after an unfortunate accident a week earlier with a girl, who shall remain nameless. She really *was* nameless, I found her wondering around near the bins outside my house and well…………anyway, moving on.

I looked in the mirror, my glasses had been straightened and the gaffer tape holding the lenses in had been replaced with clear cellotape. My shirt had all matching buttons and I had made a special effort to polish my trouser zip. 'Looking sharp' I thought.

We had arranged to meet en route. I would get the Metro at Shields, Benny would embark at Bede near the midget farm and Graeme would meet us at Jarra metro, 'Jarrow's Premier Metro Station'. I counted the money in my wallet over and over to make sure I had enough to see me through the night and after what seemed an age of flicking through notes and various denominations of copper and silver I was happy, £4.83 pence! Excellent! We were going to start at 'Trillians Rock Bar', move to a few other bars round town and finish with last orders at 'Twatters'. However; things went from bad to worse and we hadn't even reached Newcastle yet. As the Metro pulled in at Bede station I noticed that there seemed to be a bit of a kafuffle on the platform. As I looked closer I noticed about six or seven inspectors wrestling with what at first, looked like a midget! It suddenly dawned on me as I noticed the bright green underpants that it was in fact our new bass player, Benny Crumpton! Not a midget. Although Benny was only about four feet tall - apparently he wasn't a midget, he was just small; well that's what he claimed anyhow. He made up for his lack of height by standing on his toes constantly jutting his chin out all the time. The doors opened and I heard him shouting at the inspectors as he threw wild punches at anyone in a peaked cap.

'f**k off yu bag of bastads.........the machine wasn't werkin!!!'

A packed Metro train looked on in disbelief as he scrapped and wrestled, squeezing out of the inspectors grip with his lardy body. At this point he saw me,

'Aaalreet mate...I'll meet yus up there, am in a bit bother... get me pint in.....lager'. And with that, he disappeared in a wave of black uniforms. The Metro doors closed and the train pulled away. When Graeme got on at the next stop, Jarra, I told him the full story.

'Oh well, just us two then!' He said philosophically.

We got to Trillians at about seven and Graeme got the round in as I didn't have enough money. The place was 'buzzing', loads of lasses, great music and healthy toilets. Our mission was simple. Get pissed and plot the future of Pants. This time next year we wanted the DJ in this bar to be playing Pants music all night, well, at least a couple of songs anyway, and every juke box in every cool bar round the country to be full of Pants. It was our dream, it was our destiny, it was fate and nothing could stop us; except possibly a power cut.

‘Oi Oi!’ was the cry from the other end of the bar. It was Benny, he had made it! He looked a bit bruised....and stretched but he was here. Once more he was wearing nothing but green underpants as he stood in front of us.

‘What happened?’ I enquired as Graeme got the round in.

‘What yu on aboot?’ he replied in the broadest Geordie accent imaginable.

‘The inspectors and all that?’ I said, a little confused at Benny’s seemingly erratic and sudden memory loss. Then; to my amazement he proceeded to deny everything and claimed I was making it up!!! Graeme handed him a pint and asked how he was. ‘What’s it got te dee with you like?’ came an overly confrontational reply. Graeme was understandably shocked at this and became momentarily speechless. Benny then drank his pint in one go, threw the glass on the floor, walked up to the DJ, called him a ‘bell end’, punched a lass full in the face, spat on a nearby table and started on the bouncers. We frantically tried to break the fight up and work out what the hell was going on! The next thing we new, a strange van pulled up outside the bar. It wasn’t a police van either. It was brown and very old fashioned looking. A tired looking old man got out the van and came over wearing overalls and rubber gloves. "BENNYYYYYYY", he screamed. At this point Benny Crumpton, our clearly mental bassist, stopped in his tracks. The bouncers released him and time seemed to stand still for a second...only it didn't.

'Sorry Mr Chissler', was Benny's strangely meek response.

'Get in that van.... NOW', ordered the old man, and with that, Benny sloped off and climbed into the back of the van. The back doors had a small logo painted on in gold lettering which read JMF. It then suddenly dawned on us, 'Jarrow Midget Farm!' That bastard was a midget after all! He had us duped. Apparently Benny had been given a weeks release to buy some onions and not came back; he had nicked a bass and came to our audition. This also explained how he was such a good bassist. It's a little known fact that midgets can play bass guitar. It's in their DNA apparently. It's very similar to how you often get blind people with exceptional hearing or the even less known fact that badgers can make custard. His medication also made him paranoid and volatile, which of course explained his behaviour, drinking a pint in one? Not good.

It had been an eventful night and Graeme hadn't even bought my kebab yet! So we decided to finish the night off in style by getting extra large donner Kebabs with extra chilli's and marmalade sauce. Both Graeme and I decided there and then that we weren't going to bother with a bassist and Howard Trowl, our unofficial manager will have to like it or lump it. There was no room in Pants for midget bass players, or any other four string jockeys for that matter. So it was settled and with that another chapter closed in the rise and rise of Pants.

PART V
PANTS OPENING SLOT

Benny Crumpton was now long gone. A faded memory consigned to the back passages of time and space, where midgets dwell and still continue to puzzle top scientists with their strange and unique bass playing abilities to this day. Although rumours that he had been seen playing for the JMF Brass band out side various Jarra Fruit based emporiums continue to circulate. As for me, and my rock & roll buddy, Graeme "cheese" Bucket - things were looking up. The songs we were writing had a freshness that only a young and exciting band could write. My drums were no longer an old pair of trousers my mam forced me to play, but a real drum kit with real cymbals instead of Jaffa cake boxes. Graeme had purchased a new and altogether more powerful amplifier, which he had bought from 'Six String Jensen's - Jarrow's Premier Guitar and Altogether More Powerful Amplifier Emporium', situated not far from 'Jarra Cake' and about half a mile from the midget farm, where Benny dwelled.

During a particularly fruitful and creative session at the rehearsal complex we tightened up 'Pants' to new levels. Songs such as 'Patchy Flannels', 'Slap my Slacks' and 'Windy Corduroys' were all written this day and a very excited Howard Trowl, *our unofficial manager*, announced that he believed we were ready for our first gig.

'Boys! I reckon you're ready for your first gig,' he proudly announced. We agreed. I personally couldn't wait to put Pants on stage and Graeme got so excited by the prospect I think he pissed himself, although I might have made that bit up. Pissing himself that is. Not the excited bit. He *was* actually *very* excited indeed.

Newcastle had a fervent and exciting live music scene at the time, before all the venues and bars were criminally turned into cinemas, car parks, wine bars and potato shops. We weren't ready for Trillians or Twatters yet. But there were plenty of smaller bars catering for live music with a healthy student/rock clientele. We tried our luck with them all. The first bar we tried was a skuzzy little place called The Dog and Turnip, ran by a small man called Arnold Parsnip. He appeared from behind the bar looking like he hated the world, wearing a mouldy old Glastonbury '83' T – shirt which seemed to be held together with dried sweat and crisps. His disheveled look and slightly balding face didn't really bother Graeme or me. We just wanted our first gig.

'So; you want me to put Pants on here! - On a Friday or a Saturday night'?

'Yes'! We both replied in unison.

'What sort of stuff do you do'?

'Ermm, rock with a melodic edge and unique twist with a post modernist collage of guitar based acquiesce of drums, overdrive and sonic indulgences of pure ethereal sound scapes', was Graeme's reply. I was impressed with his response to an often-tricky question that anyone who's ever been in a band hates being asked; Very impressed. He had been practicing for his first NME interview and thought it sounded cool.

'Aye… its sort of rocky….with a rock edge….its canny rocky really', was my slightly less impressive reply.

Arnold stared at Graeme in a distrusting manner that made me feel uneasy. Although he may have actually been looking at me, we couldn't tell, as Arnold was clearly boss eyed. Had we blown it?

‘Have you got a demo’? He asked. Shit! We hadn't thought of that. Basically he wouldn't give us a gig unless he could here us first *or* if we had already played a few gigs and built up a following! There was a compromise however. If ’Pants’ could get a support slot with another band, that would be our way in. Yes!

A local band called Outrageous Jelly had been on the scene for about a year now and had built a small but loyal following compromising of mainly their student mates and local window cleaners. We got the tip off that they were booked to play Turnips and were looking for an opening band. We got their contact number from Arnold and gave them a ring. It was on!! They happily agreed to let ‘Pants’ open for them. I had to bring my own sticks, snare drum and cymbals, *no Jaffa cake boxes*. Graeme was to bring his own bits and pieces that he needed. Everything else was provided. No problem.

We were booked on our first gig in less than three weeks time and on a prime Saturday slot.

During the weeks leading up to the gig we practiced like mad, it was literally non-stop never ending Pants, until at last the night of the gig was upon us. We arrived at Turnips nice and prompt. The rude egotistical vulgarities of the rock and roll lifestyle hadn't seeped into Pants yet and we were keen to get things right. I had checked my gear four or five times to make sure I had everything. Graeme boiled his strings, as well as his T – shirt and I wore my best socks and polished my glasses. 'Outrageous Jelly' were already there and set up; their singer introduced himself and the rest of the band to us. They were a four-piece rock band based in 'Squidley', situated just outside Newcastle city centre. They were canny lads with good hair and clean trousers. I remember the drummer's name, as he was utter shite. His name was 'Smedley Shite'. I think. To be fair he was very friendly and didn't mind lending me his drumsticks as I had forgot mine. We were due to go on at about 8.45 and play no longer than half an hour. That suited us as we only had about half an hours worth of material. So myself, Graeme, Graeme's girlfriend 'Constance Stains' and Howard Trowl hit the bar. Howard got the round in, which was handy as I had had forgotten my wallet.

'I'd like to propose as toast,' announced Howard.

'Here's to the beginnings of a world of Pants'! And with that we all finished our lagers in one, we then got another and another followed by Jack Daniels chasers and more lager followed by lots more - I think. I remember Constance in particular had got very, very drunk. We were in the corner near the toilets as Graeme was throwing up and we were due to go on in about 10 minutes! Whilst comparing nose hair she started to act very strange.

'Me and Graeme aren't that close you know'. She drunkenly whispered.

What's she on about? I remember thinking

'We don't *do it* very often'. She continued in a very conspiratorial manner.

I was wondering where Howard was as this was getting uncomfortable. He was on the bandit. The bandit was the nickname given by regulars to a funny looking bloke with a moustache and sombrero who often drank in Turnips.

'He's always upstairs strumming his one string banjo'. She continued to whine.

We were due on stage now so thankfully Constance removed her hands from my trousers where she had accidental left them and I made my way to the floor area in the corner of the bar which pretended to be a stage. Graeme was thankfully recovered and re-appeared from the toilets. Show time!

Unfortunately the proceeding thirty minutes or so are nothing but an embarrassing blur as we were very drunk and basically fucked up every song we played. Nerves and excessive alcohol intake had gotten the better of us and even our best and newest songs 'Squeaky Walk' and 'Stretch em' Sideways' were a shambolic mess. During this forgettable dogs dinner of a set I fell off the drum stool twice and Graeme threw up again. Constance, our one and only real *rent a fan* had fallen asleep and Howard was still on the Bandit. Pants were a right mess. However; what had started as a major disappointment, we ended up being grateful for, because as luck would have it, there wasn't actually anyone there to witness it. I had forgotten to tell anyone, put posters up or advertise it in any way, neither had Graeme because he thought I was sorting it, but I thought Howard was sorting it. Added to this was the fact that 'Outrageous Jelly' were in fact utter rubbish and had absolutely no following of any kind, made it little wonder that 'Turnips' was pretty much empty that night. To be fair we should have guessed by the early clues. Firstly, there was only one bar maid working that night. Secondly, the gig coincided with the annual Window Cleaners day trip to Ipswich and not only that, we noticed that Outrageous Jelly's posters had been vandalized with comments like *shite* and *utter shite* and *total shite* and *shite with shite on*. Not a very popular band it seemed.

We had learned our lesson. Never again were we to get that drunk before a gig. Or play with *shite* bands with no fans. Also I was very wary of Graeme's girlfriend Constance Stains. The last thing we needed was a *Yoko Ono* situation before we'd even got off the ground. But this was all character building and was to help make us stronger for the rigors of the music industry, which we were destined to be a part of. The short-lived Benny Crumpton era and the gig that shall always be referred to as the *Turnip incident* were soon to become distant memories.

PART VI
PANTS GO LARGE

Over the next six or seven months 'Pants' gigged non-stop and the 'Turnip' incident was now well and truly behind us. We managed to blag support slots all round Newcastle with local well to do bands such as, 'Walter Windthrift and the West End Wellies', a weird combo consisting mainly of Tuba players - but very rocky where we went down a storm. 'Windy Corduroys' seemed a particular favourite that night. Pants also supported 'The Badger Sniffers' who played a very eclectic mix of old school punk, and skiffle. Again we rocked and I remember Graeme was on fire that night. He lit up a cigarette and accidentally set his hair on fire. He had clearly used too much hairspray and the lighter caught his nostril hair, spread up past his earwax and ignited his freshly bleached hair. The crowd loved it as they thought it was part of the show. Howard *wanted* it to be, but Graeme pointedly reminded him that he only had enough hair for about two gigs. We also played a gig at 'The Worthy Wellington' with a singer called, 'Muffty Ringworm'. She was a singer - songwriter type with no band as such, who played a lot of ballads with soul-searching lyrics. It was a strange mix of vocals and trombone. To be honest, we blew her off stage.

After all these gigs 'Pants' were getting tighter. Not only that, but we noticed there was a few familiar faces coming to see us regularly. Could Pants be getting a small following? It seemed so. 'Outrageous jelly' had unsurprisingly split up and it looked like we had filled the void for the window cleaners. Also 'bus conductors' were starting to appear at our gigs. These were exciting times for 'Pants' and me and Graeme were riding on the crest of a wave, admittedly a small wave, the type you get in medium sized puddles on a windy day, but none the less; a wave.

Now all these support slots were fine but we needed to break out on our own. We needed our own gig desperately. Howard Trowl, our unofficial manager agreed, but he thought we best play safe at first and play locally around South Shields.

'Boys…I think you best play safe at first and play locally around South Shields!' he exclaimed. Now there wasn't much of a live scene in Shields or Jarra as it was mainly wine bars with karaoke and *Monkey Mud Wrestling* nights. However, there *was* a bar called the Turtles Head which had live band nights. Luckily for us there were a number of dates available and we could have any Saturday over the next month. We picked one and we were off. This was going to be the big one; our first headlining gig.

The night of the gig arrived and Howard picked me up with my drums in his beaten up old 70's ambulance converted into a tour van. This van/ambulance didn't have a reverse gear so he always had to be careful where he parked it. Nor did it have proper brakes, Howard tended to use the handbrake and gears to stop and slow down. The indicators weren't working and the back nearside tire was flat. The windscreen wipers were dodgy and merely smeared the rain and the heating didn't work. Also the wing mirrors were cracked and the exhaust had fallen off, so it was a massive understatement to say we were all mightily relieved when it passed its M.O.T otherwise transport was going to be a major problem for getting our gear to gigs. Graeme however; had just passed his cycling proficiency test and had decided to cycle to the gig.

Previously his mother wouldn't let him ride his Raleigh chipper anywhere until he had passed the test and after the third attempt he had eventually managed it. He had bought his bike at 'Betty's Jarra Bike and Biscuit Outlet - Jarrow's Premier Bike and Biscuit Outlet', two years earlier and couldn't wait to ride it. Howard and I agreed to take his gear for him and meet him there.

Everything was set up and ready. All we needed was the support of our mates and local musos. As time ticked by we watched anxiously as the bar slowly began to fill and by 9 O-Clock it was pretty much full to capacity. Nearly 25 people had come out to see Pants that night, proving that our hard work was beginning to pay off. Show Time……..

Even though I had to adapt some of my drumming because I had forgotten my Hi – Hat cymbals we managed to open our set with a rip-roaring rendition of 'Stretch em Sideways' and continued to play our hearts out to an appreciative audience. Some of the window cleaners were in and I spotted a couple of bus conductors tapping their feet, not quite in time with the music, but still tapping none the less. Even Howard Trowl was watching and enjoying us, swinging his beret with gay abandon. We rattled through 'My

Exploding Zip' and 'Slap my Slacks' with such confidence it was without doubt the best we had ever played them. We had also written some new songs by now which we played for the first time. 'Dirty Crease' and 'Inner thigh Blues' were two such songs as well as an anthemic number called, 'Pockets of Love – *can you feel it*'. Constance Stains, Graeme's girlfriend who had arrived late due to not being able to get a bus, (staff shortage apparently), loved it, although I noticed she was watching me and not Graeme. I decided not to worry about it as I was enjoying myself too much.

Now also enjoying the gig was a certain young man called Dudley Longbottom. Unbeknown to us, Dudley was an A & R man whom had accidentally stumbled into the Turtles Head after getting lost. He worked for a small independent record company called Strangely Brown Records and was supposed to have originally travelled up to see a band from Sunderland called, 'The Odd Smells', however; there had been rioting that night on Wearside as their only cheese pasty shop, 'Sunderland Pasties - Sunderland's Only Pasty Shop' was closing due to a shortage of onions. The locals hadn't taken the news well and decided to take matters into their own hands, so riot police had cordoned off the whole surrounding area. On his way back home Dudley had driven into South Shields by mistake and ended up in Turtles. Our good fortune as it turned out because he was impressed; Very impressed. He introduced himself to us at the end of the gig.

'Boys… I'm impressed; Very impressed!' He dramatically exclaimed. Dudley needed a demo to take back with him, have a good listen and see what his boss thought. We were frantic! We didn't have anything, as we still hadn't been in a studio to record any of our songs. He told us not to worry and get something to him as quick as possible. He passed on his contact number and details and asked us to keep in touch. This could be it!!! Bloody hell! We thought. 'Pants' were on fire and on the precipice of potential fame and fortune. Graeme pissed himself with excitement…*I think.* I nearly fainted, *but Constance caught me* and Howard got four quadruple Jack and cokes in to celebrate our first breakthrough; Next stop? The studio!

PART VII

BIG NOISES FROM SMALL PANTS

Neither of us had slept well that night. For me, it was the prospect of going into the studio soon to record a demo and the reaction of Dudley Longbottom from 'Strangely Brown' Records. The whole buzz we got from the nights gig at 'The Turtles Head' was still too much and my head was swimming. For Graeme it was a dodgy chip butty which had given him the right royal shits all night and he was never off the toilet. Added to that, his girlfriend Constance Stains had drank too much again and threw up all over his 'E.T *The Extra-Terrestrial*' duvet cover. Despite this, he was still in a good mood the next day. He had been to 'Brilliant Blankets - Jarrow's Premier Blanket, Duvet and Pillow Case Outlet' and bought himself a new Duvet cover, but this time he had opted for the more stylish 'Battle Star Galactica – Cylon Attack' design.

We met up at the rehearsal complex at about 7 with Howard to discuss our studio options. As it happened we had made a bit of money through all the gigs we had been doing and this could help pay for the studio session. Howard pulled out a small bulging potato bag, emptied the contents onto his desk and gave a loud "TA DAAA!" A load of coins and notes splayed across his desk like a bank robbers haul. Graeme and I looked in amazement. We had no idea we had actually made any money and were well chuffed. Howard had been keeping it as a surprise for us for a Christmas shopping trip to 'Trouser World' or to help pay for any gear we might desperately need, but thought now is as good as any time to give it to us.

'Boys… Now is as good a time as ever to give it to you' he said. Howard started to count the money and after about twenty minutes he eventually finished.

'How much have we got'? Graeme excitedly asked.

'Thirteen Pounds 43 pence' announced Howard. 'Minus expenses, like petrol, windscreen wash and stain remover'.

Fair enough, we thought. In the end we actually owed Howard Trowl enterprises, (as he now called himself), four pounds and 71 pence.

‘Boys…you owe me four pounds 71 pence…. Sorry… Tell you what; just call it four pounds‘.

He was a good bloke Howard. But it didn’t help our studio situation. We needed at least a hundred quid for a day’s session in ‘Ronnie Tubbert’s Recording Studio and Custard Distribution Centre - Jarrow’s Premier Recording Studio and Custard Distribution Centre’. This was situated about two hundred yards from the midget farm and left of Fish village. I had already sold all my second hand socks in Sunderland the previous week and spent the money on new socks, a box of Jaffa cakes and gaffer tape for my glasses. Graeme had just blown his cash on his “Battle Star Galactica – Cylon Attack” duvet set. Bollocks.

Howard then announced that ‘Howard Trowl Enterprises’ would stump up the cash in advance on any future moneys accrued by ‘Pants’ *including the 71 pence*, but the four pounds would be added on to the debt at an interest rate of 48% per calendar day.

We were saved. Graeme and I hugged Howard with genuine gratitude and instantly rang Ronnie Tubbert to book a session in his studio. We were booked for the following Saturday, 10 am till 8pm for a fee of one hundred pounds and 71 pence. That included free custard.

We decided to try getting three songs down and after much debate; we chose to record 'Stretch em' Sideways', 'Squeaky Walk' and 'My Exploding Zip'. Although it was a close run thing and it took us ages to decide which songs would impress Dudley Longbottom the most. Graeme was keen on putting 'Windy Corduroys' down and I wanted 'Pockets of Love...*Can you feel it'*, but we couldn't do them all. We chose the three that we believed gave Pants the most impact.

That week we rehearsed like mad getting 'Pants' tighter and tighter, until we new we could confidently record our songs on Saturday. We were as ready we could ever be and couldn't wait to let rip in the studio.

On the Saturday morning Ronnie greeted us at the studio entrance. He was a friendly man who bore an uncanny resemblance to a space hopper, (The popular bouncy rubber toy from the 70's that you sat on) - but with legs. He showed us round his studio. It was fantastic, like something from Star Trek, but in musical equipment and sound recording form instead of made up computerized space ship stuff. Also, there was no captain Kirk.

Marshall, Vox, Fender and Crumpet amps were dotted all around the live room, (Crumpet amps went bust due to marketing problems, but now make some sort of bakery product apparently). The recording desk looked like something out of Star Trek as well, except there was no lieutenant Ahuru. Top of the range monitors were everywhere, a grand piano, a not so grand piano, various percussion instruments and a top of the range Drum kit complete with cymbals. *This was handy, as I had forgotten to bring mine.* The walls were adorned with framed photographs of famous, Iconic bands like U2, The Rolling Stones, Metallica, The Beatles, The Sex Pistols, REM, Abba, The New Seekers and Ronnie Tubbert & the Trumpet Troubadours. Apparently Ronnie used to be in a band but had to pack in after a serious accident caused him to put on loads of weight. He was on his bike and crashed into a hot dog van. The record company didn't want fat singers, (*unlike today's more enlightened times)* and dropped him. Shameful.

Along side prints of famous custard brands there were also pictures of singers and solo artists like Hendrix, Madonna, Elvis, Stevie Wonder, Kate Bush, Engleburt Hummperdick and Josh Sausage. Josh

Sausage was a local lad who had had a one off number one hit back in 1972 called 'Bulging Love'. He had become a bit of a local hero apparently, although know one actually remembered him, except of course Ronnie. This is where Josh Sausage recorded the single with a certain young Ronnie Tubbert at the mixing desk, not long after becoming a bit of a fatty and getting dropped from the record company for breech of contract - *'clause 84b. Stay slim at all times and don't get Lardy'.* He had this photocopied and framed for some reason. I asked him if any of the other famous bands had recorded here. Apparently they hadn't, although Stevie Wonder had used the toilet once after getting lost from the rest of his band whilst on tour in Belgium. It was a bit embarrassing by all accounts as he had run out of toilet roll. Hence, Stevie Wonder's little known nickname of 'shitty arse Stevie' or as his band called him, 'Chocolate arse'. For obvious reasons the record company hid this from the media, but we now knew the truth.

As well as all this, there was a whole gallery of other photographs of various musicians ranging from famous Welsh saxophonists to Bongo thumpers and spoon fiddlers. I was in heaven. Graeme was so excited he shit himself. Although that may have been the chip buttie he bought again from the previous night.

Pants were tuned, focused and tighter than Benny Crumptons pubic curls. We managed to record all three songs as planned and Pants were no longer studio virgins, but well soiled studio sex machines. The session could not have been more perfect, we thought we should keep the outtakes including the one where we secretly recorded Graeme having a chip induced shit and using it as samples of a drum roll and cymbal crashes. It worked! We also had time to do a skiffle version of 'Slap My Slacks' just to release the tension. Ronnie Tubbert loved us and truly believed that Pants would be riding high before to long. He turned round to Howard and said.

'Howard… I believe your Pants will be riding high before to long'. To be fair, he did a great job in mixing us. He managed to squeeze a lot out of Pants that day and I'd never worked so hard. Graeme played the best he'd ever done with some rip roaring guitar work, despite the smell of chip shit. I bashed those drums like my life depended on it, although technically it did; Ronnie said he'd 'Fuckin' kill me' if I broke his drums. Thankfully I didn't. We finished recording and mixing at ten o - clock exactly and our first Demo was complete. We packed our gear away, (well Graeme did), grabbed our free custard and left. The songs in order were:

'Squeaky Walk'

'Stretch em' Sideways'

'My Exploding Zip'.

Next was to copy it, bag it and send it off to Dudley, as well as few other record companies, just to see if anybody else wanted to have a sniff of Pants. It would have been foolish to only try one record company Howard advised. So with that, we were on our next epic adventure in the rise of PANTS.

PART VIII

A whiff of something big in Pants…

Once more it was a series of restless nights for both Graeme and me. We had made numerous copies of our demo and sent them off to all the movers and shakers in the music industry. Dudley from 'Strangely Brown Records' had his copy, as did a few others including Barney Butterhole from 'Moist Records', Charlie Farns Barnsworth at the NME, and Matilda Wetgrip at 'EMI records'. We also sent a copy to Eric Sponge from 'Ferret Entertainment Industries'. On top of this we gave a load away to our family and friends. Plus, we were selling copies at the Jarra Bus Depot, (Jarrow's premier Bus Depot) as well as all the local window cleaners from whom we had a keen following.

However, nearly a month had passed and we still hadn't heard anything back from anyone, although we did receive a polite rejection letter from Graeme's Gran. It simply read, 'What's this shit'?

We decided to send them out again but this time we put a contact number on the sleeve and the difference was immediate. I remember Matilda at EMI was particularly interested in getting into 'Pants'; however our instinct was that Dudley Longbottom was the man. He had phoned Howard and told him he was literally 'blown away' by what was coming from 'Pants', as was his Boss 'Shadwell Brown'. They wanted to travel up to see us live as soon as possible. It helped that we had had a few nibbles from other interested parties including EMI; someone called Ronald Rhubarb from 'Soggy Cushion Entertainments' and an interesting offer from 'The Hot Beef Dip and Boiled Onion Exchange'. The Hot Beef Dip and Boiled Onion exchange was situated in Gateshead not far from the 'Tramp Wash Centre'. Its owner was a chap called 'Bernard Dripping' and he wanted to set up a record company with 'Pants' as his first signing. The label would be simply called 'Boiled Onion Records' and he was to be the MD. But the biggest surprise was that head of A&R was to be Constance Stains! Constance worked for Bernard and this is where Graeme had first met her whilst buying a new effects pedal for his guitar from Bernard, * who also happened to be a friend of Howard Trowl. It also just so happened, that Bernard used to be in the *music Bizz* as a guitarist back in the sixties and was always keen on getting back into music somehow. Constance had given him a copy of our demo and he apparently loved it. Although; we doubted his sincerity because he showed no interest until he found out that other record companies were also interested. Also, he was a fat lardy arsed onion-smelling twat.

Constance had been plotting all along to get more involved as soon as she realized that big things were happening in Pants and she saw the band as a ticket into the big time instead of boiling onions every day. However, Graeme was visibly growing tired of Constance now. She was always interfering in band affairs and insisted on playing Jaffa Cake boxes on our demo, (We edited her out of the final mix, but she didn't notice). He was also sick of her constantly ruining his Battle Star Galactica Duvet cover, not to mention her oniony smell. She had once asked to be backing vocals but she couldn't sing and took the huff when we said no. However, she could actually play saxophone a bit and was desperate to play in the band, but we didn't want or need sax . Even Howard had insisted this was to be a sax free band.

'Boys... This is a sax free Band' he warned after he once caught Constance polishing the bell end with Graeme. It was a difficult time for Graeme as she was his girlfriend and he didn't want to upset her. But Pants were the most important thing in our lives and Constance Stains was fast becoming both a hindrance and an irritation.

She wasn't stupid though and had sensed that Graeme was going off her and this was why I think she tried it on with me. I remember when I first saw her she stood out from the crowd. She was on stilts. Despite this I did think she was quite sexy and without her glasses, she was beautiful. I wondered if she had any friends of equal or possibly better measurements, but alas no. That's what she told me anyway, so I was a bit uncomfortable when she suddenly started giving me attention, giving the odd wink, smiling at me seductively behind Graeme's back and flashing her fanny in the carpet shop. Graeme was my best mate and the band meant everything to us. There was no way I was going to blow this for a fumble with Constance, despite her flirty intentions and freshly combed nose hair.

Later that week we had a short band meeting in 'The Socks & Kegs' pub, which was a two-minute walk from the rehearsal complex. We always went there for a pint after a practice session to unwind and discuss songs or gigs. It was also a midget free bar, which was handy because we didn't want to bump into Benny Crumpton. A lot of bars in Jarrow still served midgets but there was always trouble at the end of the night due to excessive chin jutting and some landlords and landlady's had had enough, including the manageress of 'The Socks & Kegs', Hilary Sock. She had put a sign up outside the door, which simply read "CAN ALL MIDGETS JUST FUCK OFF". She was an uncompromising woman with a well-maintained moustache, but served a canny pint.

During the meeting we decided that there was no way we were going to sign a contract with a none existent record company with boiled onion connections, despite Howard suspiciously trying to convince us that it would be a good career move and Graeme definitely wanted to finish with Constance. They weren't even having *hide the sausage* (as Graeme called it) anymore, which is why he filled in the lonely nights by strumming on his one string banjo and writing new songs.

Despite all the personal turmoil in our lives, (Graeme with Constance) and me running out of Cheese flavour crisps, we were very excited with all the attention we were receiving from record companies. We had a gig booked at Twatters the following Friday and Howard had phoned Dudley to let him know. He promised to be there, as did Charlie Farns Barnsworth from the NME. Things were certainly moving at a fast pace because this time next week we could have our first national review and a record deal. Bloody hell!!!! Graeme was so excited he shit himself again and I bought myself some new gaffer tape for my glasses, (a stylish new purple colour).

It was to be an exciting week and the gig was to be our most important ever. It coincided with a local bus conductor strike and it was also apparently a national window cleaner holiday, this meant a huge section of our fan base would be free that night. This was to be an exciting turning point in our career and it was it also pancake Tuesday the following week. Good times ahead. ?

**See Graeme's bit for full account and pedal info.*

GRAEME'S BIT:

I often get asked about the equipment we used back in those early days and how we got the sounds on that first demo tape. As already mentioned, my amp was a powerful sounding valve affair purchased from 'Six String Jensen's' situated in the district of Jarrow. My guitars for that session were a beautiful pair of custom hand-built, solid chipboard Flying Y's. They were made by local guitar repair expert Les Muffin, who lived on the farm with Mr Chissler and had his own workshop just near the special needs Dwarf wing. Those Flying Y's were similar to the well known Flying V design except they were shaped like the letter Y. Attendees at early Pants gigs will remember seeing me onstage with a Jensen amp and a pair of Y's. Powerful stuff!

In the early days of Pants, long before our studio session, Howard Trowl had encouraged us to experiment with sounds. He advised me to try a few effect pedals to fill the Pants sound out a bit and add a more contemporary vibe to the music.

‘Why don’t you boys try a few effect pedals to fill the Pants sound out a bit and add a more contemporary vibe to the music‘? He asked.

‘This bloke will sort you out’, he said, as he scribbled a name and address on a bit of paper. It turned out that Howard had a mate who used to play guitar in the old days.

Bernard Dripping had been a guitarist in the sixties in a little known club duo called ‘Dripping and Peas’. The line up consisted of Bernard and his cousin, Simon Peas. A poor act by anyone’s standards, they told crude, sexist jokes and sang vulgar, obscene versions of popular chart hits with the words changed. The working men’s clubs of Northern England loved them.

Now, Bernard had given up on the glitz and glamour of club land and moved into the catering trade. He had started out with a hotdog van. All was going well until some idiot had crashed his bike into the back of it. Luckily, Bernard was insured and he used his compensation to start his empire: Bernard Dripping’s Hot Beef Dip and Boiled Onion Exchange. This was the address Howard had given me. Apparently Bernard had an old fuzz box that he no longer used and I was dispatched to go and buy it from him.

'The Hot Beef Dip and Boiled Onion Exchange' was situated in Gateshead, a short Metro ride from Jarrow. Gateshead in those days was renowned for ill-mannered people with bad breath and shabby sportswear, come to think of it, it still is. Bernard Dripping was expecting me. As soon as I entered the shop, he extended a greasy, onion stained handshake then ruffled my hair and belched in my face.

'So, Your Howard Trowl's young mate, are you? Well, I've got something for you son!' Then, from under the counter, he produced a battered old fuzz pedal.

'That's yours for a fiver son, it's a good 'un that, very rare!' And indeed it was, it was a vintage Kegtone Soundmincer, I'd never seen (or heard) anything like it. It was to become a cornerstone of the Pants sound. U2's The Edge had his Echo Chamber, Johnny Marr had his Tremolo effect, Noel Gallagher had his Overdrive Box and now, at last, I had The Kegtone! MY sound, the sound of Pants! We were set!

Just as I was about to leave the shop, a second fateful event in the story of Pants began to unfold.....

'Mind if I gaan for the bus now Mr Dripping'?

It was the most beautiful voice I had ever heard. I

turned to see where it had come from, and then I saw her.

'Aye Constance, get yer sel away pet'!

She was only a Gateshead beef dip assistant but I knew from that first moment she was the only one for me. I looked at her name badge; it read 'Constance Stains', for that was her name and then, in one single glorious motion, she pulled out her hair clip, shook down her flowing, curly hair and removed her spectacles.

'Why Constance, without your glasses… your beautiful' I spluttered.

'Cut the shite big nose, I'm parched and it's YOUR round'!

And with that, I knew I would never look at another woman again in my life. It's true; Constance said she'd 'break my fuckin' neck if I so much as LOOKED at another lass!

So that's how it happened. I was straddled with a lass right from the word go. Deka and me had the hottest band in the area just getting off the ground and Constance was there straight from the off. Sticking her nose into our Pants business like some demented, Gateshead based Yoko Ono. Little did we know how much shit she would stir in Pants! What a stinker!

Part 9
PANTS GET BIGGER

The national widow cleaner and bus conductor strike had made the 6 o-clock news that evening and as I watched the telly with my mam, my mams mam and my mams mams mam, and my brothers mams mam. I couldn't help chuckling to myself. Apart from the fact that I had just let a silent but deadly one go, I believed the strike had been deliberately called to coincide with our gig so that all the local window cleaners and bus conductors could be there. The union leader of 'The Window Cleaners, Bus Conductors and fish Biscuit Manufactures Confederate', or "W.C.B.C.F.B.M.C" for short, Chub Butkoffski, was a local man, whom I'm sure I'd seen at one of our gigs once. (The fish biscuit manufacturers were more into R'n'B, so they were less likely to be there). I couldn't wait. Twatters was going to be packed, so Charlie Farns Barnsworth and Dudley Longbottom were surely going to witness a brilliant gig.

I was incredibly excited as I loaded my drums and spare Jaffa cake boxes into Howard's van; he had already picked Graeme up with his gear and we were on our way. Twatters was one of the main music rock bars in Newcastle and had a reputation for hard drinking, loud music, uncompromising clientele and soft toilet roll. If you went down well in Twatters, you could go down well anywhere, and one thing is for certain; Pants were determined to go down well.

The venue could legally hold 200 people or 600 midgets. Unfortunately they still served midgets because every three years there was a bassist's convention held there and midgets made up about 40% of the bass playing population in the area, so to be fair, Twatters had no choice. They also held trombone conventions every six months and midgets also played trombones as their second instrument, although not as well as bass. The chances of Benny Crumpton being there were high if Mr Chissler let him out at weekends, which he usually did. We just had to hope he didn't know about the gig, as neither Graeme nor I could be bothered with any potential midget grief.

We loaded our gear in and set up for sound check. Howard was excited as we began to power up,

'Boys… I'm excited' he exclaimed. There was a house PA supplied and an engineer to do the sound. His name was Colin Mould, a small stocky, cocky ex-jockey, in his late 40's who had, *seen it all*, *been there*, *done that* and had four T- Shirts to prove it. He was actually wearing them! One said, 'SEEN IT ALL'. Another said, 'BEEN THERE'. The other said, 'DONE THAT' and the fourth T-Shirt said 'AND THIS IS THE PROOF'. After the sound check which took longer than normal because I had forgotten my drumsticks, we settled at the bar and ordered a massive load of triple Jack Daniels and coke, but without the coke. Thankfully, Constance couldn't make it because the buses weren't running. She wasn't bothered anyway by all accounts because she thought it was really cloudy outside and it looked like it was going to thunder and rain. In fact, it was actually a clear warm night; it was just that her windows were really dirty. Graeme was relieved because he wanted to finish with her, but didn't want to do it that night. Also, he quite fancied the barmaid at Twatters who was giving him the eye. The eye belonged to her friend who also worked there. As well as the false eye, her friend only had one leg, and one arm was smaller than the other due to a slight bit of humpage of the shoulder. She also had really massive ears. On top of all this she was quite a large young girl with bright ginger hair and brown teeth. I'd heard word that she quite liked me, but I wasn't interested because she lived in Sunderland.

We sat at the bar as it slowly filled. There was a definite buzz in the place; Twatters had notoriously dodgy electrics as everything went through one plug socket. Either way, it was cooking up to be a good night. Graeme and me watched anxiously as the punters came through the door in dribs and drabs, (although to be fair, some were wearing normal clothes). We were looking out for Dudley Longbottom and his boss from 'Strangely Brown Records' as well as Charlie Farns Barnsworth from the NME, as they were on the guest list. The guest list was quite large and included a lot of our friends, as well as some of Howard's wife and family. His wife was a strange woman called Kleb. She didn't believe in sex after marriage so their family was rented from 'Jarrow rent a Kid', (Jarrow's premier rent a kid and whelk soup agency). Anyway we found out a bit later that it was actually free to get in Twatters, so the guest list didn't really matter, but still... We were also a bit nervous of

Benny Crumpton arriving. There were a few midgets already in and were getting stuck into the Quantro and Ribeaner with vodka jelly chasers. I was praying that they wouldn't get all pissed up and start excessively jutting their chins, as it could spoil the night.

It was getting close to stage time and there was still no sign of Dudley or Charlie from the NME, but thankfully no sign of Benny either. Suddenly Howard pointed towards the door and rasped, 'There's Dudley'! Sure enough, as promised he arrived, with five minutes to spare. Charlie from the NME hadn't arrived though, which was a bit disappointing. Although know one had actually met him, or knew what he looked like, or knew anyone who knew him either for that matter.

Despite the excessive Jack Daniels, dodgy electrics and Midget pogoing we played a blinder. The barmaid was winking at Graeme throughout the set and loving it. I think her mate was waving at me as well, but I couldn't quite tell. It didn't matter though because the place was rocking; quite literally as it happened because the foundations were crumbling and the management hadn't got them fixed yet. We didn't care; we were in rock & roll heaven, playing all our faves including – 'Stretch em Sideways', My Exploding Zip', 'Patchy

Flannels' and my new favourite, a very punky anthem called, 'Smells like Teen Cheese'.

The window cleaners were going berserk and waving their donkey jackets in the air like they just didn't care - *arr hu, a hu... arr hu hu hu.* The bus conductors were jumping around all over the place and going mental, loving every note and every beat we played. The Twatters regulars were also caught up in Pants mania and jumping about, slightly out of time, but still getting off on the Pants groove. But more importantly that night, Dudley Longbottom was transfixed. Howard Trowl was smiling from ear to chin and everything was going to plan. Or so we thought. Amid the cheering and clapping boomed this loud, yet strangely high-pitched voice.

'Yuzz are fukin shit man... yu fukin twats'. It was Benny! None of us had noticed him come in and he had made his way to the front of the stage carrying his trombone. He hurled abuse at us at the end to try and spoil our night.

'These fuckas don't like midgets'! He shouted, trying to galvanise support from the other Midgets who were already there and had previously been enjoying themselves without a care in the world.

'They're fuckin midgeyphobes they are…I got sacked just for being small….. AND THEY'RE BASTARD SHITE'! he yelled, and with that he blew a triumphant clarion call into his trombone.

Suddenly, all the midgets started jutting their chins excessively and ran towards the stage whooping and hollering. Luckily it took them a while to get there because of their short legs, but they were not to be messed with and we took refuge in the dressing room. What followed was a mass brawl, because the window cleaners jumped to our defence, as did the bus conductors. The bouncers try to break it up, but to no avail. There were arms and legs flying all over the place, the occasional ear and some small toes. It was utter chaos, not unlike a bar fight scene in an old western. The barmaid that Graeme fancied was screaming for it all to stop as glasses smashed and tables went flying. The barmaid, who fancied me, joined in the fight. Howard Trowl instinctively went to protect the gear on stage and the Bottle of Jack Daniels that was also on stage for the band. While Colin Mould, the sound engineer, put on another T-Shirt, which simply read, *I've been in a fight*!

As the dust settled and the police carted off the Midgets, including Benny, back to the farm, we surveyed the damage.

'That doesn't look good' I sighed. When the barmaid with one leg got out of my way it was even worse.

'SHIT'!!!! was the cry from Graeme and me. The place was wrecked, with broken glass and tables everywhere, my drums were wrecked and the jaffa cake boxes crushed. Graeme's guitars were smashed into two pieces and one had even been nicked. His amp was toppled over and smoke was coming from the back. Howard appeared with the bands bottle of Jack Daniels,

'Fancy a drink boys'? He enquired.

'YOU'RE FUCKIN JOKING'!! Shouted Graeme; understandably not in the best of moods. We couldn't believe Howard wanted to sit and have a drink. Our gear was wrecked or stolen; Dudley was nowhere to be seen, so bang goes the record deal, we were accused of being midgeyphobes and we'd probably never get another gig in Newcastle ever again!

'Yes... let's celebrate'!!! I said sarcastically.

‘Why not boys’? replied Howard very calmly. Graeme and me looked at each other in disbelieve. What a twat!

‘What you on about’? I enquired, barely able to hold my temper.

‘BOYS…. HE FUCKING LOVED YUZ’

‘EHH‘!!!!

‘Bollocks to the fight man. It had nowt to do with yous. Dudley and his boss thought you were fuckin brilliant and he wants to sign the band’.

There was a long pause as Graeme and I tried to digest the news.

‘Seriously’! we both cried.

‘Aye’!!! Howard replied.

It was on. It was bloody on! At last all the hard work and ironing had paid off. We were about to get a record contract….with a record company to, not a string manufacturer like what happened to a rival band (Socks) a few months ago, nothings been heard of them since….But PANTS were about to get the real deal. Not only that but apparently Charlie Farns Barnsworth from the NME was there after all and by all accounts was very impressed. He had been stood at the back behind the dartboard near the knitting machine all the time. Pants were getting bigger!

PART X:

LASS PACKED IN

We had celebrated long and hard right through the night, much alcohol had been consumed and all the crisps, nuts, scratching's and rhubarb flavour yogurt had been eaten with much gusto, including four large marmalade chilli kebabs with extra flakes. We prepared ourselves for a new life. A life of sex, drugs, soft furnishings and as much Cheese as we could handle.

The contract we were about to sign seemed pretty straightforward. 'Strangely Brown Records' would give us some money in return for us writing and recording some top-notch songs. They would then release them top-notch songs, sell them, and in turn; 'Strangely Brown Records' would make some money, then; we could get even more money if we sold lots! Brilliant! We got a specialist lawyer to check the contract over on the advice of Graeme's gran. 'Smiggins & Smeg Law Firm and Toilet Roll depository ', (Jarrow's Premier Law Firm and Toilet roll depository) checked it out.

It was fine, especially clause 1 which read;

'From here on in - PANTS will write and record some top-notch songs in return for some money'. That sounded pretty good to me.

We signed the contract outside an 'Eel Pie and Mashed Turnip Shop' down that thar London. It was a symbolic gesture, not too dissimilar to the Sex Pistols infamous contract signing outside Buckingham Palace. We had ran out of tube fare so we got as close as we could, we also went the wrong way, TWICE! Then got lost. It didn't dampen our spirits though and on the way back home we celebrated some more by getting a tattoo, which read, *I'm Strangely Brown.* That was a bit of a mistake. It was meant to say; *today we signed to Strangely Brown Records and got some money.* Luckily for Graeme and me they weren't permanent and as long as we kept washing our arses, the tattoo would fade.

Later that week the NME was out and Graeme excitedly travelled to Shields to buy a copy. There wasn't a newsagent in Jarrow anymore, because due to popular demand, it had been replaced by a Custard shop. Ironically; although there was a newsagent in Shields, there wasn't a custard shop. So I had to travel to Jarrow every time I wanted Custard.

I remember shaking as we anxiously turned to the live review pages. We were in! It was at the bottom of the page and not very big, but we didn't care. We had our first national review!!!! It read:

PANTS EXPLODE IN TWATTERS

Tonight! The red mists of time and motion permeated the acquiescent sound scapes of colloquial ambiguity with a pure melt down of juddering dissonances and tonal beauty, punctuated with raw emotional thrusting. This comes to pass in the fulsome form of utter PANTS. 9/10.

Charlie Farns Barnsworth.

This was a pivotal moment in the bands history. The review was everything and later that day back at the rehearsal complex Howard was well happy.

'Boys! I'm well happy', he announced, however; one person who wasn't happy was Constance Stains.

Earlier that day Graeme had finished with her and she didn't take it well. Mainly because of the way he did it mind. He sent her a condolence card, which read

'Sorry to here you've lost your boyfriend' Cheers Graeme.

I remember Constance storming into the rehearsal complex full of thunder. Although she blamed that on the curry she had the previous night.

'YOU BASTARD'!!! she screamed at Graeme

'EHH'!! was Graeme's indignant response.

'You can't finish with me'!

'Yes I fucking can'! Graeme replied, more than a little pissed off at the embarrassing scene. Howard and me grabbed some crisps and took a seat.

'You're a liar, a shit, and shit in bed and shit at making cheese sandwiches and you've got shit socks'!! Constance had screamed.

Graeme tried the gentle approach.

'Sorry, I didn't want to hurt you, its just that I no longer find you physically attractive and you've wrecked me Battlestar Galactica Duvet cover with your oniony sick'. That worked. She punched him full in the face and knocked him out. I went to get some more crisps as Constance then started to kick him a few times in the bollocks. Eventually she stopped and announced that she was going to get Bernard Dripping from the 'hot beef dip and onion exchange' to fuck the band up. Howard looked a bit nervous at this announcement for some reason and tried to plead with Constance to keep Bernard out of it.

'Please keep Bernard out of this' he pleaded, but to know avail and with that, she was off in a cloud of rage and curry smelling bottom gas. Graeme came round, clenching his trouser grapes and in some considerable discomfort. Why should we be bothered about Bernard Dripping? We enquired. Howard then told us the shocking truth. It was to shake the very foundations of our fledgling career. It was to rock the local music scene to its core and put Howard Trowl in a new light. This was bad; Very bad indeed.

It transpires that unbeknown to us. The hot beef and onion exchange was merely a front for Bernard's whelk smuggling operation, which had grown into an international concern. Also, Constance was involved in much of the dealings and in charge of operations north of the Tyne. Howard was also implicated and was apparently in charge of operations in South Tyneside. With Howard as our manager, PANTS were inadvertently involved. The Jarrow rehearsal complex was a secret Whelk washing centre and the money used to pay for our first demo was in fact, dirty whelk money! Howard had been in deep debt and had owed the 'Jarrow rent a kid and Whelk soup' agency a lot of money; Bernard had bailed him out and now owned Howard and by implication – PANTS. This explained why Howard was keen for us to sign for Bernard Drippings record company and why Constance was always trying to join the band! What could we do? Apparently it was Bernard who had power over the band now and 'Strangely Brown Records' had been dealing with Bernard in negotiations. We had known nothing about it. We should have read the contract properly, or got a proper lawyer, either way; this was dodgy. No wonder Constance acted the way she did. She was a fucking gangster. That night, myself, Graeme and Howard hatched a plan; a fiendish plan to cut Bernard out of our lives.

PART XI:

A Whiff of Whelks in Pants.

The shock of realising that Pants were inextricably linked with an illegal whelk smuggling operation and that a fat lardy arsed beef dip and boiled onion seller, along with his assistant *and Graeme's ex*, 'Constance Stains' were at the heart of it was bad enough; But coming to terms with the fact that these odious people owned a significant chunk of 'Pants' due to managerial incompetence was very hard to take.

We liked Howard and despite his odd ways, his peculiar taste in hair and his penchant for young Mexicans, he was a good bloke. He had waved the 71 pence we owed him and didn't make much of a profit out of us when we gave him money for petrol and stain remover for his van. We even got a £5.00 a month trouser allowance and the £600 'Beard tax' he said we owed him seemed perfectly reasonable. He also helped us record our first demo and even bought us cheese crisps and custard when we ran out, although his offer to write some lyrics for us had been politely rejected by Graeme.

LADY OF THE NIGHT: by Howard Trowl

Here she is, the lady of the night
I can see her coming; she's wearing red tights
Oh she looks fine, I wish she was mine
If I was her bus, I'd always be on time
I know she wants me, I can surely tell
Coz I've had a bath and no longer smell

Oooh Oooh lady of the night
Oooh! Oooh! Lady of the night: Take it baby...

I quit my nine to five, and I feel alive
I'm better than her ex, he was called Clive
On the floor, up against the door
Arr baby I can't take no more
On the floor, up against the wall
Arr beby nar, I can't take it no more.

Oooh Oooh lady of the night
Oooh Oooh lady of the night. Take it bitch...

We felt that some aspects of the lyrics didn't quite suit the band, although Graeme quite liked the last chorus.

That week we had a meeting pencilled in with Dudley at 'Strangely Brown Records'. It would have been in ink, but for some reason we weren't allowed pens. This was an important pre-scheduled meeting to discuss marketing strategies and our first potential single release. We were booked into 'Chubbington Road Studios', not far from Abbey Road Studios as famously used by 'The Beatles'. Apparently it's where Billy Ray Syrus recorded his unsuccessful follow up to 'Achy Breaky Heart' - 'Dumpy Lumpy Bot'. We were also supposed to be discussing potential TV appearances on programmes like, MTV2, Later with Jools Holland and 'Cheggers Kitchen of Rock'. 'Cheggers Kitchen of Rock' was a new programme about to start in which Keith Chegwin introduced new and exciting rock bands in his kitchen, whilst cooking cheese and onion Flan.

However, at the meeting there was to be a new agenda. This could be potentially damaging and a massive risk. Could we trust Dudley? For all we knew he was in on the whelk smuggling racket and running the 'That Thar London operation'. He could be best mates with Bernard Dripping and if so, our plan would be scuppered.

We had discussed long and hard into the night how we could free ourselves from Bernard's onion like grip. The first idea was to simply sack Howard. Easy!

Howard then reminded us that Bernard would simply take control of Pants himself and we would be even worse off. Also, we were now signed to 'Howard Trowl Enterprises' and would owe him £20.000 in compensation if we sacked him. Graeme and I were confused. I didn't remember signing that contract and neither did Graeme. Apparently we did though. Howard reminded us of the night he took us for a drink and a curry at 'Jarra Curry' Jarrow's premier Curry and shoe outlet. We had got so pissed that we signed a beer mat that basically said Howard was our manager and it would cost us £20.000 to get rid of him; The sneaky clever twat. It was a good curry though so we felt it was fair enough.

There was however another option. It was a risk and it needed the full co-operation of Dudley Longbottom and Strangely Brown Records.

What if Pants split? Bernard couldn't be involved in the band if it didn't exist! Confused? Well it was simple really. Pants would Split and go solo for a while. Then, dramatically get back together soon afterwards under new management. It was the classic cowardly trick often used to get rid of unwanted band members. You dissolve the band, and then get back together a short while later, but without the unwanted member: Brilliant!

We arrived for the meeting at the head office of Strangely Brown Records, (It was actually the only office but it sounded good). I was so nervous I forgot to put my glasses on and I just thought I was pissed, Graeme WAS pissed, and Howard hadn't returned from the toilets after lunch in a swanky Tapas bar.

We sat with Dudley in his office and explained the whole story to him, the dodgy whelk smuggling and Howard's problem of accidentally having to give Bernard ultimate control of the band. Dudley listened with concern, amazement, shock and mild disinterest, depending on which part of the sorry tale we were on about. Howard turned up a little later looking a bit flushed. He confirmed the whole story and then told of our plan to save us all.

Dudley thought about it,

'Boys, I'm going to think about it', he said. However: He slowly began to warm to the idea. It was simple. Pants had caused such a stir, that the news story of a split would generate a lot of publicity. Even more so, if we were to go solo for a while. It didn't matter about the songs at this point. Just build enough credibility to make it believable. We were saved. Dudley was on our side and wanted Pants to be whelk free.

The plan was simple. Announce to the music media that due to high tensions and strain, Pants had split. We circulated the breaking news to all the top music industry media including, NME, Kerrang, MTV News, Potato & Trombone monthly and Cheggers Kitchen of Rock. It worked. The headlines were sensational and varied. These were just a few of that caught our attention.

PANTS SPLIT!!! (The NME)

AFTER A BRIEF RISE, PANTS COME DOWN. (Melody Maker)

PANTS EXPLODED, NOW THE BOTTOM HAS FALLEN OUT. (Kerrang)

PANTS FLARE UP CAUSES MASSIVE RIP. (MTV News strap line)

A BIG MESS IN PANTS. (The Shields Gusset)

POTATO SHORTAGE CAUSES CONCERN WITH NORTHERN TROMBONISTS. (Potato & Trombone Monthly).

It worked. Howard contacted Bernard Dripping with the news, naturally he had already heard and wasn't too happy but there was nothing he could do about it, so apparently he had decided to concentrate on whelks, his Beef dip and boiled onion exchange and a new venture - Hedgehog breeding.

The next step was for Strangely Brown Records to release a couple of solo singles from Graeme and me. We had to be careful not to damage Pants, so; the singles would be released in South America and Wales only. We gathered some old outtakes from our session in Ronnie Tubberts recording studio and custard distribution centre then re-mastered them for release. Next Graeme and I did a photo shoot for our sleeve cover and we were away.

Graeme was marketed as a hunky rock God, aimed primarily at the hot-blooded South American teens. I however had problems with my marketing strategy, as I wasn't sure about my image. It was explained to me that there was a gap in the Welsh market for 'Cake Drumming'. I had never heard of it, but apparently it was very popular with older women. Fair enough I thought, let's go for it. The singles were simultaneously released in the chosen territories with no mention of Pants, otherwise our credibility could be damaged, but it was enough to convince Bernard that it was real. Graeme's song was an instrumental eclectic mix of guitars and disco beats called *Cracking One Off'*. Mine was simply me, doing a sound check in the studio, re-mixed and called *Cake drumming* - (*The drumming for cake makers in the Welsh valleys*). Unbelievably, Graeme's single was a massive hit amongst the gay community of southern Peru. However my solo effort bombed and sales of Welsh cake plummeted, after what was described as a blatant attempt to cash in on the burgeoning cake scene of Northern Wales.

I couldn't wait to get back in Pants and start again proper. Graeme was offered a tour of Peru but thankfully turned it down, because despite his gay success, he also wanted to get back in Pants.

We had done it; pulled off a cunning scam to off load our unwanted whelk smuggling gangster. Next thing to do was reunite, with a new contract, a new manager and a triumphant single. Howard's days were numbered though, not only was his wife growing suspicious of his Mexican fetish, but Dudley believed that Howard had to go, even if it meant a pay off.

PART XII

PANTS LET ONE GO...

The unsavoury incidents that had recently fell into Pants were now well and truly behind us. Whelks were a thing of the past and Graeme had almost forgotten about Constance Stains. However, he still received the occasional letter and phone call where upon she begged him to take her back. She had promised to never be sick on his duvet covers again, kick him in the bollocks, or eat raw chilli before she went down on him. She had also packed her job in with Bernard Dripping and was now working at Trouser world. Graeme was tempted to take her back at this development. Staff discount at trouser world was 15%. But thankfully he held firm. Graeme was adamant that he didn't want Stains in his life; Or Stains in Pants for that matter.

But the biggest development was the sacking of Howard Trowl. He had completely arsed up the whole whelk affair and nearly crippled the band with his dealings with Bernard. Also, he was generally very inept in the way he handled the band, that's what Dudley told us anyway. So, Strangely Brown Records paid Howard off, although the £600 'beard tax' was apparently made up. Graeme and I went off Howard when we heard of this as we had always thought him to be wise and fair. It shows how wrong you can be. We heard later that Howard had left his wife and his rented children and had used the money he got from Strangely Brown Records to set up a moustache shop near a boys school in Mexico called Muchos Mustachio's.

We however were back on course and ready to cut our first release. Pants were booked to appear on '*Cheggers Kitchen of Rock*,' '*Jools Holland*' and a Norwegian show called '*Smell my Smeg*'. An alternative rock show screened late at night in Norway featuring the best of British music. Apparently it had over 330 viewers and Dudley reckoned it was worth doing for the experience of playing live on TV. We were on a big promotional drive to sell our debut single as the newly reformed PANTS. The single was due for release in March (just in time for the Christmas rush) and MTV needed a video. We were moving forward at tremendous pace and everything seemed a blur, although that was more to do with me forgetting to wear my glasses again.

Our debut single was to be 'Squeaky Walk' with 'Stretch em Sideways' as the B-side. These were personal favourites of Dudley Longbottom who reckoned they could really break 'Pants'. I looked forward to seeing our video on MTV, Top of the Pops and *Sponge with Delia.* Sponge with Delia was Delia Smiths Sponge and Music Show and was meant to rival Cheggers Kitchen of Rock. Delia would basically introduce new videos of up and coming rock bands in between showing everybody how to make sponge.

The video featured Graeme and me in a posh trouser shop somewhere down 'That thar London' walking up and down the 'Cotton Slacks' aisle whilst miming to 'Squeaky Walk'. I played on a marching drum and Graeme mimed the chords with his guitar. All we did was walk up and down the isle for three and a half minutes. It wasn't much fun, nor was it glamorous. I wanted to do something much more exciting. I had suggested the 'Corduroy and Action Slacks' aisle and Graeme was keen on doing a scene in the 'Flared Flannels and Velvet Dungarees' aisle, but the director insisted that it had to be the 'Cotton Slacks' aisle or his vision would be compromised. Unfortunately we didn't have much creative control in our early days so we had to make do. In hind site the director, Hector Fish was right because the video looked well good with the cotton slacks giving an eerie back drop to our song and the miming was nearly spot on. Hector was to direct all of videos from that point on, (well nearly all).

After the singles release we waited with baited breath to here of our chart position. We had been on a massive promotional push and the video was featured twice a day on MTV. We had been on both 'Cheggers kitchen of Rock' and 'Sponge with Delia'. We had appeared on 'Look North'... Twice! We had also been flown over to Norway to perform on 'Smell my Smeg' and were booked to play live on Jools Holland. These were exciting times for Pants indeed. I remember myself; Graeme and Dudley huddled round his transistor radio in the office to listen to the charts that Sunday. The DJ announced the count down to number 1.

In at 40 it's 'Cream Pie' with... Oops! I couldn't help it.

At 39 it's 'Silky Sensations' with...I love your nose.

We were getting nervous. Either we hadn't made the top 40, or we were charting higher than expected.

Some major artists and their chart positions were being read out and there was still no mention of 'Pants'.

Down 4 places to 35 its 'The Soiled Carpets' with...Stop! My Knees are Hurting.

Straight in at number 34... We held our breath. Was this Pants?

'Muffty Ringworm'...with... I Need Some Rubber

Bloody hell! That crap singer we supported ages ago in the 'Worthy Wellington' was in the charts with some mad trombone and vocals ballad. We hadn't even realise she had been signed up!

Up one place to number 33 it's that fantastic all girl band, 'Lasses Lamin' with...Fresh Air up My Thighs.

AAARRRGGG!

Straight in at number 32 it's a debut hit for 'PANTS' with...Squeaky Walk

WHOOOOOO HOOOOOOOO!!!!!!! We couldn't believe it. We had charted in at 32. All the hard work had paid off and it was worth having to eat Chegger's cheese and Onion flan after all. MTV started playing our video three times a day now and we were actually starting to become genuinely famous! I could tell because when I went to buy some gaffer tape for my glasses the shopkeeper insisted that I didn't have to pay.

'No sir… it's on the house', he said as I tried to hand him the 50 pence.

'You're in that band aren't you'?

'Yes. Yes I am' I replied calmly.

'I saw you on Delia Smiths sponge programme' he said, a little excitedly.

'Well you can have this gaffer for free, just give me a mention sometime and it's yours'.

I was flabbergasted; I was getting free gaffer tape just because he had seen me on the telly; Brilliant! So a big thank you to 'Ernest Frontbottom's Gaffer Tape & Pudding Spoon Outlet' Jarrow's premier gaffer tape and pudding spoon outlet.

Graeme too was enjoying the fripperies of fame. He had just signed a sponsorship deal with 'Kegtone effects pedals' and was getting all his guitar stuff for nothing. On top of that he was getting cheese delivered daily by a local dealer who reckoned he could get Graeme any cheese he wanted, including Edam! He just had to give him the nod.

Yes indeed, doors were opening for Pants, as we were on the up.

PART XIII

TOP OF THE POPS, TOILETS, GRAVY & RETURN OF A MIDGET.

‘PANTS’ were riding high and the excitement of breaking the top 40 with our debut single ‘Squeaky Walk’ was impossible to describe. Well actually, it is quite easy to describe if you’re an accomplished writer instead of a bum faced pissed up drummer, but hey! What can you do? However, things were to get even better for Graeme and me. Our TV appearances on ‘Sponge with Delia’, ‘Cheggers kitchen of Rock’ and our ‘trouser shop’ video being looped on MTV three times a day had increased our profile to such a degree, that we had reached number 23 in the charts after only a couple of weeks. It was an exciting time to be in ‘Pants’. Added to all this, radio one was now playing our song on a more regular basis instead of just late at night on the ‘Bobby Buttons’ show. (Bobby had taken over from John Peel, but for some reason wasn’t as successful). Our single was also being aired on the award winning breakfast show with ‘Crispin Soils’.

This was a hilarious show that featured Crispin and his sidekick 'Comedy Colin' talking endlessly about rice pudding and chips, in between playing the odd song. Hilarious! Also; to our amazement, we had out sold 'Cuthbert & Dibble'.

'C & D' as they liked to be known, were a popular rap/pop duo that formed after quitting a children's programme called 'In Bernie's Crack'. The show was based in a large house renovated into a smaller house called 'Bernie's Crack', ran by a bloke called Bernie Crack. Basically, kids would hang around the house, solving mysteries in and around their local estate whilst eating crisps.

Next was the call from Top of the Pops. Dudley was very excited as he called us into his office.

'Boys…I'm very excited', he exclaimed.

'YOU'RE GOING TO BE ON TOP OF THE POPS'!!!!!

The three of us were jumping for joy, yelping and whooping for what seemed like ages. In actual fact it was about 30 seconds.

We couldn't wait to tell our family and friends. At the time Top of the Pops was the pinnacle of music television and it was every bands dream to appear on what was basically a British institution. Graeme rang his Gran, as his mother didn't have a phone.

'I'm not watching that shite' was her terse response. Fair enough I thought.

The next day we arrived at the BBC's Top of the Pops studio for rehearsals and mime instruction. We were then shown to our dressing room. I was really nervous, as was Graeme. We wondered who else was on the show that week and it wasn't long before we found out. 'Cuthbert & Dibble' weren't on as they were falling out of the charts, but there were a few exciting big names appearing along side 'Pants'.

I remember our dressing room didn't have a toilet so I had popped out to use the public ones in the corridor. As I sat on the Lav and waited for that mornings Gravy and weetabix to evacuate from my bowls, I heard the cubicle next to mine suddenly rattle into life. 'Bollocks' I thought. I hated it when there was a stereo 'plop' situation. I squeezed my buttocks and held on; hoping whoever was in the next cubicle would be quick and then leave. I heard the tell tale sound of a belt unbuckling, followed swiftly by the sound of trousers sliding down thighs, then…

‘WHOAHHHHHHHHH Splash! ‘OHH AHH!....
AHH’ SAY THAT’S BETTER‘!!

I recognize that voice! I thought.

‘BEAT THAT MATE’ he shouted, banging on the cubicle.

Bloody hell! It was MORRISSEY I was having a plop contest with Morrissey! I remember what happened next very well.

‘I’ll try’ I nervously replied.

I let go and released the satisfying sound of ripping cardboard followed by a swift double splash. Then a followed a ‘light squeaky paper tear’ followed by another splash.

‘EEH! NOT BAD SONNY JIM’ Shouted Morrissey through the cubicle in his distinctive Manchester drawl, albeit slightly camp. Then what followed sounded like ‘two dozen’ marbles being dropped simultaneously into a bucket of water.

‘OH MY WORD.... I NEEDED THAT’ Morrissey exclaimed.

‘LAST TIME I’M EATING VEGGIE CUSTARD, he continued.

‘I can’t beat that Morrissey’, I conceded desperately holding my breath. Clearly an excessive vegetarian diet can create a right stink.

‘How do you know who I am’? He had asked a little less animated.

‘I recognized your voice’ I replied. At this point I heard him rip the toilet paper off and begin to wipe his bottom.

‘What you doing here’? I enquired, still slightly in shock.

‘Having a shit’, he replied.

No I mean…on top of the pops’

‘Oh I see; well I’m promoting my new single… *Arise, arise my lovely Sprouts, my lovely Cabbage’.*

‘Nice one’ I responded, desperately trying to sound cool.

‘Are you in a band or something’? he asked, still wiping.

‘Yeh. They’re called PANTS. I’m the drummer’.

‘That’s splendid. Well, good luck’ and with that, the toilet flushed and he was gone.

It was so surreal it had taken a while to sink in and from that moment on, Graeme and me always referred to Morrissey as, ‘Shitty Arsed Mozza’.

We were to be the third band on; following a quirky pop band called 'Salty Smells' who were currently number 11 with their fourth hit '*Hey baby, you outa wash that chin'*. We were to be followed by a solo female artist called; 'Kate Meringue' who's single '*Withered Onions'* was pushing to be number one. 'Shitty Arsed Mozza' was closing the show with a spectacular performance of his forthcoming single, *'Arise, Arise my lovely sprouts, my lovely cabbage'* complete with massive orchestra and a small allotment complete with turnip patch and baskets of sprouts dotted around the stage, which he would occasionally kick into the audience whilst animatedly whipping his mic lead during the rousing chorus. The rehearsals went well and the host was award winning hilarious radio one DJ 'Crispin Soils' who's rice pudding based banter had us all in stitches. He was a lot fatter and trampier in real life than I imagined. He was also only about four foot tall and Graeme noticed he was wearing Green underpants. You couldn't miss them as he had tucked his shirt into them and they were riding high above his jeans.

'Bloody hell!' I exclaimed. 'Do you reckon he's a midget'? Graeme looked hard at Crispin.

'You know what! I think he is' he replied. Graeme and me had bad memories of midgets and were more than a little weary of them, so our mistrust in Crispin was well justified. After the run through of 'Squeaky Walk' Crispin came over to us.

'Hello boys. I'm Crispin Soils…Award winning hilarious radio one DJ. I'm sure you've heard of me'.

'Erm… yeh. Hi' Graeme replied a little nervously.

'I like your song; I've played it a lot on my hilarious award winning radio show'

'Yeh, thanks for that' we answered with genuine appreciation.

'Is this your first time on pop's'? Enquired Crispin

'Aye, it's canny like'

'Well don't be nervous, you'll be fine. There should be plenty of gravy, cheese and some custard in your dressing room'.

'Aye, it's spot on. Cheers'. Graeme replied.

Crispin seemed a nice bloke and Graeme and I both began to relax in his company. I wondered which midget farm he came from, as there must be some big ones down in 'That Thar London'. Crispin paused for a moment then quizzically asked,

'Why don't you don't have a bass player'?

Graeme and I both hesitated for a moment at this potentially embarrassing situation. We couldn't tell him about Benny Crumpton, our previous midget bassist and the trouble we had for fear of insulting him. This was a politically difficult moment.

'Erm…we prefer the sound we get with just guitar and drums', replied Graeme. Good answer I thought.

'You got summit against bass players'? Crispin retorted. I sensed this was starting to get out of hand as a frosty atmosphere between us developed.

'No. We just like our sound the way it is' I pleaded.

'Well I reckon you've got summit against bassists. All bands need a bassist. Is it coz midgets are the best bassists'?

'No. Honest'

At this point Crispin started to jut his chin in our direction in what was clearly an overly aggressive manner. Shit, this was really getting out of hand I thought.

'Have you got summit against midgets an all'?

'No. Honest……. it's just that we like our sound the way it is. I've got nowt against midgets either. I grew up near a midget farm', pleaded Graeme.

‘AHH TELL YOU WHAT…YOU FACKING GEORDIES ARE A BUNCH OF NORVAN CANTS YOU ARE… NO FACKING BASSIST! NO FACKING BASSIST!!! AAHLL FACKING PUNCH YA IN THE BOLLOCKS YOU BAG ‘O’ CANTS‘.

We both backed away at this alarming turn of events. Crispin clearly was a midget with even more mental problems than Benny! How did this happen? What next? Then suddenly a large voice boomed through the studio.

‘CRRRRRISPIN’. It was the director of ‘Top of the Pops’.

‘I warned you to stay away from the bands’

‘Sorry Mr. Feltch’. Crispin calmed down and looked very sheepish.

‘Check your contract. NO FRATERNISING WITH THE ARTISTS’

‘I know. Sorry’, and with that Crispin walked off back to his dressing room.

The director apologized for Crispin’s behavior and to make up for our distress sent for some extra custard to our dressing room. It appears that Crispin had graduated from Cockfosters Midget farm in north London a few years back and became a successful bassist and DJ, so they let him stay out. But every now and then he would have a relapse if something triggered his past. Our lack of a bass player unfortunately sent him off again. It didn't affect our final performance though and our Top of the Pops debut was a huge success with near perfect miming. All our friends and family were proud and congratulated us, well, all except Graeme's Gran who apparently watched 'Hetty Wainthrop Investigates' instead.

CHAPTER FOURTEEN:

THE CAULIFLOWER GROWERS SOCIAL CLUB

After our successful Top the Pops appearance 'PANTS' had became a household name. We were treated as celebrities everywhere we went. 'Jarrow Bun' Jarrow's premier bun shop treated us like royalty when we popped in for some buns and I never had to put my hand in my pockets once when I visited 'Ernest Frontbottom's Gaffer Tape and Pudding Spoon Outlet'. However; despite our success, we still wanted to live locally as 'That Thar London' didn't have quite the same ambience for us as Jarrow and Shields. London certainly had far superior trouser shops and the largest onion exchange in Europe, not to mention the bewildering choice of cheeses. But we felt more at home with our family, friends and smaller trouser shops.

However, we were to be parted from our beloved bun shop and various local cheese wholesalers, as 'PANTS' were about to embark on a tour. This had been arranged for some time and a number of venues had been booked around the country culminating in an appearance at Glastonbury. We were to promote an upcoming album we had been recording and this was to be our first major tour. We had been rehearsing for weeks and working out the set order. The set was to be:

Squeaky Walk
Patchy Flannels
Stretch em Sideways
Smells like Teen Cheese
My Exploding Zip
Pancing Queen, (re-worked Abba cover)
Slap my Slacks
Can you smell Gas?
Belt up or Fall Down
This Charming Pocket
My Soggy Turn Ups
Suspicious Stain
Inner Thigh Blues
Windy Corduroys
Room for Mushrooms
Chaffed Rubbings

Cracking one Off (Full band version)

We were really looking forward to the tour and Dudley was sorting the final preparations and finer details. I remember Graeme went shopping for a whole new wardrobe. He came back later that day with a brand new Pine one which he bought from 'Jarra Wardrobe and Teabag outlet' (Jarrow's premier wardrobe and teabag outlet). It was complete with wrought iron handles and larger storage space. His previous wardrobe only had one door and could only fit two medium sized socks in it; also there was no room for trousers of any description. He was a happy man.

One thing Pants needed was a road crew. This was something we hadn't really thought about as we were used to setting up our own gear. The PA and lighting rig, complete with roadies was hired for the tour, but we also needed a drums and guitar technician, somebody who looked after and set up our personal equipment.

A long American chap called 'Chuck Weinerstienercockerleiner' or 'Steinercockerweinersey…' for short was hired in for me. He came highly recommended and in the past had worked with famous drummers such as 'Sticks Malhoon' the drummer from 'Silky Sensations' as well as 'Keith Spoon' who had a brief rise to fame in his own right by appearing on a reality TV show called 'Celebrities Sitting Down'. During this period he was tub thumping with famous Jazz saxophonist Arnold Cribbins and his band, 'Arnold & the Creamy Shorts'.

Also, he had been the drum roadie for 'Larry Sock', who was the drummer in the international multi-million selling rock band 'Mega Beard'. Needless to say his CV was impressive.

Graeme was introduced to a short chubby man who funnily enough lived near Jarrow. His name was 'Harry Witless' and despite his strange tendencies to wear tight leather shorts and sport a strange shaped moustache, which he wore rapped round his ears, there was very little he didn't know about guitars. He had a massive collection, which he kept under the bed. But apart from his goat porn, he was also the proud owner of about thirty guitars, many of which were rare and vintage. Ironically he wasn't a particularly good guitarist and spent most of his time needlessly replacing the strings and buffing his nuts. Harry was a canny bloke who constantly regaled us with stories relating to previous tours he'd been involved with. Including going to Japan with 'Celine Dion' who apparently got so drunk that he had to carry her all the way back to the hotel in his bum bag whilst fighting off autograph hunters and Mafia style Triad gangs who reckoned she owed them drugs money; Then having to climb forty flights of stairs because the lift was broken at the hotel, which in turn he had to break into because apparently they locked the doors at 11.30. Then when he got her to the room, she was so grateful she gave him the best blowjob he had ever had whilst snorting cocaine and eating onion truffles out of her bum crack. And that was just the half of it!

Later that week we were off. Our first gig was at 'Ipswich University of Art, Design & Cement mixing'. I don't mind admitting I was a bit nervous, but at least I didn't have to worry about forgetting my drums as 'Steinercockerweinersey' had it all under control. There was a top of the range drum kit with polished cymbals, all set up, tuned and ready there for me to play every night. It was a world away from Jaffa cake boxes and the old pants that I used to play on. Graeme also had the luxury of not having to worry about his gear as Harry had set up his guitars, amp, onion holder and effects pedals to perfection, although his tendency to stand at the front of the stage with an unusually large torch pointing into an unusually large pizza box that he munched from whilst we were playing was something we had to address. Harry was a very frustrated roadie who yearned for fame in his own right but was held up by a singular and unfortunate lack of talent or charisma in any form whatsoever.

Our first gig was a stormer. It had sold out and was at its full 83 capacity, Dudley agreed that we should have played a bigger venue but the 'Willie Mandela's Blind, one Legged Black Lesbian Lounge' in the student halls of residence was all that was available at the time. The tour moved on…town-by-town, city-by-city and Pants were riding the crest of a wave. The rider's at most venues were spot on, everything we requested was there for us in the dressing room at each venue we played. I was in heaven. Limitless cheese, buckets of custard and as many Spam nibblets as we could handle. However, one night we played a gig at 'West Grimdon Conservative, Protestant and Cauliflower Growers Social Club' and it was nearly a nightmare. Despite selling out weeks in advance, the chairman didn't want us there, as we clearly had no interest in growing cauliflowers. This was a stipulation at being allowed into the club and it included every single fan that bought a ticket. There was pandemonium outside the club that night as hundreds of Pants fans turned up but couldn't get in unless they were a protestant, conservative cauliflower grower! A compromise was reached however. If they all brought a cauliflower they could get in. Dudley quickly drove off to Grimdons all night cauliflower dispensary 'Arkrights 24 hour cauliflower dispensary' in the town centre and came back with nearly 200 cauliflowers, which he duly distributed to our fans gathered outside the club. Everybody was happy and ironically it made the gig just that bit more special. It was very reminiscent of 'The Smiths' triumphant Hacienda gig in Manchester during their earlier days where upon hundreds of fans waved gladioli in the air during each song. With us, it was a lot of cauliflowers being thrown about; great days. Although disappointingly, the rider was nothing more than a couple of cauliflowers dipped in vinegar and lager.

The tour was over and deemed to be a great success. We had made a lot of new friends, caught some interesting infections and sold nearly two thousand Pants T-shirts with the bands logo 'PANTS EXPLODING NEAR YOU!' in either traditional black or snazzy yellow. There was one show we had yet to do though. Yep! It was our first Glastonbury appearances. Our tour ended just in time for us to finish with an appearance at this famous festival on the main stage on the opening day. We were third on the bill but our single success had made our lowly appearance even more special. It seems that window cleaners and bus conductors bought a third of tickets sold for this day. Our original 'Pants Army' had stuck with us all through our early days playing small bars and biscuit factories and had come out in force to see us at Glastonbury. The headliners that day were to be 'Splendid Curtains' an all girl indie rock band who only a year earlier were opening for American Art rockers 'Curious Cucumber'.

I was excited and nervous, as was Graeme. The toilets back stages were in perfect condition and even had proper toilet roll paper, and at least I knew I wouldn't be having any Plop contests with Morrissey! The inner sanctum back stage was awash with all the top names in rock. Splendid Curtains were there, as was the singer from REM, 'Michael Stipe' (the rest of REM were in another tent making nettle tea apparently). Over in the far corner playing Cribbage were indie punksters 'Helmet Juice' who were opening Glastonbury. There was also a smattering of comedians and supermodels that enjoyed hanging back stage including 'Heidi Cummings,' a stunningly beautifully and elegant Austrian model who had all the men back stage turned into a gibbering wreck. Apparently she had spiked their drinks with dodgy acid. That said, she seemed perfectly nice and approachable. I remember trying my luck.

'Hi, would you like a drink', I calmly enquired.

'Yes, that would be very nice. But not the punch…I pissed in that', she replied.

BLOODY HELL!! I was buying Heidi Cummings, the world's most desirable woman and supermodel a drink! And she wasn't throwing it in my face.

'So are you enjoying it so far'? I asked. I couldn't believe how calm I was being in the face of such ethereal beauty. Magnificent breasts as well.

'Yeh, its cool' she replied.

'Vot are you doing here then'? She continued in her cute Austrian accent, tinged with a bit of American. This was going better than I ever could have dreamt.

'This is how it starts' I thought; this is the company Graeme and me were keeping now, the bright lights, rock and roll, endless parties with the rich, famous and the beautiful. I was in heaven. I could see us now; me! Deka Pimpkin, from the industrial North of England, Heidi Cummings from the farmlands of Austria, united in our quest for love. There had been many famous couples over the years - John Lennon and Yoko Ono, Mick Jagger and Jerry Hall, Billy Joel and Christine Brinkley, Richard & Judy, Sooty & Sweep and soon it could be Deka Pimpkin and Heidi Cummings added to that list. It all made sense! And why not! I was in an up and coming successful band, I had most of my own teeth and made fantastic sprout toasties.

'I'm in Pants', I announced with pride.

'Erm… well I'm in a dress. Well done, good for you'.

And with that she was gone in a wave of musty perfume and flowing locks.

Graeme had been watching enviously from the other end of the bar.

'How'd yu get on'? he asked excitedly.

'I'm not sure, I think she likes me but I don't think she's heard of Pants'.

We got another round in and began to drink. Ten minutes later Harry arrived, his access all areas pass illuminated by a small torch and hanging with pride round his neck. He was walking with a slight limp and smiling from ear to nose. 'I've just fucked Heidi Cummings'!! he announced with pride."BOLLOCKS".

PART 15

PANTS: ALBUM RELEASE

Our tour had been a major success culminating in a memorable show at Glastonbury, although I'll remember it as much for blowing it with Austrian supermodel Heidi Cummings as much as anything else. Neither did Graeme or I actually believe Harry Witless, our deluded guitar tech, had been anywhere near her Austrian Alps as he had claimed.

'I'm tellin' yu bonny lad', he argued.

'She was well up for it…you're only jealous'.

We ignored him and continued watching 'Cooking for Sooty' on the tour bus telly. 'Cooking for Sooty' was a clever cookery programme that featured the famous glove puppet 'Sooty' - cooking for starving African children.

Dudley however was too excited, he couldn't concentrate on cookery-based programmes as he was constantly thinking of ways to expand Pants and make us bigger.

‘Boys… I want America to see Pants in all their glory’ he announced.

This took us by surprise and suddenly Sooty’s ‘Custard and onion Gumbo’ was no longer of interest to us. Even Harry shut up for a second.

Our album was due out that week and early indicators were that it was going to sell well. We had also been tipped the nod that a few reviews were very favourable.

‘I’ve been putting the feelers out about doing a short college tour of America’, he explained.

‘We’ll do about 30 shows and try to get Pants buzzing State side’.

I was up for it, as was Graeme. Even the goat porn Harry had slyly slipped into the DVD player hadn’t distracted us from our excitement.

Later that week, we arrived back home and started to prepare for our album release and the impending tour of America. I missed the tour bus; it was nicer than my house and even had a flushing toilet! Not something I was used to. Graeme had visited his Gran who slapped him for not telling her where he had been the last few months and even though he had explained about the band, the record deal, and the tour she still expected him to be round every Sunday, Tuesday, Wednesday, Thursday and the occasional Friday for Cheese toasties and sprout dip, sometimes on a Monday too, Saturday as well if she asked; (a Bucket family tradition apparently).

'You're not still with that shite are you'? She would moan, stirring a fresh pot of dip. His mam was far more understanding of the situation however and would let him off on a Sunday. However, family shenanigans were not that important compared to our first album review. Our debut album 'Chaffed Rubbings' was due out that week and the press had already received their advance copies. These were anxious times for Graeme and me as bad reviews could easily see the bottom fall out of Pants. We had fretted for hours over which songs to put on the album, and along with our producer, 'Chub Cribbins' decided on what was to be our first 12 songs the world would hear, except deaf people of course who probably wouldn't hear us, or be into us anyway for that matter as we didn't have the technology for music that could transcend acute deafness.

The first reviews were out and NME was the first to give us a full feature.

"When the first big release from Pants landed on my desk I was a bit sceptical. Indeed I wasn't sure what to make of it. Pants have had a troubled start to their career to date: Accused in some quarters of being anti-midget and uncompromising in their demands for better quality custard. Not to mention drummer Deka Pimpkin very publicly being linked with Supermodel Heidi Cummings and apparent all night sex and biscuit parties back at a famous hotel, where they notched up an 'onion nibbles' bill of over thirty pounds!

But Pants have astounded me with their unique sound and smell. The opening opus 'Squeaky Walk' leaves you in no doubt whose boss, and that man is Graeme 'Cheese' Bucket - with a bludgeoning guitar onslaught of sonic incomprehension that leaves the listener both breathless and gasping for air, as Pants let rip. 'My exploding Zip' for me, is a modern classic along the lines of 'Paper Laces' 'Billy Don't Be A Hero' and top duo, 'Johnston & Johnston's' eponymous, 'Whey Hey We're the Johnston's', which if I remember rightly was number 1 for 68 weeks. Of course it would be churlish to suggest that 'My exploding Zip' could reach those Heights, but with this album I can confidently predict that Pants are on the rise and will only get bigger, indeed explode!!! But seriously, with timeless melodies mixed with pure rock sensibilities in songs such as 'Slap my Slacks', 'Suspicious Stain' and the title track itself,' Chaffed Rubbings' Pants are in no mood to slacken.

I implore you for the sake of your creaking record collection, buy this album; you'll not regret it. I for one can't imagine my life without Pants". 9/10

This was a pivotal moment in our little bands career. We had had favourable reviews in the past for live shows and the NME had been championing us for some time, but never in our wildest dreams did we expect such a fantastic response. Other music mags were also very positive, one describing our album as the best debut since, 'Now that's what I call Music One'. As for 'What Window' the window cleaner's bi-monthly newsletter and 'Tickets Please', the bus conductor's weekly magazine, well…they just went wild in their '*Pops*' section. 'Trombone monthly' was a little Luke warm due to the lack of brass instruments featured, but strangely seemed to enjoy our use of the Monkey Skull in 'Room for Mushrooms'. Only 'Shoe Lace World' gave a bad review, describing the album as an insult to the world of music and the worst debut since 'J. S.

Bach's' 'Harpsichord of Fire'. Oh yes, and Graeme's Gran thought it was utter Shite. Despite this, things were looking very good indeed.

The tour of the US of A was now confirmed and we were in full album promotion mode. It had just been released stateside and early indicators were favourable. We weren't quite ready for Madison square gardens, but it was looking good. So 'Pants – The American Leg' was underway; Yeeharr! And so forth.

PART 16:

The American Leg, Yeehaar! *And so fourth*

We arrived at JFK Airport early Sunday morning feeling a little more than worse for wares. Me, Graeme and Dudley, our manager had been hammering the badger juice on the plane over and it had kicked in big time half way across the Atlantic. Although the complementary Otter scratching's hadn't helped. Graeme had disappeared for a short while during the journey only to return smiling from ear to neck.

'I've just joined the mile high club', he proudly boasted followed by a knowing wink. I was a tad confused with his general aura of self-satisfaction as he sat back down and continued to drink his badger juice and fanta. Only a week earlier I had sent off my application for 'The Goat Cheese and Custard Club' (South Shields Branch), but you didn't see me bragging about it. I put it down to the high altitude and alcohol.

At the airport a grinning imbecile greeted us. I found it strange that American airlines would employ retards at the front line of passport control, but hey! What do I know? However the questions proved more than a little strange and a few of them had me a bit worried.

'What is the purpose of your visit sir'? My answer of 'Introducing the youth of America to Pants!' wasn't such a good idea in hindsight. I was off to a bad start as I think I rubbed her up the wrong way, which isn't an advisable thing to do to someone who is clearly a retarded lesbian. However my attempt at good old English humour was nothing compared to the following question.

'Have you ever committed acts of genocide'? Now I was happy to be quite experimental in the bedroom but this was a bit personal I thought. Tip (Always keep a Bunsen burner next to your bed). Graeme too looked a little confused. Dudley stepped in,

'Just say no boys'.

'Erm…No' I replied, still confused.

'Are you a terrorist? Or do intend carrying out any acts of terrorism'?

I was sorely tempted, I really was. I decided to put on an Irish accent

'Oh! good God no! God bless ya, I'm only here for the craik and potatoes so I am, but I am tempted to blow up the white house while I'm here…. so I am…don't you know…so it is'.

Two days later I was released. Luckily for the band there were no actual shows missed as it was mainly settling in. Our first port of call was at radio KBLNNMH. An interview had been set up at a college radio station which played mainly rock and indie mixed with the occasional bit of country. The DJ who ran the late night show was called Chuck Sloshelwang III. He was a ridiculously loud and overly friendly chap with a lisp, who spat everywhere when he talked. He also had chronic wind and bad breath. This was our first radio interview and when we entered the studio we nearly gagged, both Graeme and I frantically waved our hands in front of our noses to trying to divert the smell but it was to no avail.

'Hey you guyssshh…Welcome to our little sshtation, I'm Chuck SssLoshhsshelwang'

'Hi' we replied holding our noses.

After we acclimatised the Budweiser's came out and we settled in ready for the interview, which was going out live. Amazingly when Chuck was on air he didn't lisp.

'AAAAALLLLRRRRIGHT their rock dudes welcome to KBLNNMH home of the rockinest coolest sounds this side of the Atlantic. We've got a great show for you tonight folks featuring *grrrrreat* sounds from the likes of 'Spoon of love'; 'Eggy Guffers', 'Britney Beaveritch' and a *terrrrrific* new band all the way from the UK called 'Pants' CHECK…IT…OUT…. WOOO YEH! We'll be *rrrright* back after these following messages'.

With that he cut the mike, pressed the commercials play button and let loose an almighty rasping trouser trumpet which fare well shook the foundations of the studio. Twenty minutes later the adverts finished and our single 'Squeaky Walk' was cued and ready to play.

'AAALLLLLRRRRIGHT NOW…. Welcome back to KBLNNMH, the home of the best new music on the planet. ARE YOU LISTENING OUT THERE RUSSIA'?

Graeme and I just sat opposite utterly bemused, holding our noses.

'Ok dudes and dudettes, as promised here's the debut single from Britain's finest new export

PAAAAANTS…. out on Strangely Brown Records, Its rockin, SQUEA….KY…WAAALK. YEH'!

And with that our song kicked in, it sounded good I don't mind saying.

After it finished we were primed and ready. Interview time, Dudley started to look anxious, this was our first live interview and what we say in the next five minutes could have a massive baring on our success or otherwise in America.

'WHOO YEH! That was BITCHIN! MAN, ok I've got PANTS in the studio with me now, so it's a *BIG* KBLNNMH welcome to Graeme and Derek …Hi guys welcome to America'.

'Hello there' we replied simultaneously.

'First of all can I just say I think you guys are AWSOME *MAAN'*

'Thanks very much' Graeme replied

'So where did pants meet'?

'Outside Jarra bun, Jarrow's premier bun shop. It used to be a trouser shop; it's where Graeme used to hang out.' I answered. The DJ was a bit confused.

'A BUN SHOP'? He responded, 'Erm…OK YEH… WHOO…. LETS HERE IT FOR THE BUNS'.

He continued.

‘I noticed you guys don’t use a bass player, was that a conscious decision or was it a happy accident in Pants’.

We had to be careful here as America had quite a large midget population and bass players were plentiful, as were tuba players. The growth of tuba players had apparently increased by 34%, matching the levels of obesity that had also increased so fat midgets were even more common in America. In England trombone playing midgets were common but in America it was Tubas that fat midgets could play as well as bass, *not* trombones. There were so many subtle differences between the two countries but this was the main one.

Chuck leaned forward in anticipation of our answer; I got a bad feeling he was setting us up.

I looked at Graeme and he looked at me. I knew he was thinking the same. We angled for our usual answer to this politically tricky question.

‘Well…it’s simple really. We just prefer the sound we get as a two-piece…. and we get more money ha ha’! I answered trying to lighten the mood.

‘I see’. Chuck replied, not picking up on my joke.

‘I heard you’ve got a problem with midgets, is that true’?

'No not at all' Graeme responded, 'We just prefer it that way'

'Well over here in the U…S of A …we have a lot of midgets who happen to play bass and who might not believe you. What have you got to say to our midget listeners!'?

We were getting a bit miffed now and what started as a friendly interview was turning into a witch-hunt

'Tough' Graeme angrily replied.

'What about introducing a Glockenspiel to the sound of Pants', Chuck asked.

Dudley was frantically trying to cut the interview and it was only later that we found out why.

'Well we like the sound the way it is…I doubt the Glockenspiel will give us the sound we need' I replied, a little confused and angry with this stupid DJ's questioning.

'SO…Have you got something against ginger dwarfs as well'?

Apparently ginger dwarfs made up two thirds of the Glockenspiel playing population of America. We didn't know that and Chuck had set us up for more controversy.

‘BOLLOCKS TO THIS‘! Graeme shouted, threw down his earphones and stormed out of the studio. I followed.

‘Well there you have it folks. Another limey band comes over here with their questionable values and can’t handle it when the questioning gets tough. I for one have never been so disgusted since the Beatles last set foot on these fine shores. I’ll be back after these messages…. YEH’!

That hadn’t quite gone to plan I thought. Later we found out that the owner of the radio station was a midget and we were well and truly set up. Dudley had no idea. We should have guessed mind as all the toilets were really low and pictures dotted around the studio were all of famous midgets such as ‘Toots Malhoon’ and ‘Corey Stumpington’ from ‘Toots & Stump’. They were a famous American ‘bass and tuba’ duo that had a hit back in the early 70’s. These were by all accounts the early influences of later drum and bass artists. Also; all the pictures were only about waist high on the walls. I kicked myself for not noticing the clues and Graeme kicked Dudley. This could go either way, we could be ruined with the American leg of Pants dead in the water before it even started, *or*... Kick us off great style like the infamous Sex Pistols ‘Grundy show’ interview. We were soon to find out.

PART 17:
PANTS BIG IN AMERICA

After our disastrous radio interview, midget sympathizers boycotted our gigs and we were greeted at some venues by demonstrations and near riots. I remember one day, as our tour van pulled into a small but popular venue in Austin Texas called 'The Fisted Redneck' we were pelted with rotten tomatoes, apples and blueberry pie, as well as an assortment of corn based snacks and burgers. Massive placards were waved at us that were less than complimentary about the band, 'DOWN WITH PANTS!' – 'MIDGETS DON'T NEED PANTS' and 'JESUS HATES PANTS!' These were just a few of the slogans directed at us. Ironically the gigs themselves weren't too bad as a hardy bunch of fans braved the demonstrations to see us. 'Squeaky Walk' was doing quite well in the indie charts and we had built up a small but loyal fan base. However we were victims of politics further into the tour as the Governor of Massachusetts was running for election and he needed the midget vote. Apparently

26% of the population were midgets so he banned us from the state and our shows were cancelled. This bad publicity however only increased our profile and more and more people were interested in having a good look at 'Pants'.

Later that week we learned that our single had made it into the billboard top 20.

'BOYS…your single has made it into the billboard top 20' announced Dudley, unable to contain his excitement.

'BLOODY HELL!!!!!!!!' Graeme and me shouted, equally excited.

'What number?'

'Number 20' Dudley replied.

This was it. This was BLOODY IT!!! We had done it! PANTS were big in America!

That night we celebrated long and hard and we invited all our new music biz chums along to help us get utterly twattered. Dudley organized a large VIP area at LA's famous 'Whiskey a Go', just off Sunset Strip. It was similar to 'Whiskey a Go Go' but a little smaller. Among the guests was a selection of rocks finest. 'Motley Crue' turned up but left shortly after the sausage rolls ran out and 'Ozzy Osborne' made an appearance, but later we found out he only wanted to use the toilet. That said, among the luminaries who did stay and enjoy our hospitality was 'Stumpy Van Halen' the younger brother of 'Eddie'. Elton John's Sock roadie and a selection of models and reality TV stars such as 'Gordon Trumper' who had apparently just won channel 9s new hit show 'Talentless Twats'. There was also a smattering of minor celebs that would turn up at any party to get their picture in the magazines such as, 'Mandy Dwindle' who was desperate to resurrect her fast fading career as a daytime soap actress after she got caught masturbating in the Cream fingers isle of 'World of Cake - LA's Premier Cake, Bun and Hand Grenade Outlet'.

It was all too facile and false for Graeme and me, Dudley seemed to be enjoying it though and Graeme's guitar tech 'Harry' was hopelessly trying to cop off with a young singer called 'Avril Shlopp' by pointlessly trying to impress her with his multi angled Swiss army belt, which did everything except keep his trousers up. Graeme and me sneaked out of the party with a couple of girls and went back to the hotel to have our own private party, which we did…several times. The girl I was with was called 'Penelope'; she was a cute as a button on a fluffy baby cat and incredibly sexy with all her own teeth. I don't mind admitting I was fantastic that night; I gave her all my best moves. Mind you I did tend to practice a lot on my own. Penelope complimented me on my well-kept toes and especially enjoyed the trick with the Bunsen burner. Graeme got off with a 'ginger haired' Scottish girl called 'Morag' who had borrowed Penelope's spare teeth and I do remember that she had a pair of massive melons. She had nicked from the buffet table earlier in case we got hungry (*boom boom*). She too was also ridiculously horny; if you dimmed the lights and squinted a bit. 'On the floor, up against the door, arr beby narr, can't take no more' was the cry and I didn't even need a shoehorn.

Eventually and all too quickly the tour was all but over and our attempt to break Pants in America was a hit at the first time of asking. The promotions and dodgy Midget ran radio stations had paid off. Out of the 48 shows that we were booked to perform only 12 were cancelled due to irate midget demonstrations and our single had reached the top 20 before falling back down. Despite the success we were getting homesick and I was desperate to get back to Blighty. I was missing my friends, the weather and the simpler selection of cheeses. Graeme felt the same and once more, we had been informed that there was a new trouser shop opening in Newcastle called 'Flannels 'n' Flares' that sold the latest line in 'Activity Pants'. This could rival anything that 'That Thar London' had and we were determined to be at the opening party as our celebrity status almost guaranteed us an invite. Besides, we felt that we had neglected Britain for too long in search of the Yankee Dollar. Dudley wasn't happy. He wanted to stay longer as he thought we had a good chance of cracking South America, not to mention Canada who he believed were ripe to be exposed to 'Pants' after 25 years of Rush's 'Spirit of Radio' being number one.

We got our own way and later that week we were on the plane back home. JFK Airport New York direct to JFK Airport – Jarrow, 'Jarrow's Premier Airport and Underwear Import Facility' the JFK stood for 'Jarrow's Fine Kegs'. Funnily enough we always wondered what the JFK stood for and not many people in Jarrow realised that. There were plans for an airport to be built in Hebburn Town as well, but the site had previously been earmarked for a new 'Tramp Wash Centre' similar to the one in Gateshead, only bigger.

‘Pants’ were back on home soil, ‘soiled pants if you like’ and we were determined to be bigger than ever. We wanted the world; we wanted hit after hit. We wanted a permanent dressing room on ‘Top of the Pop’s’. We wanted that stupid midget radio one DJ ‘Crispin Soils’ to beg for forgiveness and most of all, we wanted a pair of ‘activity pants’ from the new Trouser shop in Newcastle.

PART 18:
PANTS ON RICHARD & JUDY

We had been back in the UK for about a month now and had settled back into the old routine. The new trouser shop in Newcastle 'Flannels & Flares' had lived up to all our expectations and the 'Action Slacks' isle was indeed a joy to behold. Graeme was keen to do another video there for our next single but the manager wasn't keen to be associated with rock & roll types.

'I'm not keen to be associated with rock & roll types' was his blunt reply when Dudley enquired about the possibility.

After the disappointment of not being able to shoot our next video there had dissipated, Dudley called for a meeting to discuss our impending interviews on 'Richard and Judy' as well as another appearance on 'Cheggers kitchen of Rock' and a new music show on channel 5 called 'Noel Edmunds's Pop 'n' Beards'. This was supposed to be a new and exciting rock show designed to rival 'Cheggers kitchen of Rock' where instead of food and rock music, Noel explored beards and their uses from the last two hundred years. In-between these segments he would interview bands both new and established. The original concept was to only feature bands that sported beards but after the 'ZZ Top' slot was finished they struggled slightly and only managed a couple of 'folk' acts, one called - 'The Crumpled Tank Tops' and another called - 'Sweats Munroe and his Horn Pipe Trio'. Needless to say Edmunds had to expand the original idea; however exploration of beards from the last 200 years was a sound concept which kept the show running for three years!

'Now listen, Richard & Judy's the tricky one' Dudley warned us, ever more cautious after our American radio disaster.

'What's the problem?' I asked, 'Surely it'll be harmless? A couple of easy questions and then mime to our single'

'No, No, No,' Dudley shouted, exasperated at our general easy going approach to our impending appearance on day time televisions most popular magazine, pipe and slippers show.

'They're a couple of right twats…honest!'

'EH!!!' was our reply. I watched a lot of Richard & Judy during my formative years and I found them to be really jolly and friendly to their guests.

'Now listen carefully' said Dudley in a whisper, almost as if he feared being over heard. 'They play good cop, bad cop', Graeme and me listened intently.

'First, Richard will suck you in'

'OOER!!' I couldn't resist and Graeme and I fell about laughing.

'NO MAN…SHUT UP, THIS IS SERIOUS' Dudley shouted.

'Richard will…Erm…be nice to you, ask a couple of safe questions like where you met, what's your favourite soap, do you prefer your socks steamed or boiled etc.. Etc...You know the typical crap.'

'Aye…Definitely steamed' Graeme and I replied.

'You'll then go off air, and Judy will suddenly turn into a right bag of twats on you.'

'How's that like!' I asked.

'WELLLLLLLLL' continued Dudley. He then began to tell the story of Terry Waite's appearance whereupon after a series of nice and complimentary questions relating to bravery, endeavour and the human spirit, from Richard. Judy then launched into a tirade of abuse relating to a waste of tax payers money! And what did he expect 'stupid old duffer interfering with 'rag head' businesses and worse! With all the cold and hungry people in the world, at least he got free food and because he was tied to a radiator, he didn't have to worry about being cold at night!

Phil Collins also appeared one week and he too didn't expect the hard ride from Judy! Apparently after a series of nice safe questions from Richard about baldness problems and what a great song 'Sussudio' was. Judy launched into him big style, called him a fat baldy cock and claimed that the only reason he went on any charity show, especially 'Children in Need' was to promote his new crap single. Strangely enough though - Phil actually agreed on that point and didn't see the problem! Judy was right. He *IS* a cock.

We were warned though. There was a strong chance that Judy would bring up our midget problems.

We arrived at the studios early in the morning and were greeted by Judy Herself. She was wearing nothing but a see through negligee and hot pants. Richard then made an appearance as we sat in the green room drinking custard. He was wearing what looked like little more than a thong and a rubber vest cut off at the waist.

'Hi guys. Is everything ok?' he politely enquired,

'Yes thanks' we answered.

'We'll see you at 11.50, ok?'

This was very strange. Here we were, sitting in the green room at ITV drinking complimentary custard, while Richard and Judy looked like they had just been to an Amsterdam fetish party!

Other guests on the programme that day were a couple from Chiswick who had adopted a stoat. Someone called Frederick Shrimpton who had the largest collection of cabbages in the North West and finally, celebrity chef 'Gordon Dudbury' who was as famous for his sexual innuendo's as much as cooking and had a show called "Dirty Duds in Your Kitchen' which had been a massive hit for BBC 2.

We were to be on following a piece about 'summer fashions for amputees.' A more conservatively dressed Richard summarised.

'So there you have it folks. Tank tops can be a very handy piece of knit wear to have in your wardrobe. After the break we'll be talking 'Pants'...The band that is… who've just come back from a tour of America and courted some unwelcome publicity. See you soon'.

We took our place on the sofa while Richard and Judy adjusted mikes and barked last minute orders at the studio staff and camera men. A few minutes later we were to be interviewed on telly…LIVE!

'On air in…..5...4...3...2….' whispered the studio manager as the familiar Richard and Judy theme tune reverberated through the monitors. I remember being quite nervous as I had never been on telly before, Graeme wasn't too bad as he had had experience of television. Not so long before this appearance he had appeared on the local news giving his opinion on the opening of a new hyper market specialising in 'cardigans' called 'World of Cardigans'. This was to be Jarrow's premier cardigan retailers and apparently the biggest in Europe. I remember Graeme being quite vocal in his enthusiasm for the place as Jarrow had been crying out for a cardigan specialist for some time.

As predicted Richard was niceness wrapped in a basket of warm friendliness with simple questions about our preferred tea time treats, favourite colour and love of socks. He gushed over our album and pretended 'very convincingly' that he was a fan of

'Pants'. Judy sat off camera steely eyed looking at us with a mild scowl and half a breast showing just to put us off guard. She then joined in with devastating effect.

'So what's the situation with midgets then? Because I had heard that there were some problems with your attitude towards the little fellas.'

Fuckin hell! This was getting tiring now and the bandwagon was now in top gear.

'We don't have a problem with midgets at all!'

Graeme replied with surprising calmness. He then turned to the camera.

'……and we would like to clarify once and for all on national television that neither me nor Deka have anything against height challenged people of any race, colour, hat size or religion.'

That, we thought was the end of that. Judy wasn't impressed though.

'Well with respect Graeme, it's easy to come here and say that - but your bands actions tell me another thing altogether.' Richard then interjected,

'Tell you what…why don't we get some midgets in and we'll send the guys out on a bonding session in….I don't know….say a furniture shop somewhere and see how they get on! Or….no no no…. I've got it!!' he gushed excitedly. 'They could perhaps sing backing vocals on your next single.'

This was getting out of hand.

'Yes…and you could release it on mini disc!!!.....get it? Mini disc…..because they're midgets…midgets…mini??...ha ha'. Richard was clearly impressed by his own improvisational crapness.

'Look man. It's all a load of bollocks' I shouted and with that I tore off my little bug mike and stormed off set in dramatic fashion. Graeme followed although not before whispering a polite, 'Thanks for the custard by the way…..it was lush.'

Dudley was exasperated, and stood with his head in his hands. You could tell he was pissed off. We didn't go looking for controversy; it just seemed to follow us around. Not unlike Donny Tourette's, lead singer from rockers 'The Towers of London' who famously pumped on 'Never Mind the Buzzcocks' causing no end of controversy. Indeed it was a moment that almost rocked the establishment to its knees.

Things were getting on top of us and I wondered how much longer the band could survive. We needed to get away and get away quickly.

PART 19
WE GET AWAY AND GET AWAY QUICKLY

After our disastrous appearance on 'Richard & Judy' me and Graeme were more than a bit concerned that our image was going a bit banana shaped. Banana shaped was a bit like pear shaped but more 'bananary' in overall look and feel, which is pretty bad in a fruit, based 'comparison type analogy' of our TV appearance.

We had decided a holiday was in order. We had made quite a bit of money after our recent successes and the Richard & Judy appearance fee alone would pay for a pretty good jolly up. Later that day we were booked. One week in Dibblins Caravan Park. This was a quiet, little known Caravan Park not far from Butlins and an ideal retreat for pop and rock stars such as ourselves. Indeed; many famous faces had stayed there including the one from 'Take That' whose name know one can remember, The bassist from 80's sensation 'Brother Beyond' and a chap called Albert Fish, who was the keyboard player from 'Flock of

Pigeons'. 'Flock of Pigeons' were a very successful 'Flock of Seagulls' tribute band who were doing very well around the East Surrey pub and club circuit. In fact other members of the band had made a handsome living plying their trade - and 'Wishing' (If I had a photograph of you) was always a popular choice every other Friday at 'Crimpers Night Spot and Fun Bar', where they had a residency. Albert, or 'Stu' as his mother liked to call him, had taken to the drink really badly after a particularly vitriolic interview in the 'Crimpers' monthly news letter, 'Crimpy Gossip'. The interviewer had apparently accused him of miming. He had spent the weekend at Dibblins Caravan Park and it cleared his head completely, indeed, he was a new man. He had decided to leave 'Flock of Pigeons' and form his own tribute act, 'Short Back & Sides' - a tribute to 80's pop sensation 'Haircut 100'. However they weren't very good by all accounts and disbanded after just four days. It seemed that Albert *or* 'Stu' had his head cleared so well that he forgot how to play the keyboards. Attempts to sue Dibblins Caravan Park failed because apparently, there was no evidence that he could ever play them in the first place! Also 'Dibblins Caravan Parks' lawyers produced witnesses that were willing to testify that Albert *or* Stu was in fact 'Utter Shite' and was in fact simply miming to pre-programmed keyboard patterns.

These were tricky times for pop and rock stars, even wannabe pop stars like Albert *or* 'Stu'. Gossip columns hounded our every move. For instance when we went shopping; the paparazzi were there. It didn't matter whether it was for run of the mill stuff like 'Cheese' or even designer clothes from fashion outlets such as 'Diggery Flannels', 'Marcel Du Chiggley's World of Underpants' or even the very exclusive 'Wayne's Shoes' (where David Beckham had once been snapped). As for Mr David Beckham himself, he apparently denies ever being in 'Wayne's Shoes' and in fact there is NO actual photographic evidence of Mr Beckham and his lovely wife purchasing a pair of flip flops - as claimed by the owner and manager – Wayne Shoe. Although the suspicion is that Beckham literally was snapped there, or more accurately - a life size cardboard cut out of him modelling a pair of trainers was.

In the typical British press tradition we had been built up and now the knives were out to cut us down.

We had moved from being NME darlings to tabloid gossip fodder and the cooler music rags didn't seem interested in us anymore. Instead, all we could expect was pithy inaccurate sound bites and bitchy unimportant reviews in tabloid papers such as 'The Sun' and 'The Mirror' that frankly didn't have a clue about me or Graeme, never mind the inner most workings of 'Pants', the band we had formed and still very much loved. The Richard & Judy debacle had only fuelled our problems, so to say this week was a welcome break from it all was a massive understatement. We were staying in caravan number 2, next door to caravan number 7 where Albert *or* Stu had stayed and opposite number 18 where Ozzy Osborne was said to have holed up during a problematic Black Sabbath period of drugs, booze and recreational crosswords. It was surprisingly roomy and had all the mod cons you would expect in a Caravan of this size and class; there was a table and three chairs with cushions. A very pleasant looking ironing board cleverly tucked behind the fridge, which in turn was situated next to a clean and modern oven which featured two gas hobs, one large one, for woks and such like and the other for milk pans. Our biggest concern was of course, did it have a grill? The answer was thankfully yes. There were of course two beds of equal size, 5 feet by 1 inch, complete with tasteful duvets. Although Graeme had a hankering for his 'Battlestar Galactica Cylon Attack' set which he still missed to this day.

Now to stock up the fridge!

I remember a knowing look had spread across Graeme's face with this suggestion. 'Are you thinking what I'm thinking?'

'Aye' came the reply. So off we trooped.

An hour or so later our little fridge was bursting at the hinges with all sorts of Cheese. Plus a small bottle of milk.

Later that evening we decided to check out the sights and sounds of Dibblins Caravan park. Neither Graeme nor I were here to 'dry out' or go 'cold chicken' through miss use of drugs, (unlike a certain Aled Jones who by all accounts went a bit crazy with the white powder not long after 'The Snowman' became little more than a distant memory in 'pop' history). No; for us it was a simple get away, to unwind, blow out the cobwebs, escape from the unwanted glare of publicity and perhaps finish a 'Junior traveller' crossword or two.

We started at the club house bar and grill which was handily situated next to the Dibblins Caravan Park Kebab shop, which in turn was next to the Pizza take away along from 'World of Curry' – '*Curries you know and love from all over the world*' (to give it its full and proper name) and Dibblins China Town which featured no less than Three Chinese takeaways; 'Wok on by', 'Noodling About' and 'Adolf's Chop Suey House'. We headed for the bar and ordered ourselves 4 massive Jack and cokes, each. We then took ourselves a nice little table near the window well away from the toilets, surveyed the surroundings and soaked up the atmosphere. It was a plain but tidy bar with more than an ample selection of beers, wines, spirits and whelks. Portrait photographs adorned the walls and some were even of famous people, however most were of the landlady who we later learned was called Dave. She was a strange looking woman, Jet black hair, with a fierce face sporting a large ginger moustache. She was under the misguided comprehension that she was some sort of model and wanted everyone who visited the bar to know who she was and to be somehow impressed. There was also the occasional photo of her shaking hands with the odd famous face that had visited over the years, including 'Emu' but not Rod Hull, Basil Brush, the drummer from Herman's Hermits and the bassist from Queen - which I only new because he was wearing a Queen T-shirt and holding his bass guitar. There was even a picture of Famous ex - England, Newcastle and Liverpool footballer 'Peter Beardsley', who really did have an odd face.

It was my round but I had left my wallet in the caravan so Graeme subbed me 20 quid and I duly headed for the bar. As I patiently waited to be served there was a sudden rumpus as the all too familiar sound of crashing tables and the thunderous echoes of drunken tomfoolery filled the bar. To my astonishment it was the bassist and tuba player from 'Damp Sensations'. They were absolutely paralytic, falling all over the place and bumping into the walls as they stumbled their way towards the bar.

'Damp Sensations' had had a couple of top 20 hits a few years back, their most famous song, 'Puddles of Love' had reached number 7 and had momentarily catapulted them into superstar status as they appeared on every TV show possible. However; a very public split had ended their career. During a performance of

'Puddles of love' on 'Cheggers Kitchen of Rock' the bassist and tuba player had had a massive fight with the singer, guitarist and glockenspiel player. It was mayhem; with fists, feet, drum sticks and Gibson Les Paul's flying all over the place in a blur of fevered and frenzied fighting. It wasn't pleasant viewing for anyone connected to their band but I thought it was hilarious, as did Graeme. We never did find out what the fight was about, all anyone new was that the band split, never to be heard from again apart for the odd mention on the radio. They made it to the bar without falling over again and the bassist who was the smaller of the two and with his chin resting on the bar rail, shouted his order to the barman. Four pints of lager were ordered and while he waited he turned to me and slurred.

'Whaa da Fook are you looking at?...... Ya Specky twat!' He was almost identical to 'Benny Crumpton' - but not as obnoxious. It was a little eerie and brought a few sudden flashbacks of our early troubles with our one time bassist. Graeme had sensed the trouble and came over to help out if things got a little out of hand. Although by coming over I mean hid behind the fruit machine. Suddenly, his aggressive manner abated and an attempt at a smile cracked his oily features.

'Aaaahhhhh! I know yous…..Hey Eddie! Com 'ere. Its them two from Pants' he shouted to his equally inebriated friend, whilst pointing at me and in the general direction of the fruit machine. It seemed that the tuba player was called Eddie and was almost as small as the bass player who constantly jutted his chin forward in an aggressive manner despite acting altogether more friendly.

"Ow' do fella's. P… P..Please to meet your acquaintance" and with that he presented his hairy arm to shake my hand. He to, was short on height and was clearly an American. Of course it all figured, 'Damp Sensations' had not only one midget in the band, but TWO. This may have explained the problems. Graeme and me gave a quick knowing glance and decided without explanation, that it would be wise not to mention troubles from our early days.

That evening we shared more than a few drinks with Eddie and bassist Rodney and found their company surprisingly pleasant, despite the smell. We also found out why 'Damp Sensations' split. It seems that the other members of the band had planned a bonding trip to Disney land without consulting Eddie or Rodney. This in itself may have been fine, however; the trip also included rides in the park which had height restrictions and the other members of the band hadn't taken that into account. This had been a bone of contention for sometime and a simmering hostility eventually boiled over that day on the 'Cheggers show'. Apparently during the performance the guitarist turned round to Eddie and mouthed the words 'Big Dipper', then winked. Eddie clearly thought he was taking the piss so decided to lamp him one with his bell end. The rest, as they say is history.

The hours seemed to melt away as we drank our way through copious amounts of lager, Jack Daniels, vodka and Whelk wine. We were constantly laughing as we shared and compared tales of our rock and roll lifestyle and without realising we had developed a friendly rivalry, trying to out do each other as each story seemed more and more implausible the further the night wore on. Eddie claimed to have slept with TWO women in one night whilst on tour and he reckoned that he didn't even know their names! Rodney tried to gazump him with a story involving leather, vodka, cocaine, a travel hairdryer, a small pudding spoon and a warm glass of lemsip, as well as THREE girls all of whom worked for B & Q. Graeme and me just sat back and laughed. If only Harry was here I thought, he'd have a few tall tales to tell and no parachute would be needed. We were still in the bar and it was gone 2 o'clock in the morning and we were all feeling a little worse for ware. We were also feeling a bit hungry and had eaten the bar out of nuts, crisps and whelks.

'Let's get a chinky! shouted Rodney in what seemed an over excited manner, almost as if he was calling a nation to arms.

'KEBAB!' shouted Graeme, even more excited.

'CHINESE!' I counter suggested, with equal enthusiasm.

'EVEN BETTER!' Rodney shouted back at me.

'Pizza?' suggested Eddie a little more sedately.

Half an hour or so later the four of us stumbled out of 'World of Curry' clasping carrier bags dripping with an assortment of curry dishes. Graeme had gone for the ever faithful King Prawn Vindaloo, chips, Nan bread, Pelaw rice and custard slice. I opted for the 'less bowel exploding' Chicken Korma, Nan bread and strawberry tartlet. Our new Rock 'n' Roll chums Eddie and

Rodney both shared a Liver and Onion Balti with a side order of mince.

'Now THAT'S good eatin!', exclaimed Eddie.

My memories of what happened after that are vague despite remembering in detail what we all had to eat. But it was when we got back to their caravan to share in some post curry lager drinking that things are even hazier.

All I know is that both Graeme and I woke up late the next morning with traffic cones on our heads and no trousers on. Also we were outside on the grass, no where near our caravan and Eddie and Rodney, our new vertically challenged rock 'n' Roll buddies were gone. Vanished into thin air along with our trousers, wallets, (well Graeme's wallet) and left over curry. The BASTARDS we thought. We also thought OWWWW! As I know if Graeme's head was anything like mine, not only would he have better luck with girls but it would be pounding with the mother of all hangovers.

We had been done; done with the old 'make friends, get em drunk and nick their trousers' routine. This was particularly annoying to me as it was the third time this had happened and I still hadn't learnt my lesson. What was even stranger is that our trousers would never have fitted them as they were most very definitely midgets. What made it even more galling was the fact that it was only our first night! We decided there and then that we'd be a little more careful from here in and go easy on the alcohol - or at least some of it anyway.

PART 20:
BINGO!

The following evening we had both sufficiently recovered to continue without throwing up and spoiling a perfectly good carpet. Graeme trooped off to the hole in the wall. He was dying for a piss and I had been in the toilet ages. While he was out he also visited the cash machine as I had forgotten my card and we were in need of some readies for the rest of the week. It was annoying that midgets would still be giving us grief after all this time no matter where we went; even a nice little retreat like 'Dibblins Caravan Park' wasn't midget free. Still we were determined not to let it spoil our holiday.

Our plans that night were to be simple. Bingo! The nations favourite pass time and biggest recreational employer of blotter markers and pink cardboard. In Dibblins Concert room there was Bingo played every other night and tonight *was* another night! When Ozzy Osborne stayed he had cleaned up by all accounts. But apart from his part time job as a mop and bucket technician - which he took for extra cash, he also won the flyer three times and got no less than five full houses, winning a total of forty eight pounds, a shoulder of lamb, a large sirloin steak, four red onions and a jar of apricot jam. A time in his life I bet he'll never forget.

We got there nice and early in order to get a seat near the front which also happened to be near the bar and toilets, (I was still feeling a bit delicate and didn't want to be caught short). Graeme got the round in and I settled into my gaming mode, marker ready, ears pinned back and glasses perched on the end of my nose. There was no real benefit to having my glasses there I just thought it looked cool and I could pretend to be wearing bi-focal's. In reality it was a crap idea and I couldn't see so I gave up on the plan. Graeme arrived with the drinks and we surveyed the room, checking to see if there were any midgets about; there wasn't. However; we did see Andrew Ridgley of Wham fame. He was sitting by himself looking a sorry sight if I don't mind saying. He had his marker in his hand poised and ready for action, hovering millimetres above the bingo card and it looked like he meant business. I remember thinking 'He hasn't come here to lose'. Further along from him sitting on a massive table designed for four people was 'Meatloaf', who was obviously by himself, but he had brought with him five massive Tupperware boxes filled with sandwiches and crisps and they took up the rest of the table. Graeme noticed that he was looking longingly at the lamb shank sitting on the prize table by the stage. They were all taking it very, very seriously. I also spotted Michael fish the weather man and John Craven from Newsround and Country File fame. (It wasn't just rock and pop stars that stayed here). They too, had a very serious business like look on their face as they sat patiently waiting for it to start. It was also very noticeable that they too were by themselves, except John Craven who had a pet 'good luck' tortoise by his side munching on a piece of brown lettuce, well at least I presumed it was lettuce.

8 o'clock on the dot the bingo started and an eerie hush descended on the surprisingly drab concert room.

'Eyes down and 'ere we go….quiet please'

I couldn't help sniggering as it all seemed surreal to me. I'd never played bingo or been to a bingo hall before and I just couldn't take it seriously. At the next table a couple scowled at me and told me to Shhh! I didn't recognise them at all so I presumed they were average run of the mill holiday goers. If they new who I was I bet they wouldn't be so prickly. I made a mental note not to give them an autograph when they realised their horrendous error. Which I was sure they would, possibly. Later on.

'Cheese & Chive.... twenty five' the caller continued.

'On the floor.....Number four'

'Stinky puddle...number eight'

'Two fat chimps........thirteen'

'HOUSE!' a shrill cry boomed out from the other end of the room.

'Flippin' heck! That was a quick round' said a genuinely astonished and not altogether happy Graeme. I wasn't either as neither of us had even blotted one single number. I craned my neck trying to see who the winner of a small tub of rhubarb was. I *did* recognise her but couldn't put my finger on it.

'Who's that?' I asked Graeme. He in turn craned his neck to get a better view of the winner.

'That's Carol Vorderman!' exclaimed Graeme, more than a little excitedly. And it was! Carol Vorderman had won the rhubarb and seemed very pleased with herself. Only four numbers called and then a house? It seemed to me that the sultry brunette star of mathematical based TV shows had been very clever and worked out every possible combination before hand in order to win the tub of rhubarb. Meatloaf seemed particularly upset. Graeme agreed with my suspicions.

'If this was Vegas' I asserted, 'She'd be thrown out of the casino for card counting…… or something like that'. Graeme once more, agreed with my assertions.

However we had no time to dwell as the full house was starting and the clammy but very professional looking bingo caller was in full throttle.

'Two brown socks..............Eleven'

'Kinky. mutually based oral sex designed to give both partners simultaneous pleasures as yet untried by those of certain religions, weight or living in parts of America………Sixty Nine'. With that a couple of wolf whistles rang out across the room, followed by quiet sniggering.

This was hopeless, we hadn't one number between us and it looked like Vorderman was blotting away. Even Andrew Ridgley seemed happy with his progress and gestured the looser sign at me with his fingers on his forehead when he caught me looking. I wasn't happy about that and was pretty sure if George Michael was with him he'd be a lot friendlier or at the very least better mannered. Apparently George Michael was at the high stakes horse racing and country karaoke night in the main bar - at a different caravan site.

The night wore on and neither Graeme nor I got anywhere close to a full house. The best I got was two numbers – and one of them was wrong. Graeme faired slightly better and managed about five numbers but we were no where near winning, unlike Carol Vorderman who not only won the Rhubarb, but the lamb shank that Meatloaf was after. He wasn't best pleased I can tell you and he stormed off like some sort of winged marsupial with devilish intentions, peddling as fast as he could on his Raleigh chopper, although that wasn't very fast as he had flat tire. Andrew Ridgley won a flyer as well. He deliberately brushed passed me clutching his jar of pickles with what can be best described as the most a arrogant look of self satisfaction I'd seen in a long time. I so much wanted to punch him that I felt my fist twinge. The anger swelled up inside me and fuelled with alcohol and an overwhelming sense of injustice I made my move, however; just I was about to let fly there was a sudden unmistakable sound of a smashing pickle jar followed by an almighty crack. It was Carol Vorderman laying into him with such ferocious venom and fury that he started to cry. It seems that she was one number off winning the pickles and wasn't too happy that Andrew Ridgley had got there first. It was a blur of fists, brunette hair, white slogan embossed t-shirts and cream coloured cashmere tops as Carol Vorderman ripped into him. She punched him exactly twelve times in the face, twice in the gut and once in the back of the head. I counted five kicks in the shins and a further three hit their target right between the legs. For his part Andrew Ridgley landed four blows to Carols head, one kick in the stomach and two rips of her hair in a vain attempt to drag her to the floor, but little else. Carol had won by eight head punches and seven to the body. A total of fifteen hits or kicks altogether. Andrews hair pulling didn't count. After the dust settled a polite round of applause echoed round the concert room as Carol simply dusted herself down, straightened her top and combed her hair. Meanwhile, holding a silk handkerchief to his nose and noticeably limping, Andrew sloped off in disgrace, with no pickles. Carol didn't get the pickles either mind as they were smashed but it was a point of principle – and one that both Graeme and I heartily applauded. John

Craven had won nothing which was a shame, but Michael Fish shouted for a line and got himself a nice packet of mince. But the night most definitely belonged to Carol Vorderman whose mathematical prowess had seen her win almost every prize there was to be had, including the kudos she had earned just for kicking the shit out of Andrew Ridgley by a grand total of fifteen blows to five – Richard Whitely would have been proud. This was something I had really wanted to do but to be fair, in hindsight; she had done a far better job than I could have.

Later that night, me and Graeme settled for a Chinese from 'Adolf's' and went back to our caravan. As we greedily munched away at our assorted meat and special fried chips with five spice gravy we decided that we had had enough. It was only the second night but we had exhausted all the possibilities that interested us. Also we weren't best pleased that we had, or rather Graeme had had his wallet nicked, and we both had our favourite trousers, trousered – Also to add insult to injury, we had lost at bingo which neither of us were keen on, or very good at for that matter; we just weren't in the same league as Carol Vorderman, nor had we the ruthless will to win of Andrew Ridgley or Michael Fish.

Added to this, we found out that the club house bar was closed for refurbishment and although it was planned that it would re-open in two days, Dave had put a notice up claiming that it would now be closed for up to six weeks due to a Whelk shortage. Sod it we thought. Let's go home and find out what Dudley had planned for us. We had some new some ideas and perhaps a single could be released, maybe a small tour or a couple of festival gigs? Either way we were out of here. And we hadn't even used the grill.

PART 21:
IS IT A CORGI?

We arrived home late the next day after more than a few visits to the lavatory, it seems that 'Adolf' wasn't using the freshest ingredients with his 'assorted meat and special fried chips with five spice gravy' after all. A meeting was immediately set up with Dudley to discuss our next move and check on sales and marketing possibilities. There was no denying we had fallen from grace slightly and were no longer flavour of the month. A new band called 'The Turnip Crisps' were now the new darlings of the music press and were being tipped for all sorts of awards, including the Mercury Prize, MTV's best new comers and the very prestigious, 'The Sponge with Delia's Special Mix Award'. We had never been nominated for any of these awards which rankled slightly. Thankfully Dudley was still very much behind us and had no intention of letting Pants slip down. At the meeting we discussed a new strategy amongst many other things, although a twenty minute debate on whether we should have chocolate hob knobs or caramel fingers with our coffee wasn't the most productive use of our time.

"REMIX!" announced Dudley very excitedly; wiping chocolate hob knob crumbs from his mouth, his eyes wide open and his hands gesturing animatedly like a demented film director painting a scene to his actors. I remember Graeme and I looked at each other slightly bemused.

'Sorry? - What do you mean?'

'It's all the rage!'

We still didn't quite grasp what he was on about. Dudley then explained.

'We get one of your singles remixed for the clubs....give it a 'hip hop groove type vibe.'

I leaned forward trying to take it all in. Graeme seemed a little unsure about what exactly Dudley was trying to turn us into, but after much debate, discussion, argument, punch up and quiet discussion again, Dudley tried to explain the concept to us.

'Ok boys, its simple really'. He leaned forward. 'We choose one of your songs, re-master it, re-mix it and add some drum machine grooves and keyboards, the odd sample thrown in, a bit of cool rap maybe?…Erm….re –do a video and repackage the lot as a brand new song with new image, the lot!'.

And with that he sat back in his chair with a very pleased look on his face. Imagine the sort of face that says 'I've just invented pleasant sounding bagpipes' and you'll get the idea.

Neither of us were exactly over the moon about being replaced with computerized drums and keyboards and I was especially worried about the new video/image idea. I had spent ages honing my look and I had managed to bag a sponsorship deal with 'Sticky Moments Gaffer Tape – The Gaffer that's Well Sticky' so naturally I wasn't keen on being re-branded. There was also the possibility of legal action unless their Gaffa tape was clearly seen on videos and television appearances. Graeme's double sock and chip's deal was unlikely to be affected apparently, but mine? Well that was a little more complicated.

Either way we were understandably unsure about this new direction we were seemingly being forced to take. However; the hard facts were that sales were dwindling, our image was tarnished and TV appearances were fast becoming few and far between. It seemed that we were becoming more and more of an irrelevance as each week passed and even Graeme's Gran had stopped writing abusive letters to every radio station complaining about us. Action was needed, Dudley knew this, his secretary knew it and Ernest Frontbottom from the 'Gaffer Tape & Pudding Spoon Outlet' - Jarrow's premier gaffer tape and pudding spoon outlet knew it. If the truth be known I should have guessed, because when I had visited his shop - where my celebrity status had previously afforded me free pudding spoons; he suddenly started charging me the full 69 pence per spoon. At first I thought I had perhaps upset him with my gaffer tape sponsorship, but it was nothing to do with that; it was simply that I just wasn't hot news anymore, certainly not enough to get free spoons, or any other preferential treatment for that matter.

Graeme too was suffering under the fickle hand of rock celebrity. A simple night out with his mam to celebrate her birthday turned into farce when he attempted to get in 'Jumbo Johnsons Rock Night' at 'Jumbo Johnsons Night Spot and Waffle Dispensary' down Newcastle's popular Quayside. Ordinarily he would simply waltz up to the door, no queuing, give a cheery smile to the door staff and he was in for free.

Not that night though. He got stopped, his mam ID'd and he had to pay the full 50 pence admission. And all this after being told he'd have to wait in the queue with everyone else, (although to be fair, there were actually only four people in the queue at the time). This was a timely reminder that we were no longer rock Gods at the top of our game, not to mention an embarrassing moment for Graeme. His mam was less than impressed apparently and decided to go home, leaving Graeme on his own. Then; and just to rub it in, the waffle bar had shut.

WE'LL DO IT! Why not I thought and Graeme was determined not to have another 'Jumbo Johnson Rock Night - Waffle free' situation occur ever again.

It was decided that 'My Exploding Zip' was the best song to do. It seemed to lend itself for a remix with a punchy chorus and a good tempo.

Now DJ Mark Spanner was hot property at the time, re-recording and producing old cover songs in a contemporary style using the latest in studio technology - not to mention having a tasty line in designer sunglasses, hats and cardigans. He was duly commissioned by Dudley after some protracted contract negotiations (which took up the whole lunch hour), and set to work later that week on lifting new Pants back to the top.

Graeme and I were banished from the studio as Mark had negotiated complete artistic freedom and we were urged to simply '*trust him as he knew what he was doing*', we would only be called for if and when needed. Other than that we were told to stay away until it was finished. This didn't feel right; after all it was OUR song he was messing with. We decided to hole up in a little bar within eye line of the studio to keep tabs on things and to check out comings and goings. During the time it took to drink eight lagers and four double Jack Daniels with brandy chasers we saw what looked like a small group of 'gangster rap' types strut in, dripping with bling, attitude - and rain. Three brass band types clutching a tuba, trombone and a French horn - dripping with rain, followed later by a small dog, possibly a corgi but we weren't sure, I personally thought it was a cross breed but Graeme was convinced it was a thorough bred; It to was also was dripping with rain. Later on we saw a very glamorous young woman glide through the doors also dripping in bling, but not rain as it had stopped. We also noticed a pizza delivery man but he didn't go in, he was just dropping off what looked like a large flat white box, then he went. A bit later we also noticed Dudley appear, then a few minutes later he left the studio holding what looked like a piece of pizza, possibly pepperoni, possibly Hawaiian - but again we could have been wrong. This was all too much and the suspense was killing us, plus I had a strange hankering for pizza. We were both determined to hear how the remix of 'My exploding Zip' was going and who were all these strange people coming in and out of the studio…. and whose dog was it?

Later that week we were summoned to the studio. We had given up on spying from a distance as we had learned absolutely nothing except that there was a pizza takeaway and delivery shop just round the corner that did Monday evening specials - '12" Spicy clam and cabbage Neptune' for £4.99. Bargain. Basically we had gleaned nothing from our amateurish surveillance operation that could help us in any way. Besides it wouldn't have made any difference because DJ Mark Spanner had negotiated exclusive rights to almost all of the royalties accrued if this was to be a hit as well as an enormous fee for remixing it in the first place which would be repaid from OUR share which was only 7%. We felt this was a tad harsh on us as we had written the song in the first place, but as Dudley reminded us after we complained, '*7% of something is better than 14% of not much of something*'. Wise words from a man who knew the business inside out I felt.

We were eventually summoned and in the mixing room we plonked ourselves down on a very soft sofa which almost swallowed us whole while we waited for DJ Mark to play us his finished re-working of our song. Perched on the end of a very comfortable looking leather recliner chair Dudley winked at us reassuringly as Mark pressed the play button with aplomb, put his sunglasses back on and with his hands behind his head, sat back in his '*even more comfortable looking than Dudley's*' leather recliner chair. Suddenly; in a burst of surprising volume emanating from the wall mounted speakers came the sound of drums, but they weren't my drums. They were some strange mix of electronic and live drums playing a beat that I hadn't done, nor in truth would be capable of doing as it sounded a bit like someone had let an octopus loose on a strange alien drum kit which who in turn had been taught how to play by a chimpanzee. Both Dudley and DJ Mark nodded their heads back and forth in time with the groove which I had to admit was fast becoming strangely hypnotic. Graeme sat open mouthed as the beat moved on and layers of keyboards and percussion slowly joined the mix. This was a new one on us and was more than a little surprising. We barely recognised our own song as only the vaguest hint of the original pop/rock burst that we had loved playing live all this time was there. I could just make out some of Graeme's guitar way low in the mix and occasionally disappearing altogether! My drums were totally replaced and so were Graeme's vocals. Instead there was the low rhythmic pulse of what sounded like rap followed by female vocals warbling in the background in that phoney 'R n B' style that we both hated. Then there was the distant sound of what seemed to be trombone, Tuba and French horn, swamped in reverb subtly interweaving in and around the rap line and Graeme was sure he heard a dog barking as well. But to make matters worse! What really capped it off! What totally put the sprouts in the pudding – was BASS! There it was, high in the mix, rumbling through the speakers like an out of control panzer tank trudging through the allied lines in 2nd world war France. Dudley and DJ Mark were well into it, nodding there heads back and forth in time to the music that we barely recognised, and at one point I thought they were going to put their hands in the air 'like they just don't care'. I wasn't convinced and Graeme was shell shocked.

'What the FUCK'S that?' he shouted, clearly agitated.

DJ Mark didn't flinch, but Dudley was clearly a little put out.

'What exactly is your problem Graeme? This is the Scooby's Gonads' he insisted, clearly unmoved by our obvious concerns.

Graeme however had his own concerns. Firstly: the guitars were all but removed. Instead there was rapping with female 'R n B' style vocalising, keyboards. Brass instruments, BASS! All manner of exotic percussion on top of programmed drum machine grooves augmented with the occasional dog barking – possibly a corgi.

I remember Graeme being very agitated as he tried comically to get out of the giant marshmallow disguised as a sofa, on which by the third attempt - and with a little help from me pushing him from behind, he was upright, gesticulating wildly. He wasn't a happy bunny, (unlike 'Jive bunny' who were creating one of their brilliantly unique dance remixes of popular hits from yesteryear in the studio next door).

Basically 'Pants' had been ripped apart and the vision of our band that we both shared was now obliterated at the hands of some fly by night DJ, whose only talent appeared to be fiddling about with other peoples songs. Also he could programme drum machines, play keyboards, bass guitar (despite not being a midget), percussion, set up and record in a professional studio and operate a mixing console as well as being a highly respected producer who apparently has his finger on the pulse of popular youth culture and has built up a reputation for successfully reinventing failing Artists/bands. He had also passed a grade 4-trumpet exam. Dudley was adamant and no amount of protests from either Graeme or me was going to change that fact. 'My Exploding Zip' was going to be released as a single with accompanying video, whether we liked it or not.

Later that night Graeme and me checked the contract we had signed in what seemed an age ago now. How could Dudley do this? Was he even allowed to do this? We knew times were hard but both Graeme and I were convinced we had full artistic control.

Eventually we found it and there it was clause 3a.

'Should the band find itself in hard times and/or become artistically redundant, split up, or one or more of its members die under either normal or strange circumstances –Strangely Brown Records reserve the right to evoke FULL artistic control of all songs recorded and reserve the right to re-release, repackage and exploit all materials in order to make more cash in anyway the company sees fit.'

We were outdone by clever contract jargon once again. It seems that we were helpless to stop this song being released no matter what we said or did and Dudley was in no mood to play Mr nice guy. Strangely Brown Records was haemorrhaging money and more recent signings such as solo artist 'Chumley Biscuit' weren't taking off despite the money poured into marketing him as the next Lulu. It seems 'Pants' were his only bankable asset and he needed a hit from us - and fast.

PART 22:
SHABBY SPORTSWEAR

We were duly summoned to Dudley's office for yet another meeting, 'My exploding Zip' had been mixed, mastered and had been pressed almost immediately the minute we left the studios. Dudley had gone down in our estimation as the bloke we once trusted to help and guide us through our career and he now seemed as fickle as everyone else in the music bizz. Back at the office he was less bullish and almost apologetic.

'You knew the score boys' he sighed.

Graeme and I simply sat down in silence eating from a fresh plate of chocolate hob knobs.

'Look at it this way, this could be the beginning of a new chapter in Pants history' offered Dudley somewhat unconvincingly.

'We're a rock band!!!! Not some sell out one hit wonder shite that you've turned us into' replied Graeme with me nodding vigorously in agreement, trying not to spit hob knob everywhere.

This was a very uncomfortable moment for both the band and Dudley. I personally hadn't felt so uncomfortable since I accidentally sat on Grace Jones's lipstick in the green room before a TV appearance in Belgium where we were both appearing a while back. Grace Jones had often been praised for her unique sense of style and uncompromising use of makeup, but she hadn't noticed that her cherry red lippy was in fact a new shade of brown that evening.

Dudley had obviously decided that there was no point in any further small talk and cut straight to the chase.

'We.... or more accurately you; are going to make a new video for my exploding Zip' he announced very matter of factly. To fair we knew it was coming and were frankly resigned to it. Ordinarily it wouldn't have bothered us and we would have actually enjoyed it had we any faith in the song we were promoting.

Dudley then continued to explain the plans in as much detail as he thought we needed to know. Thirty seconds later he was finished giving us the details.

Apparently we were going to Gateshead to film a video. The original plan was to shoot it in New York, but to keep the budget down there was a compromise, so Gateshead it was.

Early the next Friday morning both Graeme and I turned up at the meeting point, ten minutes walk from the tramp wash centre and eerily close to 'The hot beef dip and boiled Onion exchange' where Graeme had first met Constance.

It was cold and we were tired but at least there was a catering van supplied for the crew and us, although its limited selection of tea and pea's pudding butties or; coffee with deep fried cheese and Whelks for the more sophisticated pallet was a tad disappointing, although to be fair, we both enjoyed the cheese.

The storyboard was simple enough. We were both to strut along the street in time with the song, looking as cool and mean as we possibly could. Every now and then a girl would approach us wearing very little, (but just enough to still be aired at prime time). We would take it in turns to pretend to snog them for a couple of seconds then move on. This was to last for the full duration of the song. Simple!

Apparently special effects were to be added later. This was to be in the form of our zips exploding each time we snogged a girl. We weren't too pleased with the concept it has to be said; I remember Graeme spending ages on the original lyrics. It was meant to be a bittersweet love song with heartfelt observations on the frailty of modern day relationships. Instead, the video was giving the impression that 'My Exploding Zip' was about nothing more than 'shallow bragging about sexual conquests with a series of loose women'! There was a bonus of course! We got to kiss a load of models hired in for the shoot – or so we thought anyway. In fact, only two were brought in and they weren't from a top agency either.

To save money Dudley had asked for a couple of girls to be rounded up who he had seen earlier that week hanging round the Metro centre sharing a cigarette. They were both willing to do it for a packet 20 superkings each and as much pea's pudding as they could eat. The plan was that they would wear a different skirt or top with a new wig on each appearance. As they were entering the frame from behind the camera, you never got to see their faces. This, we were told would give the illusion of a dozen or so women shaking their 'booty' in our direction. Just as well their faces weren't to be seen we thought, because beautiful, they most certainly weren't. In fact they gave us problems from the off. Firstly; they were over an hour late, then they insisted on chips and cheese pasties instead of pea's pudding, they also smoked all 20 of their cigarettes in about an hour, and then demanded 20 more each. They then announced that they had been fined by inspectors on the Metro system for not paying their fare and blamed us 'Coz they wouldn't be on the *'metty'* in the first place if they didn't have to come here for the video' So Dudley had to give them ten pound each to pay the fine. But the biggest problem was that they refused to wear the skirts and tops that had been especially bought in. They weren't told about what they had to wear until the last minute and because they weren't professionals or had any type of contract for that matter, they refused flatly and insisted on wearing their own clothes. It was too late to get some new girls in so Dudley had to give in to them. This was getting worse. Had we really sunk this low? Because of this unexpected downturn in quality me and Graeme then added to Dudley's problems and decided that we weren't going to kiss them either. A quick rewrite was in order and it was decided that girls would simply dance in front of us instead.

So in summary: the video for 'My Exploding Zip' was now a cheap misrepresentative display of misogynistic bollocks set in Gateshead, *not New York* - featuring two chav girls wearing shabby sportswear and trainers with cheap over sized earrings dangling round their 'love bite' ridden necks with foul smelling breath, dancing very badly to our song which had been re-recorded and remixed to sound like some cool New York groove *thang* that neither Graeme or I really liked anyway. Brilliant!

This was the low point of our career. There was very little money coming in, Dudley had blown all the budget for our re - launch on DJ Mark Spanners fees, session musicians and a dog, *possibly a corgi* and left very little for a top notch video or promotion, which seemed to be doing little to enhance our dwindling career. In fact Graeme and I firmly believed it would do us more harm than good, especially with the unnecessary addition of these ill mannered, foul smelling chav girls spoiling the vibe.

The cheapness and simplicity however was also our saving grace, as at least the video didn't take long to complete and at about 7.30 pm, the day was done. Both Graeme and I had strutted up and down the same street over and over, badly mimed to some unconvincing rap version of our song. Ate copious amounts of fried cheese and Whelks and watched with helpless dismay as the two chav girls changed wigs for each take and gyrated their flabby bodies for the camera, thankfully never showing their faces for 'technical reasons' (although we knew it was also in the name of good taste and decency)! This all seemed a far cry from our first foray into the world of video with Hector Fish's more glamorous and professional approach when we made the video for 'Squeaky Walk' in a trouser shop. I wondered if Duran Duran ever had similar problems whilst filming the video for 'Rio'. One thing is for certain; I bet they had a better choice of snacks in the catering van.

PART 23:
SHABBY REVIEW

We had hit an all time low and even Dudley, whom we had trusted implicitly, seemed distant and not looking after our best interests, he in turn was feeling the heat from his boss 'Shadwell Brown' because we were no longer selling in the quantities expected and neither were other artists on the roster. 'Chumley Biscuit' was a disastrous signing whom had blow his entire advance on a medium sized snail farm, then ran off to Belgium with his Welsh girlfriend refusing to do any publicity, or even write anymore songs. Then in a dramatic fit of pique he committed suicide by shooting himself in the head – twice, claiming that the popular teatime soap Neighbours had 'lost its soul'. In his suicide note he wrote,

"Neighbours has lost its soul. I can't take anymore story lines of such vacuous and irrelevant pomposity anymore - the earlier episodes had characters that were more rounded and the story lines felt relevant to my life. I know my good friend and pianist Clive insists

that I should fill the void by watching Eastenders but I can't. Neighbours is the one for me, but it's just not the same with Hilda Ogden gone and the Dingle family don't seem to hold my interest. Because of this; life just simply isn't worth living".

His girlfriend wasn't affected too badly by all accounts as she was more of an Eastenders fan and has since moved to Norway with Chumley's pianist, Clive.

Now 'Strangely Brown Records' was a small independent label and times were hard and they certainly couldn't afford to lose their investment without any return so early. They relied on the loyal following of fans of bands on their small roster who in turn fed from the kudos and credibility that the weekly and monthly mags such as the NME, Q magazine, Kerrang and 'What Fish monthly' gave. Other bands signed up before and not long after our signing such as punky poppers 'Penelope Chissle and the Crumpet Lickers' were all very good, but were a million miles from the top 40. As were 'Glorious Fudge Bucket' whose exciting and eclectic mix of Rockabilly and highland folk music had very little impact on radio daytime play lists. In short; Dudley was relying on 'Pants' to hold the label together and he would do what ever it took to get another hit, regardless of our artistic integrity or so called '*hipness*'.

The reviews however were less than sympathetic with one oily rag describing 'My Exploding Zip – Spanner Mix' as:

'*.....An outrageous attempt to gain favour with the clubbing classes, facile in its conception, futile in its release and shabby in its choice of dog. Quite why DJ Spanner got involved with these tools is anyone's guess but I suggest he wakes himself up as soon as possible with a hefty doze of smelling salts to help obliterate the foul smell of 'cash in' mixed with a generous helping of putrid trouser gas masquerading as pants. Shame on all those involved in this shambolic abortion of a record that should by rights be burned on its release before it pollutes the shelves of honest record shops up and down this fair land.*'

We tried to look at the positives from this review but decided after much reading over and over and analyzing of the clever journalistic word play, that there wasn't really much positive to take from it. Mind you; the choice of the dog, 'possibly a corgi' was what probably spoilt the finished mix and THAT was Spanners fault! Unfortunately it wasn't the only bad review either, with one paper describing it as '*...Worse than kissing your gran goodbye only for her tongue to slip into your mouth*'. Again positives were looked for, but with the exception of your gran happening to be Joan Collins, or Lulu; there seemed little to console us.

These were our first bad reviews and it hit us hard; Very hard. Dudley however wasn't overly concerned. Where as Graeme and I felt the criticism badly, Dudley's only concern was shifting units and a couple of bad reviews rarely made a difference to chart positions; although 'Dog & Hounds – the sniffers guide' was surprisingly quite positive giving it a four out of five 'bark' rating and actually applauded the use of dog - 'Possibly a corgi'.

MTV were now looping our Gateshead based video ten times a day and the commercial aspect of our song was certainly making it more palatable for your average day time radio listener. Had we sold out? Had we dismantled the very soul of 'Pants' hoping for a quick buck with a radio friendly watered down version of our song? The answer was well and truly - YES WE BLOODY HAD! Worse though was the fact that we didn't even want to do it in the first place and none of this was our doing. It was actually Dudley and

'Strangely Brown Records' that got twitchy and repackaged us for commercial gain: The bastards.

Back in Dudley's office the MTV channel was on his wall mounted television just left of the turtle tank - which always stank! Lo and behold our video was on; we sat back and watched, squinting through painful eyes as if watching a particularly gruesome horror film. It was the first time either Graeme or I had watched it and it wasn't the nicest of experiences I can tell you. I never really felt comfortable at photo shoots and as for videos? Well I enjoyed the crack and had a laugh but always felt self conscious at seeing myself, even the expensive shiny trousers and spanking new gaffer tape on my glasses didn't help my overriding fear of looking like a complete twat. Graeme wasn't as bad as me though and being the front man in the band had made him more comfortable and confident in front of cameras, especially video cameras where he always felt he could 'bust a move'; which he did, quite often.

The video was laughable and not the type of thing we would normally have wanted to do; even our earlier 'Hector Fish' directed video in the trouser shop – although also cheap, had a cooler 'indie' feel to it. This was just cheap and tacky without the cool! It looked right for MTV mind; letter box style framing, wind machine, low camera angles looking up at us rather than straight on with soft focus, although this was as much to avoid getting the tramp wash centre in the frame as much as anything else. Even the chav girls looked presentable with their backs to the camera, wearing shades. Also the fact that they were only on screen a few seconds with their odious cheap track suits, slightly blurred certainly helped. Then as each girl spun away after dancing suggestively in front of us for a couple of seconds, the special FX were introduced and our Zips exploded. Dudley had hired the services of special FX and CGI expert 'Sebastian Pittlebottom', or 'Bill' as he preferred to be called, who had apparently worked on amongst others, 'Dr Who', Star Trek', 'Blade Runner' and 'Bagpuss'; Although it later transpired that he actually only worked on bagpuss for one week - and was then sacked for giving the little puppet mice unrealistic proportions in certain areas which the producers thought 'highly inappropriate'. We never did find out where that was.

To be fair, the exploding zip effect didn't look too bad and actually looked like…well……an exploding zip! Exploding zips apart, the video wasn't great and highly unlikely to win any awards soon. It was simply a means to an end. We needed MTV coverage and the video was the only way. Three tiresome minutes later and it was all over and as the credits appeared in the corner of the screen -

'My exploding Zip'

'Pants – Spanner Mix'

'Strangely Brown Records'

We gave a little sigh, a sigh that said, I'm not happy about this but there's little we can do and besides it might make some money and at least the exploding zip effect looked OK and it could be worse we could be working in a sausage factory for minimum wage or part time in a cabbage van.'

Dudley seemed pleased and spinning round on his chair gave a cautious 'thumbs up' in our direction. Graeme offered another digit from his hand in reply - but it wasn't a thumb. Ignoring this he continued.

'Ok boys, the mid week chart positions are out tomorrow so lets keep our fingers crossed. I believe this'll be a hit!'

Graeme and I didn't answer and just continued throwing curried peanuts into the turtle tank. Tomorrow would be 'make or break' for us. If our bastardised song was looking like a flop things could be very grim for us indeed, if it was looking like it could be a hit…..things could be very grim for us indeed. The only difference being that we might be able to afford to buy some new socks. Silver linings and all that!

PART 24:
CURRIED TURTLE NIBBLETS

Later the next day I received a call from Graeme, it seemed we were looking at a possible top 20 hit despite the less than favourable reviews. Dudley was right about that at least, it didn't matter what the likes of the NME thought if thousands of kids hear the song ten times a day it will catch on. Dudley asked us in to the office for a quick meeting/celebration and even though we felt very uncomfortable with the idea we went along with it anyway.

Immediately on our arrival we were treated with a can of lager, curried turtle nibblets and a large slice of blackberry pie and cream. The turtle smell had gone, which was a relief because they really did stink the office out, in fact; so had the turtles, although we weren't sure where. The only smell in his office now was one of success - and Blackberry pie – and curried Turtle nibblets. Dudley was determined to celebrate, but more importantly, he wanted us onside.

‘Boy’s! I really want you on side’ he announced as he held aloft a lukewarm can of lager in a celebratory toast.

‘Here’s to the continued success *and* evolution of Pants!’

Both Graeme and I clanked our cans together with Dudley’s in what can be best described as ‘sufficiently enthusiastic enough to be polite’. Dudley ignored our obvious indifference and gulped greedily from his can of lager. He then continued.

‘Listen boys. It looks like we’ve got a hit to celebrate and I for one couldn’t be happier. It would nice if you could at least show a degree of enthusiasm!’

I couldn’t answer as I had a mouth full of Blackberry pie. Graeme declined to give comment as well, although that may have been something to do with the mouth full of curried Turtle nibblets he was struggling to swallow, which were surprisingly more-ish. Dudley continued regardless.

‘OK boys we’ve an appearance on Blue Peter this Thursday so let’s make it a good one.’

Now there was a time gone by where an appearance on every child’s favourite ‘tea time Sticky back plastic endorsing, pet loving and altogether comfortable, enjoyable TV accompaniment with fish fingers and alphabet spaghetti in the living room programme' - would have got me a little excited. But not now; now we had aspired to bigger things and an altogether cooler more discerning market. It wasn't that long ago we were on Glastonbury! Now this! Blue Fucking Peter!

The thought of Blue Peter opened memories of days gone by, particularly the time when my mam opened another tin of alphabet spaghetti only to find to her frustration that once again it was all 'O's and not a exciting mix of 'A's and 'B's with the odd 'Z' thrown in for good measure. Her patience had run out and she sent the offending tin back with a strongly worded letter of complaint. Two weeks later she had a reply with the offending tin returned and a curt letter enclosed explaining that she had in fact bought a tin of Spaghetti hoops! So there it was; Blue Peter with Fish Fingers and Spaghetti hoops on my knee was a strong childhood memory. As was 'Top of the Pops', and it was 'Top of the Pops' (amongst others), that I strongly associated with music not Blue Peter, which I associated with sticky back plastic and tortoises'. Neither Graeme nor I had any desire to sell ourselves out even further by appearing on a children's tea time show and that was final.

That Thursday we arrived at the BBC and made our way to the Blue Peter studios. For all intense purposes we looked like a couple of school boys being unwillingly dragged to the barbers to get our haircut, so to say we had a spring in our step would be an outright lie. We were greeted by a floor manager and shown to our dressing room, which to be fair was very clean and sturdy, with no hint of sticky back plastic, although we were warned that we would be sharing with 'Gordon' the tortoise and the Blue Peter cat 'Snuffy', the previous cat 'McClain' had been killed in a fight just three weeks earlier and some of the floor staff and presenters were still in mourning. It seems that Snuffy was sensing that he was second best and thus; was a very temperamental cat indeed, because of this we had to tread carefully.

'Don't sit in that chair' warned the slightly camp floor manager, pointing at a chair in front of a big mirror.

'That's Snuffy's.' We decided it best not to, it didn't do to upset the regular staff.

About half an hour later 'Walter Chigley' one of the presenters came in to say hello. He was a friendly young man who was no where near the obnoxious coke sniffing; womanizing egotistical fop the press had painted him out to be. Luckily for him the BBC had stood by him and he managed to keep his job. At least he came to say hello unlike Snuffy or Gordon and Graeme wasn't too impressed that the other two presenters 'Wayne Shrimp' and 'Jenny Soil' hadn't made the effort.

A few minutes later the then producer of Blue Peter, 'Clarissa Flannelette' came to see us and give us our final briefing. Myself, Graeme and Dudley listened intently as she read through the show's running order. We were to follow the segment were 'Jenny' shows how to make a 'Sticky back plastic holder' from house hold socks, glue, old cereal boxes and sticky back plastic. It was to be going out live, at tea time; so there was to be definitely no lewdness or erotic gesturing of any kind, nor was there to be any hint of mouthing swearwords or vulgar finger signs in any shape or form. If we did, not only would we lose our fee but we could be sued for breech of contract and banned from ever appearing on any BBC programme ever again, and that included 'Top of the Pops'. All we had to do was mime to our song. Funnily enough the fact that it was called 'My Exploding Zip' didn't seem to be a problem. We agreed of course, besides there was nothing we could do even if we wanted to, we had already signed the contract.

Not much later, around tea time in fact, there was a buzz about the place as Blue Peter began what seemed like its millionth live transmission. We were on standby and ready to go on at the end, following Jenny's item. Gordon and Snuffy had taken their places on the couch and were consummate professionals. Our gear was set up behind them and was almost always in camera shot as Walter, Wayne and Jenny rambled on about the environment then jumped around enthusiastically as they took it in turns to talk about the perils of eating yellow snow. A few minutes later Wayne showed the nation's children how to make nut flapjacks and it has to be said, he looked every inch the professional chef in this item. Jenny's segment was slightly off to the left and gave us the chance to get ourselves ready without being on camera. Before we knew it, Jenny had built her sticky back plastic holder and the three of them huddled together in front of the couch as Walter began his introduction of the band.

“Well that’s it for today; we hope you enjoyed the show and now to close us out, one our favourite bands, singing their new single, ‘My Exploding Cake’ its PANTS!”

And with that the three of them turned around to us, clapping wildly as the previously bright white studio lights turned to a flashing red and green affair and our song kicked in through the monitors. To be honest we both just went through the motions and gave very little to this mime, unlike our first Top of the Pops appearance where our enthusiasm and excitement made the whole occasion special. It just didn’t feel like us and the re-mix hadn’t really grown on us as Dudley had promised. There were bits I quite liked to be fair and the dog bark ‘possibly a corgi’ *had* actually grown on me a little but Graeme hated it, which was unsurprising really as there were hardly any audible guitars in the mix. Three and a half minutes later it was all over as Blue Peter’s familiar theme echoed round the studios monitors and Jenny, Wayne and Walter disappeared, as did Gordon and Snuffy. An unfamiliar crew began to dismantle our gear and we were whisked away into a waiting car. No autographs, no fuss, not even a thank you from Clarrisa who disappeared quicker than the nut flapjacks that the camera crew greedily snaffled in one go. The ruthless machine that was Blue Peter had stopped for one day only to return the next and there was no time for sentiment or niceties. Oh how we yearned for our world back, a world of gigs and rock and roll abandonment, proper riders as well and not just nut flapjack crumbs. I was depressed and Graeme wasn't too happy either. 'What next?' we wondered as the streets of that thar London blurred past the car window on the way back to our 'B n B'. The following Sunday the charts were out and just as Dudley said, the word was that we had made the top twenty.

PART 25:
MORE DOGS.

As my alarm clock shocked me into life, I realised that annoyingly; I had missed Jeremy Kyle, again; although I suppose it would help if I actually set my alarm early enough to get up in order to watch it. Another alternative of course was to record it and watch it at my leisure which was preferable as I didn't have top get up! Ah the subtle life choices that can make so much difference to the outcome of a day, or even a week or more. Now I enjoy Jeremy Kyle I have to admit. His placating, soothing, yet uniquely authoritative tones and understated presence always made me feel that alls well with the world. I also enjoyed laughing at the sub human freaks that he wheeled out day after day seemingly brought in for nothing more than the baying public to cringe at. Each morning a parade of fubugly Chav girls with unwashed hair and flabby buttocks squeezed into ill fitting shell suits, announce on national television that they might not know who has fathered some poor unfortunate baby they've spawned. Meanwhile a parade of equally monosyllabic chav 'lads' seemingly going out of there way to look scruffy argue the toss over who may or may not be the father - mainly because none of them can remember due to taking copious amounts of drugs. And who said our nations future is in doubt? Now that's top telly!

Not long after munching into a custard muffin I heard the news from Dudley that 'My Exploding Zip' had indeed made the top twenty – in at number twenty. I felt mixed emotions to be honest, I was happy that we had charted and the few quid we'd make was always welcome, but I couldn't help feeling that it wasn't really 'us' and I felt equally haunted by the 'sell out' tag. Many a time I had slagged other bands off for sounding exactly like what we did now and I don't mind admitting, it didn't feel comfortable.

Graeme was equally uncomfortable; although that had more to do with underpants he had bought the previous week from 'World of Underpants' in that thar London. In a vain attempt to make his 'undercarriage' look bigger he thought it would be a good idea to wear keks two sizes smaller than he needed. I understood the thinking but doubted it would work, and I was right. I advised him to go for at least three sizes smaller for the full effect, in fact even go for children's sizes! Although Thomas the Tank Engine underpants wouldn't really look that sexy, no matter what was in them. He decided to play safe and ended up in discomfort – And with no real enhancement effect. Still; being the consummate professional, he soldiered on.

In truth Graeme felt numb, and it wasn't his tight underwear either. We had a hit but it didn't feel real. To make matters worse we hadn't even wrote a new song in ages and the buzz had gone from the band. Unsurprisingly our top twenty entry had accelerated our media duties and a small number of telly appearances had been scheduled throughout the week; including a quick sound bite for MTV, a sad two minute interview for a new kids TV music show called, 'Popping in Your Face' and an appearance on another Saturday morning show called 'Sounds of the Crescent'. This was an updated version of 'Sounds of the Street' that was supposedly aimed at a more middle class market. It was rubbish, but we were scheduled to appear in a promotional drive to push our song further up the charts. As well as all this tedious media stuff, where we were asked the same questions time and time again, we also had a couple of press interviews but NOT the NME or Kerrang but instead with childish pop glossy's like 'Kidz Noyz' and a new publication simply called 'Kerrting' the supposed 'pop' alternative to the rockier based Kerrang. What the hell were we doing this crap for? In the blink of an eye we had turned into some dour run of the mill 'pop' band. Worse; was the fact that our original following had seemed to have moved on and saw us as little more than some sort of pop sell out and to add insult to injury, the younger ones didn't really get us anyway because we weren't pretty enough! We were basically caught between two stools and had lost all direction, although Graeme did receive a letter from his Gran saying that she thought we were much better now but just needed to sack the drummer! One interview was with 'Dogs & Hounds: the Sniffers Guide' who constantly questioned us about the use of a dog 'Possibly a Corgi' on the single and wondered if indeed a 'Yorkshire Terrier' would have made a better choice. It went as follows:

IS THERE A DODGY DOG IN PANTS?

As another chapter of this interesting but troubled band enfolds, I met up with the lads to discuss their new single; a remix of an old favourite, 'My Exploding Zip' which has just charted in at number twenty. Throughout this groovy little number you can quite clearly hear what I believe to be our old friend 'the Corgi'. Its unique bark brings a strange feel to the song which some have questioned as an odd choice. I'm here to try *and get to the bottom of this and see if there were any viable alternatives to this strange and curious breed which has often caused controversy amongst many of us across the country, including Princess Anne!*

'I noticed that during the song that a dog 'possibly a Corgi' is used quite liberally throughout. Was this a conscious decision to enhance the rhythmical flow of the song or was it simply a case of – 'oh that sounds good….put it in'.

GB: *'Well it wasn't anything to do with us really; it was mainly DJ Spanner's work'*

Are you saying that you had no artistic control of this song? Sounds a bit mental!

GB: *'I couldn't care because we didn't choose the dog'*

'Surely though you could have stepped in as the use of a Yorkshire Terrier may have been a better choice!'

GB: *'Yeh you could be right, but as I said; it was nothing to do with us'*

'I quite like the song and I'm sure it'll be a top hit, but I must take issue with the choice of dog. Of all the breeds out there I don't think you could have picked a worse one, even a cross breed may have done a more professional job, with appropriate training of course'

GB: *'Well you should take it up with DJ Spanner, he chose it.'*

'Did you not think that saying that as it's your song, that you could have stepped in at some point! After all I'm sure with a little delicate negotiation you could have used any of say.... a 'Nova Scotia Duck Tolling Retriever', or perhaps a 'Petit Basset Griffon Vendeen' or at a push an 'Affen Pinscher',....all fine dogs.'

GB: *'I don't really understand what you're saying. It's a remix of an old song and had very little to do with us. Honest! I'm not really an expert on dogs or their contribution to pop music'*

'Well I think a basic understanding would help anyone involved in music. Surely the two cannot be separated?'

GB: *'Are you talking about rock music? I've often heard that politics and music can be linked but dogs and music?*

Well it would help in interviews such as this or even our sister publication, 'Nice Tails Bi - Monthly'

Me: *'I quite like the Bernese Mountain dog'*

'Ah yes! a fine dog indeed, but I doubt its general low frequency bark would have suited the ambience of your song'

Me: *'Hmmm fair point'.*

'Are there any other projects in the pipe line that may involve dogs?'

GB: *'Well unless you count your lass. No, I'm off'*

And with that Graeme was off. This concluded our interview and I for one am more than a little disappointed with Graeme's attitude as this certainly sets a bad example to the more impressionable followers of this band.

Next week I'll be speaking exclusively to Duran Duran about 'Cavalier King Charles Spaniels' – and their influences on the writing of 'The Reflex'.

Needless to say this negative publicity wouldn't have helped our career, especially as we were still reeling from the Richard & Judy debacle. Although to be honest, I felt my own contribution was quite incisive. Dudley wasn't impressed though and only hoped that this poor interview didn't adversely affect our chances of climbing the charts. He was sure it wouldn't though as our video was still being looped regularly on MTV and top of the play lists on radio stations up and down the country. However he decided to pull the interview with 'Trombone Monthly' – Just to be on the safe side.

As for me and Graeme, we had passed caring.

PART 26:
BAKEWELL TART

The following week we had fell to number 28, despite my contribution in the interview for 'Dogs & Hounds – the Sniffers guide' magazine - and predictably our single was no longer being looped as regularly as it had been on the music channels or the radio. Graeme, seemingly unperturbed rang me to give me the news that he had written a new song and wondered if I'd fancy coming round to work on it with him. I told him I'd be round after Jeremy Kyle, about three o'clock. It wasn't strictly after Jeremy Kyle, but that was what time I would be finished watching it after successfully recording it for the first time.

I arrived about ten to six and he greeted me with a smile, a can of lager, three slices of cheese and a small Bakewell tart. In his newly refurbished 'rumpus room' he had a massive hi-fi system, and hundreds of CD's, an old but comfy looking sofa, about five guitar amplifiers… actually; after counting them it was four. He also had his guitars neatly hanging on stands and a bewildering array of effects pedals spread all over the room, both on shelves and on the floor. There was also a recorder and mixing desk, a pudding mixer, an electric piano, a mandolin, a banjo, three penny whistles, a small slightly rusty trumpet and a small vocal PA with about six microphones…actually after counting them there was only two. There was also a drum machine, (which he tried to hide from me but I knew he had it) and nestled in the corner was an ironing board. In the other corner was a small fridge packed with lager and cheese. I remember thinking that this was money wisely spent and the perfect musicians hide away, although he had skimped a little on the quality of the pudding mixer. It was all a far cry from my pad, which had little more than a drum kit, a small stool, another drum kit and a slightly smaller drum kit packed tightly in the corner next to a tea trolley – which I never used. Although I did have a natty little trouser press that I'm pretty sure Graeme was envious of.

I sat slurping from my can as Graeme burst into his new idea. Within moments of him plugging in, the room filled with a cacophony of crashing guitar chords under a searing melody played at a very fast tempo. 'Ahhh this was more like it' I thought as I greedily chomped on a very tasty Bakewell tart. Within three very short minutes it was over and as he turned the volume knob down on his guitar he looked up and excitedly asked.

'Well! What do you think?'

'Brilliant' was my honest reply as Bakewell tart crumbs spat out my mouth. Graeme was unperturbed by my uncouth table manners, besides; this was his 'rumpus room' and anything goes. Graeme wanted to get in the studio and record it as soon as possible and wanted my input with the drums and any arrangement suggestions I may have had.

'Wouldn't mind your input with the drums and any arrangement ideas you may have.' He politely asked.

I already knew what type of beat I could play as he began playing it again, where upon I simply suggested a break down in the middle section to allow the song to breathe. Graeme agreed and we started to get it together from start to finish. For the first time in a while I felt a tinge of excitement as we worked on his idea, a tinge I hadn't felt since the popular evening soap 'Emmerdale Farm' changed its title to 'Emmerdale'. This could be a new beginning for 'Pants' we thought, getting back on track, getting back to the way we used to be and enjoying our music and hopefully, reawakening our fans who had since moved on and even perhaps winning some new ones.

'What's this song going to be called?' I asked, still spitting Bakewell tart over his carpet.

'Hmmm, not sure yet. I've a couple of working titles' Graeme replied, very clearly rejuvenated by this invigorating creative streak.

'Aye, what are they then'? I enquired, leaning forward in anticipation.

'Well the songs about our troubles over the last few months and how fickle the industry is... It's like an attack on all those phoneys at the top that don't care about the music and just want to see shifting units, profit margins, bottom lines, marketable territories with target demographics. Shiny videos and plastic pop with manufactured songs that have no meaning or relevance to our lives... Over produced pap that pollutes the airwaves at the expense of REAL music and honest bands out there, doing it for real, sweating over a guitar...or a piano...creating something that's true and has feeling and depth, power and passion...Something that says...YES THIS IS MY LIFE, THAT'S WHAT I FEEL!!'

Graeme was nothing if not passionate about the art of song writing. I sat silently for a few moments as I digested his heartfelt outburst.

'Well?'

'Either – 'Spank Her Daft' or 'Jump Me Bones'

Now I didn't mind 'Jump me Bones' as it had a bit of a ring to it, but 'Spank her Daft' was a bit…well…ordinary sounding I thought.

'How about…Suck my Sack,' I tentatively suggested. Graeme pondered for a second.

'Aye. I like that' he excitedly replied. I was happy because I hadn't had much input over song titles in the past as Graeme always wrote the lyrics and consequently thought of the title.

So, we agreed over a fresh can of lager that 'Suck my Sack' was to be the title of our new single and I for one could not have been happier.

Dudley however wasn't happier, in fact he was decidedly unhappy. He was happy that we were writing new songs but unhappy with the direction we were taking. Altogether that was a 'mish mash' of happiness and unhappiness that could only mean one thing, a battle to be happiest. Both Graeme and I were determined it was going to be US sitting on the happy bus, but Dudley held our passes and it wasn't going to be easy.

'I'm sorry boys, but we're not prepared to put you in the studio at the moment and certainly not to record a song called 'Suck my Sack!' - It ain't going to happen', Came Dudley's curt reply to our request to book us some studio time. Basically the remix of 'My Exploding Zip' hadn't made as much money as he had hoped due to its short stay in the charts and he was even more adamant that 'Strangely Brown Records' were not going to waste more money recording and releasing a brand new song which would be banned everywhere and therefore end up being a flop. Even if we changed the title as Graeme suggested to the more radio friendly 'Eat some Cake', Dudley wasn't interested. He had heard the demo version and basically didn't like it. Nor did he believe it would be a hit. Things had become sour between our record label and us, but more worryingly they were no longer supporting us in any shape or form. We were in limbo and contractual obligations meant that we couldn't simply go out and do it ourselves, even if we had the financial clout and know-how, which we didn't.

Later that week we had a meeting to try and sort things out between the label and ourselves. Basically we felt that 'Strangely Brown Records' were no longer supporting us and we wanted to know why, and to see if there was anything that could be done to get things moving again.

In Dudley's office the atmosphere was very frosty and both Graeme and I were no longer prepared to play ball. The remix of 'My Exploding Zip' was a sham and the video was even worse, it had charted but not very high and then fell out of the charts again after only one week. So! We wanted to know what they were prepared to do about it, especially as they weren't interested in releasing our new song.

Dudley was surprisingly friendly as he greeted us with a small plate of assorted pickles and crisps. We suspiciously accepted his hospitality and once more sat on his office sofa, an office that was rid of turtle smell but had a slight whiff of wet dog.

He started the moment we got ourselves comfortable.

'Listen boys, I know things have been tough and we haven't been seeing eye to eye recently, but I've had a word with a few people and I think it would be a good idea to do some live shows, nothing major, just about ten or twelve dates round the country, to help kick start some interest, then we can see about releasing a new single. What do you think?'

'Why? There's no new album or even a single to promote, so what's the point?' Graeme argued. To be fair he was right, it seemed a little strange as not many bands do random tours after all.

'Its what you do best, get you going again, rejuvenate those gigging juices that you've always loved…also we've just signed a new band and we want them to support you.'

So the truth was out. It was all about giving one of the new bands on their roster some exposure. It seemed clear to us that neither Dudley nor 'Strangely Brown Records' cared about us anymore. We were yesterday's news; old hat, bent spoons and all the labels resources were being pumped into launching and promoting this new band. What could we do? In truth we had little choice in the matter and besides, after some thought we realised that it couldn't actually do us any harm. So there it was; Pants were on tour again.

PART 27:
MINCE & DUMPLINGS

We busied ourselves rehearsing for the upcoming gigs over the next few weeks and had 'Suck my Sack', which we were going to be showcasing live - tight as a Stoats pump hole, we also had another new song idea which we were desperately trying to get ready to play live, this song had the working title of, 'This Dying Planet of Fools'. Unlike 'Suck…' which was, a heartfelt tirade hitting out at the shallow elements of the music industry 'This Dying Planet of Fools' was a no nonsense rocker about drinking and casual sex and it was fast becoming a favourite of mine.

We received the tour dates and venues and it was to be a small eleven date tour of medium sized venues across the UK, starting in Glasgow and working our way down to Newcastle then way across to the North West to Manchester and Liverpool, down to Leeds, Sheffield, then the midlands with Nottingham and Birmingham, followed by a show in Oxford then that thar London, finishing in Ipswich. The support was confirmed as 'Mince & Dumplings' who had recently been signed by Dudley after accidentally catching them live at a small pork and wine bar whilst on his way to check out another band from Cornwall. He got lost and ended up at their gig instead, liked what he saw and he asked for a demo, which they duly sent. Like us they were a two-piece but had bass guitar as well as electric lead, however; they used a drum machine and samplers. I didn't like them, even though I hadn't even heard them; or met them yet. It was a point of principle, simple as that, I had my views on things and there were standards I had set myself. Now call me old fashioned but I refused to give them the time of day no matter how friendly they may be. I simply didn't like people from Barnstable.

'Mince & Dumplings' had been gigging all over Devon and got themselves a bit of a following, especially amongst 'dog breeders' and 'custard manufacturers' who were almost fanatical in their support. They comprised of Stuart Mince on Guitar/vocals and Arnold Carrot on Bass, who also did all the programming. It seems they weren't too keen on the name of 'Mince & Carrot' as it sounded a bit stupid so opted for 'Mince & Dumplings'. Arnold didn't mind by all accounts and has actually added 'Dumplings' by deed poll as his middle name. Of course their name did cause some confusion in pubs that served meals in and around the Devonshire area, as occasionally people would turn up, pay their five pounds and end up with a large plate of Mince & Dumplings with potatoes, veg and gravy, when they were actually expecting a two piece rock band with pre-programmed drums. 'Mince &Dumplings' typically thought that the confusion would gain them publicity and had no intention of changing their name and to be fair, they were right. It made the local news and was referred to as the 'Dumpling stand off'. It soon blew over though as pub owners were making money from the confusion and the band themselves even managed to get a few more people to their gigs as one or two punters would often arrive, think they were getting a plate of 'Mince & Dumplings' for a couple of quid, only to find themselves watching a two piece rock band with pre-programmed drums. Nice one.

Our first show was at Glasgow's Barrowlands and to our embarrassment wasn't fully sold out. I remember meeting the lads from 'Mince & Dumplings' for the first time during our sound check. They stood near the mixing desk while my new immigrant drum tech 'Ahoy Hoy' thumped my kick drum over and over while our sound engineer for the tour 'Walter Whumlsley' or 'Chez' as he preferred to be called, attempted to get a good sound. Half an hour later he managed to get some actual volume through the speakers and moved on to the snare. He was shite. Graeme still used Harry Witless, as not only was he his guitar tech - but also his friend now. They were back stage tuning up, comparing nuts and eating whelks, leaving me to make small talk with the 'mince boys' as we called them.

Through gritted teeth I attempted conversation.

'So how's it going?' I lamely asked. The fact that I couldn't get the thought out of my head that these two twats had usurped us as 'Strangely Brown Records' new darlings and effectively made us redundant, didn't help with my less than friendly welcome; Also they were from Barnstable.

'Yeh good thanks, quite excited if the truth be known' Arnold replied.

I resisted the urge to grill them about not using real drums as to be fair; we had had enough similar questions about having no bass guitarist. Well, I resisted for about three seconds anyway.

‘What’s the matter, couldn’t find a good enough drummer in Barnstable?’ I asked with more than a hint of bitchiness in my tone. They refused to be unsettled by my tone and answered quite matter of factly.

‘No there’s a load, it’s just that for starters they’re all about seven feet tall round our way and thick as pig shit. Also we prefer the hassle free sound of drum machines…easier to sound check!’

Of course I could have been wrong, but I’m sure I picked up a hint of sarcasm in their answer and felt decidedly uncomfortable. I stood for a few seconds thinking of a witty repost but was struggling. Damn! Where was Graeme when you needed him?

Not only was Graeme a better guitarist than this Stuart Mince but also a damn sight wittier. He had even done an evening class in witticisms which had cost him a fortune, spending over a thousand pounds on guaranteed come backs, jokes and put downs so that he’d never be out done again by cocky chat show hosts and radio presenters. At last my drum sound check was done and Graeme arrived with Harry who went off to the stage, plugged in and started checking the effects. Graeme came over and introduced himself to the ‘Mince boys’ politely asking if things were ok. To our amazement Stuart then began to complain about the measly portions of custard in the rider and Arnold 'Dumplings' Carrot wasn't impressed by the fact we hadn't sold out!

'We're only on this ere' tour for exposer and you carn't even sell out! We thought you were better than that. I don't mind admitting, I'm a tad disappointed'

Graeme and I just looked at each other in disbelieve at their cheek and arrogance.

'Probably sumfing to do with the fact that theys have no bass player in the band' added Stuart chuckling to himself.

Now they were DEFINITELY being sarcastic I thought. Graeme took a deep breath, looked Stuart Mince right in the eye and began to unleash the full force of his rapier wit, honed to perfection by his evening class training.

'FUCK OFF YOU DEVON TWATS!' and with that sauntered towards the stage to help Harry. I was impressed and also left for the stage leaving them standing alone, no doubt fuming. That was the last time 'the Mince boys' and us mixed. We never watched them play or even shared a drink or two with them. In hind site it was a shame because tours can be more fun making new friends, sharing the rider and having custard fights. By all accounts Chris de Burgh had a notorious tour where he had non-stop pillow fights with the then support band, ‘Judas Priest’. We however had ten more nights with the ‘mince boys’ as we called them, so our fun was unlikely to be in Chris de Burgh proportions. Shame.

PART 28:
CAKE & CABBAGE CONFUSION

The tour moved through Britain at a snails pace as each nights set seemed to last longer and longer, although that may have been to do with the fact that we added a couple more songs each night, including 'Suck my Sack' and 'This Dying Planet of Fools', which for me was the highlight of the night. The 'mince boys' were getting a half decent reception and it irked us a little that Dudley was watching them more than us, in fact we barely saw Dudley who was always too busy looking after our support band - the now renamed by us as *'mince and faggot'*- rather than looking after us. In fact you would think that it was them that were the headline act rather than Pants!

Each city blended into one as did each hotel room, most of the venues were similar in size and décor and it was all too easy to forget where we were. In fact I did, more than once. Actually, with the exception of the first gig in Glasgow, I forgot where we were every single night. I thought we were in Ipswich when we were in

Oxford and I thought we were in Sheffield when we were actually in Birmingham! It was only when the lighting technician pointed out to me that I had the wrong itinerary that I realised why I was so confused. I should have realised to be fair, as it is well known fact that Nottingham has no cake shops and when I thought we were in Nottingham there was in fact an abundance of cake shops, which meant we were in Liverpool. Liverpool had hundreds of cake shops but had a distinct lack of 'Cabbage retailers' as they had all been taken over by 'sportswear outlets' but when we were in Nottingham, you couldn't move for 'Cabbage retailers', which it was famed for throughout the world. It was these simple clues that I should have looked for as we entered each city. That thar London of course was easier to guess, as it stank of shit.

In truth, despite the confusion over which city we were playing in, the odious, arrogant support band that was now clearly favoured by Dudley our so-called manager and despite quite enjoying thwacking the shite out of my drum kit and the new songs, there was something missing, and it wasn't just my new rolls of gaffer tape either. Our rider was pathetic. No custard or glamorous flavoured yoghurt and the selection of flavours amongst the two bowels of crisps was poor, with one bowel being ready salted and the other being…ready salted, as I had discovered to my disappointment one night. The alcohol supplied was also quite poor with no Jack Daniels or any other such luxuries. No! For us it was a twelve pack of 'ace lager'. There was a small bowel of whelks in the corner of the dresser but little else and they never lasted long. Now although we tried not to let it affect our performances we couldn't get out of our heads that this was the beginning of the end. More tellingly than the feeble rider however were the general ticket sales, had we fallen from grace so quickly? It only seemed like yesterday that we were playing Glastonbury, (although Graeme reminded me that that was because I had been watching the video of it on the tour bus yesterday). The only gig to sell out on the whole tour was Newcastle, were we first cut our teeth as a new up and coming band. Even there it was mainly due to an abundance of guest list passes for all our friends and family who helped fill the venue. Well all except Graeme's Gran who stayed in to watch 'The Bill'.

No; things were definitely coming to an abrupt end and it was painful to accept I don't mind admitting. At our penultimate show in that thar London only six hundred tickets sold for a two thousand capacity venue, the worst yet. This wasn't helped by the fact that Dudley, or anyone else for that matter failed to get it advertised properly so the only ones who really knew about it were our fan club members who comprised mainly of bus conductors and a few window cleaners who were still loyal to the 'Pants' sound. Despite being cockney bus conductors they were just as passionate as the northern bus conductors and gave us a rapturous reception, but the barely third full venue didn't help us in our quest to go up a few gears in our performance. Neither did the slightly musty and faint odour of shit that seemed to hang in the air. Our set comprised of all our favourites with the new ones added, which we paid special attention to so that we could gauge audience reaction. It was quite favourable in Oxford, Newcastle and Sheffield, but in the rest there seemed little more than polite applause and just the odd whistle of approval, which was very worrying. Things were going from bad to worse and it was as if Dudley was hoping that our new songs would bomb to justify the labels lack of support. In Camden's 'Ian Beale Hall', after the final clang of guitar chords echoed around the room followed by a '*Faaalumpp*' on the drums - the reaction to 'Suck my Sack' was muted and met with little more than appreciative applause with barely a whistle or a whoop from anywhere. This tour was a bad idea I thought and the very fact that we had no new album to promote left it almost pointless and a waste of time. We had achieved little more than demoralising ourselves and only helped promote them twats 'Mince & Dumplings', who were depressingly getting better and going down well now.

Our final show in Ipswich faired a little better and the ticket sales were reasonable in the 'Thomas Wolsey Bingo, Badminton and Roller disco Emporium', a one and a half thousand capacity venue situated near the carpet district just outside the town centre. Once more we played our set of favourites including not only the new songs but also an improvised section where we pretty much jammed through a made up song that Graeme had previously been working on, it was like a live rehearsal and to be honest I quite enjoyed the freedom of not knowing what was going to happen next. It was also funny watching our hopeless soundman 'Walter' panicking, as he looked through his notes desperately trying to work out what was going on.

The mad thing is that all he had to do was keep the main faders up and do little else; after all we weren't the hardest band in the world to mix live. It was the best we had played all tour and the loyal fans that turned out to see us loved it. Also as I looked to the side of the stage I noticed 'mince & faggot' watching for the first time with more than a look of envy about them.

However; despite ending the tour on a bit of a high and just about getting away with coaxing some poor disabled kid to get up and dance. We knew that things were over. Strangely Brown Records and Dudley had lost faith in the band and no longer seemed interested in backing us anymore. All their resources seemed to be channelled into launching 'Mince & Dumplings', which to me was a desperate act and very annoying, especially as we had made them so much money in the past. Mind it was hardly surprising either, the new and suicidal signing 'Chumley Biscuit' had been disastrous as was the doomed remix of 'My Exploding Zip' and we were the only band ever to make real money on their roster, but we had also cost a lot and now we were fading, and fading fast. To make matters worse, no other labels seemed interested in taking us on so it seemed inevitable that we would visit the band graveyard soon. We would have our memories and still make money from royalties and there was no way we would stop playing, it was in our blood, but the vibe and excitement we first felt on our first 'Top of the Pops' appearance would never happen again. No longer would we be performing after a cheese flan special on 'Cheggers Kitchen of Rock' or no longer would I find myself having a shit in the toilet cubicle next to Morrissey. It felt weird but we knew it was right. Pants had to split.

PART 29:
PANTS SPLIT

We sat in the 'Mould & Dog' pub back in Newcastle sipping from our lager as Dudley walked in, still holding his overnight bag, obviously not keen on staying up north too long. We didn't offer to buy him a drink and just watched as he asked how much each beer, lager and soft drink cost before making his order. Ten minutes later he joined us at our little table in the corner with his half pint of raspberry juice.

'Ok boys, we've seen the lawyer and I think you'll find everything's above board.'

He handed us our copy of the contract and sipped from his drink. Basically everything would stay as it was, we'd still receive our royalties and 'Strangely Brown Records' would continue to make their money from further sales as usual. It's just that we would no longer make any new records for them, or for anyone else for that matter as it was clear that no one was interested in signing us anyway. Music had moved on and although there would always be a market for rock, too many labels wanted a quick fix, a quick profit and had no interest in developing bands anymore. The charts were a wash with one hit wonders, novelty bands and singers who basically had very little talent. Our song 'Suck my Sack' seemed very prophetic in hindsight and our only regret was that we didn't get to release it.

'So that's it then?' enquired Graeme.

'Guess so' replied Dudley just as I burped louder than I originally intended.

'It's been excellent working with you boys…. I wish it wasn't ending like this. I mean… do you really have to split up?'

'It's probably for the best, in truth we're not splitting…it's just that we're no longer going to exist as Pants', I answered, quite pleased with myself as it was one of the most succinct sentences I had put together in quite a while. Graeme agreed.

Dudley just sat and philosophically surveyed his surroundings. The 'Mould & Dog' was a quiet little bar not far from the local television studios away from the city centre and was a handy little place to come for meetings because there was plenty of privacy. Often presenters from various local TV shows would pop in for a drink after their programme so the bar staffs were used to serving celebrities.

I decided to remind Graeme that not only had I heard Morrissey curling one down, but also a number of local newsreaders and weathermen had plopped away within earshot. I found it difficult to watch the local news these days as I couldn't get the image of them squeezing out large arse turnips while I was happily pissing in the trough.

Suddenly and without warning, Dudley spat a mouthful of raspberry juice all over the table and in complete shock shouted, 'What the FUCK!!'

At the corner of the bar was a blackboard and listed half way down was 'Mince & Dumplings'.

'Since when did they have a gig here'? He asked, clearly a little put out. Of course he had done what many had done before him (mainly in Barnstable) and mistaken the food menu for gig listings. He calmed down when he realised his mistake and we all had a little chuckle, as to be fair it was quite funny. It was a very easy mistake to make of course, especially as at the other end of the bar was the ACTUAL gig listings board advertising the fact that a local band called 'Fiery

Onions' supported by 'Stuffed Trout' were playing that night. It could often get confusing I had to admit.

Two pints each for me and Graeme and another half of raspberry juice for Dudley later, we parted company. Dudley would announce to the media that we had split by mutual consent and that there were no further plans to record again with any other artists. In a nutshell; Pants were finished. Later that week the music media had a field day and although our split wasn't exactly headline news or causing widespread grief amongst legions of music lovers around the world, ala The Beatles, Take That, The Smiths and Bros, it still caught the attention of millions…well thousands of rock fans round the world. Not to mention bus conductors and window cleaners who were naturally more than a little concerned to hear of our demise. Although to be fair it seemed that their void had already been filled by the musical rumblings of 'Ched Wombat and the Wet Flannels' who had become very popular in the underground 'skiffle' scene. Of course we had split before, but this time it was for real and not just to try and hoodwink a dodgy manager either.

However the headlines this time weren't front page or leading the news story's on rock television programmes, the most sympathetic being in Kerrang whose headline in the News section read:

'FIRST THEIR ZIP EXPLODED, NOW THE WHOLE LOT'S GONE AND BLOWN UP. SURPRISE AS PANTS ARE NO MORE'

'Potato and Trombone Monthly' was the least sympathetic with a headline which simply read:

'SHIT BAND CALLS IT A DAY'

They never liked us anyway as I could never recall a good review or favourable interview in our time at the top.

So there it was; both Graeme and I sat once more in a bar while Dudley had disappeared back down to 'That Thar London', no doubt plotting the rise of 'Mince & Dumplings'. We however; sat with our memories…and a pint. Memories of a bloody cracking time, writing songs, recording songs, gigging up and down the land, meeting famous celebrities and hanging out with some of the world's most famous musicians…. as well as some of the shittest ones. We had seen America, nicked towels and finger snacks from hotels all over the country. We had been on 'Top of the Pop's', 'Chegger's kitchen of Rock' and 'Sponge with Delia'. I had had a toilet plopping contest with Morrissey – and lost, chatted up Heidi Cummings - and got blown out, while our guitar roadie 'Harry Witless' had apparently been blown off. We had been on Richard & Judy and ate some of the finest custard and cheese the world has to offer. Our moderate wealth had afforded us the luxury of buying some of the finest trousers ever designed, but not only that I also had a stonkingly brilliant drum kit. Graeme had built up a collection of stonkingly brilliant guitars, pedals, amps and ironing boards as well as a rare vintage ironing board said to have been once owned by 'Hilary Munce', who was a famous nineteenth century rambler from Merthyr Tydfil; apparently. This had taken pride of place next to his vintage 50's Gretsch which he acquired earlier that year from a blind window cleaner who was a fan of the band. He never did say how much he paid for it but a very happy blind window cleaner was seen wearing a new donkey jacket not long after the deal.

Yes indeed; we had our memories and that was one thing know one could ever take from us. Pants may have fallen, but in OUR minds they're still riding high.

BIT AT THE END

Its seems like only yesterday that I was enjoying the finer things in life such as top grade cheese, custard, oven chips, batternburg cake and an assortment of glamorous flavoured yoghurt - well actually, it WAS yesterday now I think about it. There was a sale on at Cobblers Hyper Market in the town centre and I couldn't resist. Graeme had also taken advantage and stocked up on a variety of cheeses and cake mix. The days of Pants were well gone however and everyday humdrum chores such as shopping, ironing, washing up and cushion fluffing filled our days. Now don't get me wrong; we still partied and went out for a few drinks together, it's just that it all happens in and around our home town now and not in glamorous locations on tour such as That Thar London. LA or Ipswich. But at least it was real, like our friends who weren't just a bunch of hangers on; or wannabe's who we neither knew that well, nor cared about for that matter.

Graeme had moved to cosmopolitan Shields and lived not to far from me where he shared his flat with a small cat and a half breed stray hedgehog. He still plays in bands most weekends and is enjoying it tremendously. As well as being a popular session guitarist he is also strumming away with a 'Carpenters' tribute band called 'Karen and the Cakes' *amongst others* and is still a bit of a celebrity locally. I've also been active of course and kept my drum sticks nice and sweaty over the years by jamming with numerous bands, including a Rockabilly band called 'Jimmy & the Saucepans' who are incredibly popular in and around South Shields. Graeme often plays with them as well when their original guitarist can't play, which is every other Saturday it seems. This is due to the fact it's a wash day and he has to stay in washing his socks ready for the following week. An excuse that Jimmy is suspicious of incidentally, as he believes he's actually been moonlighting, because another Rock'n' Roll type band has suspiciously appeared on the scene called 'Gordon & the Gravy Bowls', who by all accounts have a guitarist with dirty socks.

When both Graeme and me are playing with 'Jimmy & the Saucepans' we often revive a few 'Pants' favourites just for the hell of it and Jimmy to be fair, doesn't mind. Its great fun and we enjoy it, but that's as far as it will go. When we're out we often get asked if there's going to be an official reunion as it seems that there is still a little bit of interest in us, but to be honest - it's highly unlikely. Those days are gone. Pants were right for that moment in rock history and it would be hard to revive the band seriously, even if there was *massive* interest, which there isn't! As for the friends and acquaintances we have been involved with during our career, that's a different story.

By all accounts Howard Trowl is still in Mexico, but serving a prison sentence for exporting illegal moustaches. Graeme ex 'Constance Stains' still lives in the area but we never see her and has apparently started up a late night 'Onion Dispensary' in Gateshead catering for the intellectually challenged. Benny Crumpton our one time short lived and short on legged mental bassist - still lives in the Jarrow Midget Farm but is heavily sedated most days as he's broke his chin too many times and thankfully, is no longer allowed out; Except on Tuesdays when he takes advanced trombone lessons.

Dudley Longbottom switched careers and started working at a haberdashery in Finchley after 'Strangely Brown Records' went bust, not long after 'Mince & Dumplings' failed to make any impact what's so ever -

and since split. Attempted solo careers also failed apparently and both Stuart Mince and Arnold 'Dumplings' Carrot are now working in 'Burger King' specialising in Lettuce washing. 'Harry Witless', Graeme's guitar tech and friend still often hangs out with us helping out for free at gigs every now and then, but has since been offered a job as a beard and Brazilian wax technician for Madonna – or at least that's what he told us anyway. Oh! And Graeme's Gran still thinks we're shite.

We're both happy with our lives though, still playing, still partying, still purchasing exciting new trousers from time to time and generally taking things easy and I for one wouldn't have it any other way.

The End

Lightning Source UK Ltd.
Milton Keynes UK
UKOW05f2224190813

215623UK00001B/19/P

9 781782 995197

Toledo, Spain

The City of Three Cultures

A Starting-Point Guide

Barry Sanders - writing as:

B G Preston

Toledo, Spain

ISBN: 9798367920147

1st edition – January 2023

Acknowledgements: The author greatly appreciates Sandra Sanders' contributions. She provided substantial editorial assistance to ensure the accuracy of this work.

Photography: Photos and maps in the Starting-Point Guides are a mixture of those from the author and other sources such as Adobe Images, Wikimedia, and Google maps. No photograph or map in this work should be used without checking with the author first.

~ ~ ~ ~ ~ ~

Historic Toledo - with the Alcázar and cathedral standing tall and overlooking the city.

Contents

Preface: The "Starting-Point" Traveler

Some General Travel Suggestions

Introduction & Area Covered:

This Starting-Point guide is intended to help new travelers to the area explore this historic city. When coming here, Toledo may easily be visited as a day trip from Madrid or for longer stays where this beautiful city may be used as a basecamp to explore the region of Castilla-La Mancha and its many treasures.

Toledo is framed on three sides by the Tagus River
Photo Source: Dmitry Dzhus - Wikimedia Commons

Geographical focus is on the city of Toledo and the nearby Don Quixote Route into the country south of Toledo. If you stay here for several days, trips to some of the region's more noted destinations such as windmills in Consuegra are recommended and are covered in chapter 8 of this guide.

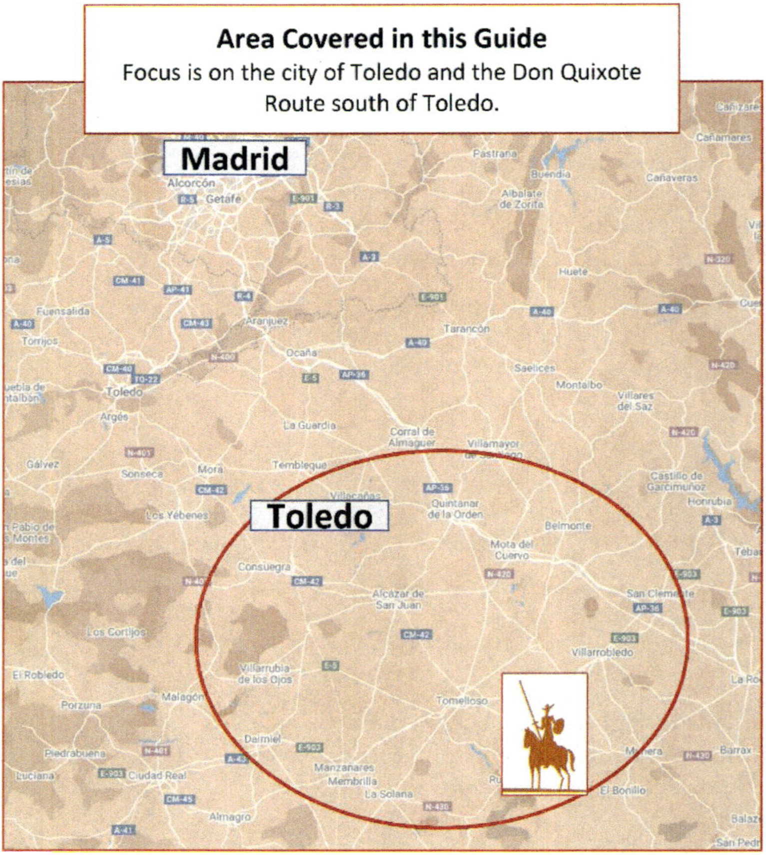

The Windmills of Consuegra
One of many great sites to tour near Toledo

The Ideal Itinerary:

If your travel schedule allows **plan on staying at least 1 night in Toledo.** Ideally, you will be able to stay as many as three nights. This is a delightful small city to stay in to explore the historic Old Town and the area nearby.

This is an area with a pleasant variety of destinations outside of town although your focus will likely be within Toledo itself. In addition to needing at least one full day within Toledo, more than one day is needed to appreciate the hill country, vineyards, and countryside.

A three-night itinerary would, for example, allow you to:

- Day 1 - arrive late morning and become oriented to the area around your lodging. Explore some of the historic Old Town and probably head out to a top sight such as the Alcazar de Toledo or the El Greco Museum. Toledo's leading attractions are described in chapter 6.
- Day 2 - spend one full day in the city to discover the Old Town and its many treasures such as the grand cathedral and monasteries.
- Day 3 - explore the area vineyards or perhaps the windmills made famous by the novel Don Quixote. The Don Quixote route provides a great selection of day trips from Toledo and are addressed in chapter 8 of this guide.
- Day 4 - after your third night here, have a great breakfast and enjoy the local cuisine then head out to your next destination.

Visit the Tourist Office:

Toledo is a popular tourist destination and the city does a good job of helping visitors. The website for the city's tourist office is a subset of the larger site covering the Castilla-La Mancha region of which Toledo is the capital. If you wish to do some research before heading here, visiting this site is a good place to start.

www.TurismoCastillaLaMancha.es or

www.Tourismo.Toledo.es

In addition, the Madrid tourist office provides details on Toledo and trips to there from Madrid as well.

www.EsMadrid.com/en/Trips-Toledo

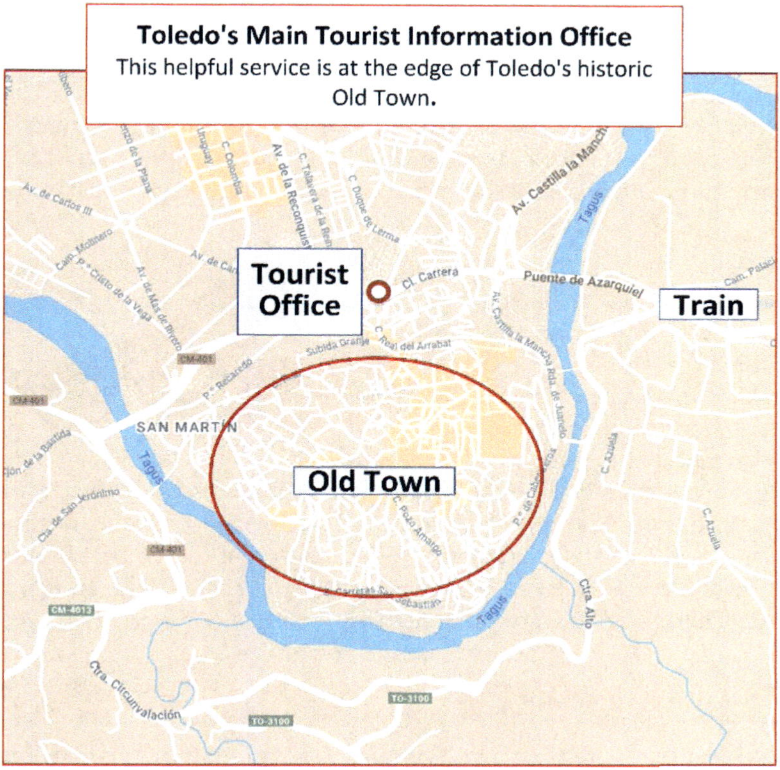

Toledo's Main Tourist Information Office
This helpful service is at the edge of Toledo's historic Old Town.

Tourist Office Location: The office is easy to locate as it sits in a standalone building just outside of the ancient city walls. If you take the bus into town from the train station, it can drop you off here. From this point, it is an easy stroll into the heart of Old Town.

The address is: Paseo de Merchan, Toledo – and their phone is 925-211-005

Among the many services available, they can provide detailed maps of Toledo which will greatly facilitate your explorations of the city. In addition, this is a good site to book a wide range of tours including valuable walking tours of Old Town.

Discount Travel Card: As of this writing, the **Toledo Card** has been discontinued. Travel cards such as this can provide some notable savings on attractions and tours. If you visit the Tourist Information Office, check to see if this program has been reinstated.

Toledo Tourist Bracelet: Another option, the **Toledo Tourist Bracelet** covers entry into seven sites within central Toledo of which most are churches or other religious buildings. Chapter 6, which covers attractions in Toledo, notes which attractions are included in this program. The bracelets do not cover the most notable attractions, unfortunately. They may be purchased at the Tourist Office or at the entrance to each attraction and the cost will be roughly €12. There is no need to purchase this item in advance.

Download some Apps: [1]

With the incredible array of apps for Apple and Android devices, almost every detail you will need to have for a great trip is available up to and including where to find public toilets. The apps range from those created by official agencies such as the Tourist Office and the regional train service. Several are put together by individual app developers. Following are a few recommended by the author. Given the popularity of Toledo, many apps are available and the ones cited here are a representative sample only.

[1] **Limited street maps in this guide.** This guidebook does not include an appendix of street maps. The apps cited here are likely to be far more beneficial as they are interactive and provide more details than a set of maps in a printed guide such as this can provide.

- **Toledo Travel Guide:** Produced by Goaz Socia. This app provides information on area hotels, restaurants, and attractions. Easy to use interactive maps are included.
- **Toledo Travel Guide in English (TOL):** Several excellent travel apps to Toledo are available but not all of them are in English. This one app does a good job of highlighting the attractions and tours here and it is completely in English.

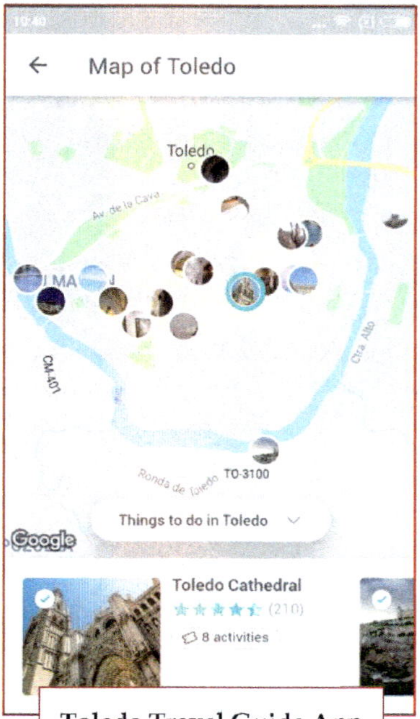

Toledo Travel Guide App

- **Bus Toledo:** Toledo has a comprehensive bus system. This app helps you learn it and understand the various routes. Strongly advised if you will be using buses to travel around the area.[2]
- **Toledo Map and Walks:** Provided by GPS My city, a firm which presents similar apps for numerous cities. Excellent use of interactive maps and suggested walks around the city and area.
- **Toledo Walking Tours:** Developed by GVAM. The app has several themed walking tours with interactive maps such as an El Greco walking tour.
- **Renfe:** This is Spain's primary train service, and the app is a must if you will be traveling by train anywhere in Spain.

[2] **Toledo, Spain Apps:** When looking for apps in the App Store, be sure to qualify your search for "**Toledo, Spain**." Without the qualifier of "Spain", it is likely that you will receive suggestions for apps in Toledo, Ohio.

Detailed route info and schedules are provided, and tickets may be purchased directly from the app.

- **Rome2Rio**: An excellent way to research all travel options including rental cars, trains, flying, bus, and taxi. The app provides the ability to purchase tickets directly online. A good alternative to this is the Trainline app.
- **Google Translate:** A must if you do not know any Spanish. This app is a tremendous help when you need to communicate with non-English speaking locals.
- **Trip Advisor**: Probably the best overall app for finding details on most hotels, restaurants, excursions, and attractions.
- **Flush**: A very helpful app which provides guidance on where to find public toilets.

The Puente de San Martín (Bridge) over the Tagus River at the base of Toledo.
Photo Source: FJM Fernandez-Wikimedia Commons

1: Toledo Overview

The City of Three Cultures. This simple term "The City of Three Cultures" sets the stage for this amazing small city. Many cities have a neighborhood or historical building which are World Heritage Sites, but rarely will you find an entire city receiving this designation. All of Toledo is a UNESCO World Heritage Site[3] and the lack of modern buildings greatly adds to this. As an interesting aside, if you look at the painting of Toledo's skyline called "View of Toledo" done by El Greco in 1608, it almost exactly matches how the town looks today.

Toledo sits on a rocky hill above the Tagus River and is framed by this river on three sides. It was this natural barrier which helped the community to grow and survive. It was even the capital of Spain until it moved to Madrid in 1560.

The town is a delightful maze to explore and working your

[3] **World Heritage Site:** In 1986, the entire town of Toledo was granted this designation due to its monumental and cultural heritage which spans over 2,000 years.

way through town is made easy by well-marked signage to attractions. Being old and built in a confined space, many streets are little more than narrow alleys. Still, visitors will be amazed to see vehicles navigate their way through lanes where it does not seem possible that traffic would be. Not all lanes and roads will have vehicle traffic. Often, you will encounter pedestrian-only routes which adds to the ancient feel and ambiance of the town.

Toledo's Old Town is a tightly packed maze of narrow lanes which can be fun to explore.

This is an ancient town on a rugged hillside which, in many communities, makes it an arduous experience to work your way through. This is often not the case here although the presence of many cobblestone lanes can be a hindrance for mobility-impaired individuals. The city planners have helped in many ways including underground escalators to help navigate between the upper and lower areas of town and to do so out of the heat.

While Toledo has numerous historic structures packed into a small area, it is certainly not the only European city structured this way. What makes this city so special is the blending of religions and cultures which was, at times, done in a relatively peaceful way. In Toledo, there was a substantial period when differing cultures were able to live together peacefully.

Toledo is pronounced **"Toe Lay Doh"**

Visitors will encounter historical treasures representing Christians, Jews, and Muslims. Often these historical sites from differing cultures sit only a few feet from one another. In some cases, there are buildings which incorporate elements of each of these cultures and their religions. These different religious groups lived side-by-side for centuries and weren't

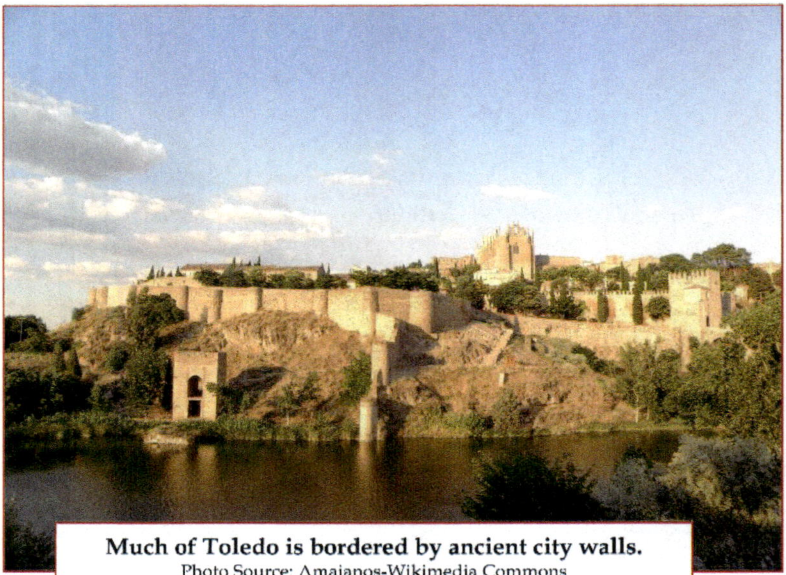

Much of Toledo is bordered by ancient city walls.
Photo Source: Amaianos-Wikimedia Commons

always trying to eliminate one another. As a result, Toledo well deserves the honorarium of the ***"City of Three Cultures."***

The Plaza de Zocodover is where many tours start and is a great place to begin explorations of Old Town.
Photo Source: Google Maps

Highlights of these different cultures are evident in such structures as:

- City walls built by the Visigoths [4]
- An aqueduct, circus, and baths left by the Romans
- An ancient bridge built by the Moors/Muslims
- Ancient synagogues built in the 15th century by the Jews and even by the Moors.

---

[4] **Visigoths:** A Germanic tribe which were powerful in the 5th & 6th century. They were a subset of the Goths who were loosely aligned with the Roman society. They claimed much of the region after the fall of Rome and held onto the area for centuries.

History and culture are at the center of everything here, even in the cuisine. **A walking tour of Toledo is recommended** as a well-informed guide will point out details of structures which would be easy to simply walk by and miss. Buildings which do not appear to have special significance could, for example, have a foundation laid by the Romans which was later added to by the Visigoths, and again altered by the Moors or Jews. At the very least, download one of the many apps which will help point out these special elements.

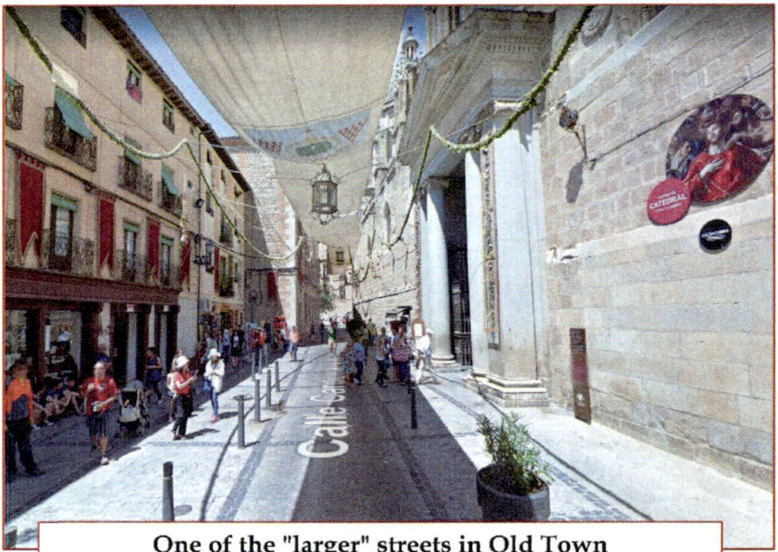

One of the "larger" streets in Old Town
Many popular areas such as this one next to the cathedral are covered to help shade visitors from the strong summer sun.
Photo Source: Google Maps

If you are not with a guide, having a map or map app with you is essential here. Open spaces such as plazas or parks to help your orientation are few and the streets are typically narrow with little discernable pattern to them. Chapter 5 outlines several sources which provide tours of Toledo. Some tours start in Toledo, many others are full day bus tours departing from Madrid

Crowds - this is a popular destination which is easily reached from Madrid for day trips. Expect to find several tour groups and lines of tour buses near the city entrance. Don't let this crowding keep you from visiting Toledo. There is plenty to see here and you are not always surrounded by throngs of people.

The Old Town

In all likelihood, most of your explorations will be in and near Toledo's Old Town. Plan on doing a lot of walking as it is nearly three-quarters of a mile square (1.2 km) and the historical sights are spread throughout this space.

The Alcázar de Toledo
Photo Source: MEH Bergmann-Wikimedia Commons

A great way to reduce this walking burden is to catch the open-air tourist train, the "Toledo Train Vision." This attraction takes riders to view leading attractions within Old Town (it does not let you off en route). Adding to this is the Hop-On Bus Tour which takes riders to the area surrounding Toledo. Details on these two tour options may be found in chapter five.

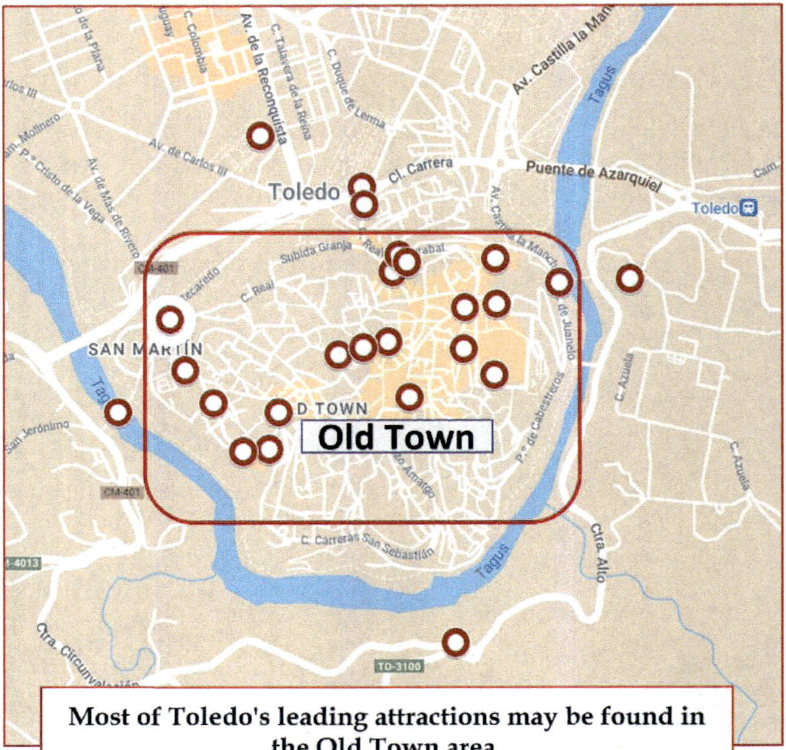

Most of Toledo's leading attractions may be found in the Old Town area.

Each circle above represents one of the citys popular attractions. These are detailed further into this guide.

The main attraction is the town itself. As cited earlier, it is a maze but an enjoyable one. Take time to explore the many lanes, most of them quite narrow, and enjoy the area's excellent wines and cuisine. Toledo has many historical sites to explore, and it could take many days to see them all. For most of us, visiting some of the leading sites, such as the Alcazar de Toledo, will be enough to provide a good sense of the power shifts and cultural evolution here.

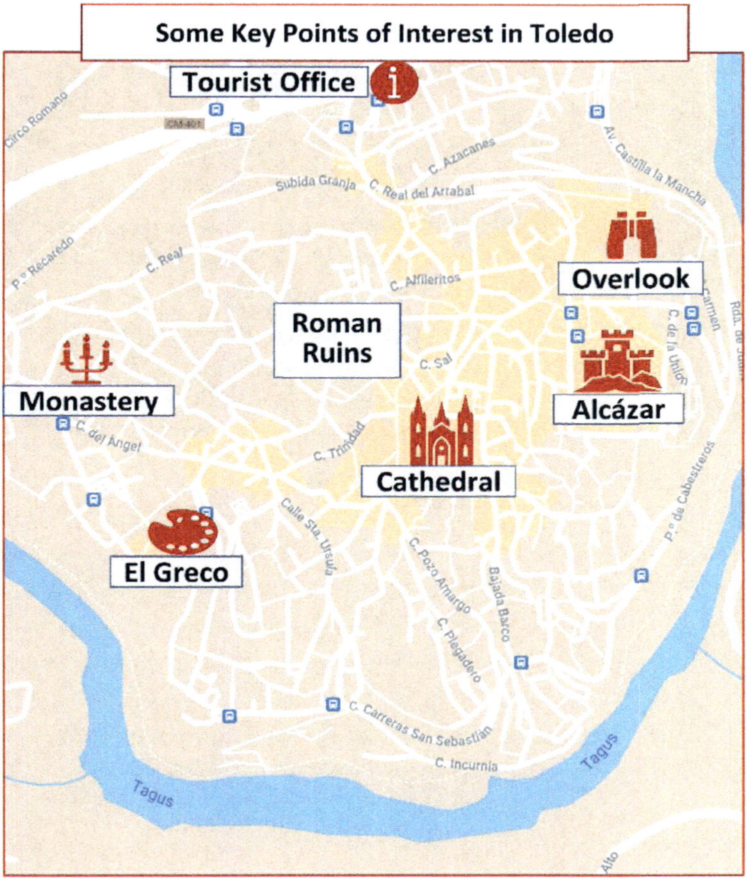

Chapter six outlines many of these cultural sites in and around Toledo.

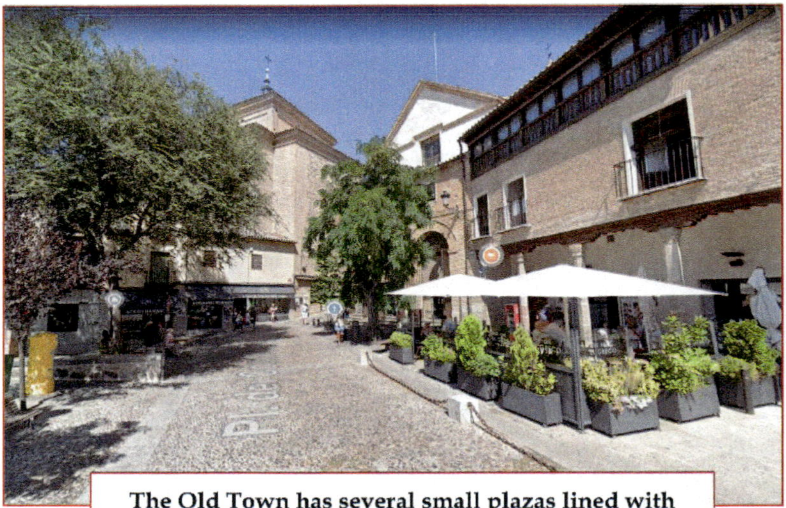

The Old Town has several small plazas lined with open-air restaurants.
Photo Source: Google Maps

~ ~ ~ ~ ~ ~

2: Toledo Facts, Climate, & History

An understanding of the area names and geography of the city and region can be beneficial. The following are a few basic facts about Toledo and Castilla-La Mancha which might prove useful.

Toledo is the capital of Spain's Castilla-La Mancha region.

- **Capital of Toledo Province and Castilla-La Mancha:** It is easy to be confused with the varying references to Toledo as a capital. In some cases, it will be listed as the capital of the Toledo Province and other resources will list this city as the capital of Castilla-La Mancha. It is both.

  An analogy can be made with the United States where Castilla-La Mancha is the rough equivalent of a U.S. state, and the province of Toledo could be thought of as a county within Castilla-La Mancha.

Much of the Castilla-La Mancha region is flat agricultural lands bordered by low hills.
Photo Source: M. Peinado - Wikipedia

- **Castilla-La Mancha**: This area, of which Toledo is the capital, is what Spain defines as an "Autonomous Community." In short, this means it has some self-governing and control much like a U.S. state has. This is a large region in the center of Spain on an expansive plateau covering much of central Iberia. It is divided into 5 provinces and Toledo Province sits in the north-west of this region. Madrid is not part of this region or province.

In geographical size, the Castilla-La Mancha region is Spain's 3rd largest but, in population, it ranks 9th so it is a largely open and uncrowded region.

- **Toledo Stats**: As of 2018, the population of this small city was 84,200. The population for the metropolitan area is roughly 280,000. The elevation of 529 meters (1,736 ft). This moderate elevation gives the area a pleasant climate year-round.

Climate & When to Visit:

As with most areas in Europe, the best times of the year are spring and fall if you wish to avoid crowds. Summer is the most popular/crowded season and, naturally, the hottest.

If you are not averse to the multitudes of tourists in the summer, or occasional frosts in the winter, there really is no bad time to visit this charming town and city. Each season certainly has its own positives and negatives, but do not hold back on visiting here simply because it may not be an optimum season.

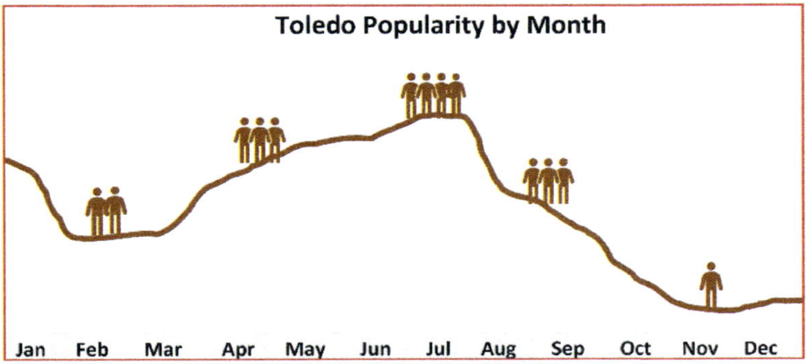

Officially, the climate here is defined as "Transitional Mediterranean." It is semi-arid for much of the year which can lead to substantial differences in temperature in a single day with cool mornings and hot afternoons. Rain chance here, due to the arid climate, is typically low and most of southern Spain has recently incurred severe drought.

Some Seasonal Considerations:

Light snow does occur in Toledo in the winter.

Winter (Dec - Feb): The winter climate in this area, which is slightly lower in elevation than Madrid, is generally cool. Rains are moderate and, when they occur, come in from the Atlantic. Daily lows (see chart on page 28) can be cold but rarely below freezing. Precipitation is normally very low.

Positive aspects of visiting here in the winter are low tourist crowds and hotel rates are at their lowest during the year. A negative aspect is that many tours and tourist activities will be closed. If your focus is on the major attractions and not on area tours, coming here in the winter is recommended.

Winter Events:[5] A fun aspect of visiting here in the winter are the leading events. One of the most notable is the Christmas market which is held in the two primary squares of Zocodover and Town Hall.

Spring (Mar-May): This is an arid area and even in the Spring, rain is modest and unlikely to hamper travel plans. Some storms from the Atlantic are likely to blow through.

Late Spring is an excellent time to visit this city and area as temperatures are comfortable and most tourist sites and tours are open. Hotel rates will be higher than in the winter. Some storms from the Atlantic may blow in but typically do not last long.

Summer (Jun-to-Aug): This area is hot and dry with little to no rain. Even with the heat, the arid climate is less likely to wear you down than more humid areas. Toledo also does a good job of providing many covered lanes to reduce how much baking sun finds its way to the streets.

This is the most popular (crowded) and expensive time to visit. On the positive side, all tours and activities will be in full operation.

---

[5] **Events Calendar**: One of the better websites for updates on events in and around Toledo, Spain is **www.ToledoSpain.click**. Once you are on the site, click onto "Events" near the top of the page.

Fall (Sep-Nov): Weather is generally pleasant with cool to warm temperatures. Rain chance is low in September and October. Most shops and tours will be open through October. Hotel rates decrease from their summer highs. All-in-all, probably the best time to visit here.

Average Toledo Climate by Month [6]				
Month		**Avg High**	**Avg Low**	**Avg Precip.**
Jan	😐	53 F / 12 C	34 F /-1 C	1 inch
Feb	😐	57 F / 14 C	37 F /3 C	1 inch
Mar	☺	65 F /18 C	41 F /5 C	.9 inch
Apr	☺	68 F /20 C	45 F /7 C	1.5 inches
May	☺	76 F /24 C	52 F /11 C	1.7 inches
Jun	😐	87 F /31 C	61 F /16 C	.9 inches
Jul	☹	94 F /35 C	66 F /19 C	.3 inches
Aug	☹	93 F /34 C	66 F /18 C	.4 inches
Sep	😐	84 F / 29 C	59 F /15 C	.7 inches

[6] **Climate Data Source:** Wikipedia.com

Average Toledo Climate by Month [6]				
Month		Avg High	Avg Low	Avg Precip.
Oct	☺	72 F /22 C	50 F /10 C	1.9 inches
Nov	😑	60 F /16 C	42 F / 5 C	1.5 inches
Dec	☹	53 F / 12 C	37 F / 3 C	1.6 inches

Some History:

Toledo's tagline of "The City of Three Cultures" could easily lead visitors to believe that the various ruling groups and religions always lived together peacefully here. Unfortunately, this is far from the truth.

There was a period during the 11th to 15th centuries where Jews, Moors, and Christians did live side-by-side and did so without continually trying to wipe each other out. This situation of having differing religions coexist was unusual and something to be praised.

As different groups took power there were, as so often is the case, power struggles and sometimes these were brutal. One of the worst examples was "The Day of the Pit" early in the 9th century when the Moorish leaders invited 5,000 local citizens to a "party" at the Alcazar palace. These visitors were summarily killed and thrown into a giant pit.

The era of the three religious groups (Moors, Jews, and Christians) living and working together came to an end in 1492, the same year that Columbus sailed to America. At this time, all non-Christians were forced to either leave Toledo or convert. This was followed by a two-century long period of persecution against the

Jews. Since that period, most of Spain has been predominantly Christian/Catholic.

In the late 16th century, the current king, Philip V, chose to move the capital to Madrid. At the time, Madrid was an unimportant town a short distance north of Toledo. With this move, Toledo's role in the region's history and overall importance greatly lessened. The population of Toledo, over a sixty-year period, was reduced by half.

El Greco's View of Toledo - 1608
Photo Source: Wikipedia

It wasn't until the twentieth century that Toledo began to grow again and gain importance. Its importance was no longer political or even industrial, it now shifted to what it is today, a national monument and historic treasure which people enjoy visiting

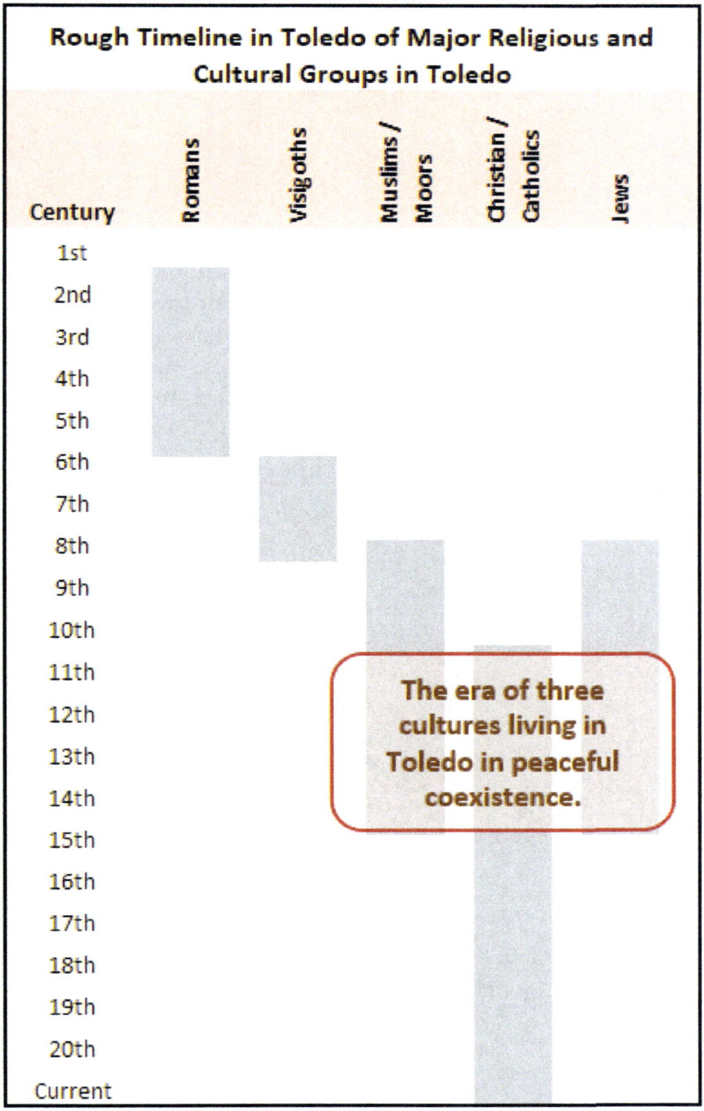
Rough Timeline in Toledo of Major Religious and Cultural Groups in Toledo
Century
Romans
Visigoths
Muslims / Moors
Christian / Catholics
Jews
1st
2nd
3rd
4th
5th
6th
7th
8th
9th
10th
11th
12th
13th
14th
15th
16th
17th
18th
19th
20th
Current
The era of three cultures living in Toledo in peaceful coexistence.

3: Traveling to Toledo

Toledo sits nearly dead center in the Iberian Peninsula, one of the reasons why this city was such a prominent town throughout the region's history. The downside is with many of the region's cities located near a coastline, Toledo tends to be out of the way to visit from almost every city with the notable exception of Madrid.

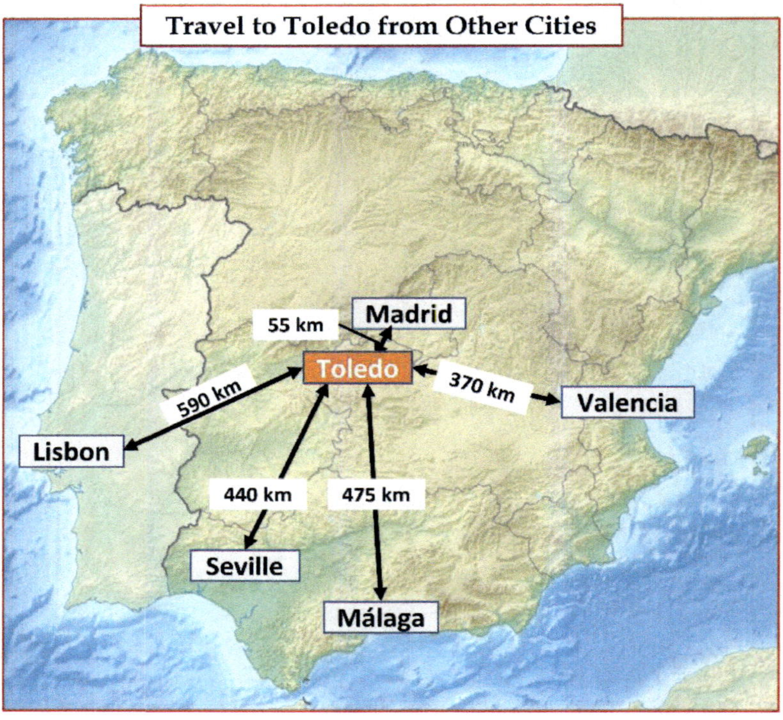

There is no commercial airport in Toledo. If you wish to fly here, the closest airport is Madrid. Train travel to Toledo from such areas as Barcelona or Valencia requires a change in central Madrid.

Travel Time to Toledo from other Iberian Peninsula Cities		
City	**By Car[7]**	**By Train**
Lisbon, Portugal	5 ½ hours	12 hours + Multiple train changes.
Madrid, Spain	50 minutes	33 minutes Multiple direct trains daily
Málaga, Spain	4 ½ hours	3 ½ hours Change trains in Madrid
Seville, Spain	4 ½ hours	4 hours Change trains in Madrid
Valencia, Spain	3 ½ hours	3 hours Change trains in Madrid

Recommended App and Website: There are many great online services to help you plan travels in Spain and Europe. One of the best is **www.rome2Rio.com.**

This service compares travel times for many modes of travel including flying, train, bus, and driving. The ability to purchase tickets is also included.

Rome2rio

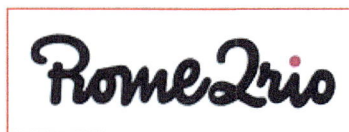

[7] **Driving Time Note**: Travel times depicted here are measured from the center of each city as the start and end points. Actual driving times will vary depending on which route you take and your starting location.

Trains from Madrid to Toledo:

The train trip from Madrid is a fast and enjoyable way to get to Toledo. This is a nonstop high-speed train which departs from Madrid's Atocha station, the primary station in central Madrid. Trains depart roughly once every hour.

This is a quick trip of only 33 minutes and the fee, at early 2023 rates, for a roundtrip is roughly €25.

Toledo's train station, built in 1858, has been classified as an historical monument.
Photo Source: King of Hearts - Wikipedia

Ticket Booking: There are several online options for purchasing train tickets in Spain, including:

- **www.Renfe.com** – Renfe is Spain's train system. This service has the distinct advantage of not having a middleman, so if problems arise or changes need to be made, they can easily be done at the station.

- **Reseller sites:** Several good options exist for purchasing travel for trains and other modes of travel including:
    - **www.Rome2Rio.com** - use for trains, buses, and more.
    - **www.TrainLine.com** - purchase train tickets for travel in most countries.

Toledo Train Station and getting into town: The train station is a beautiful structure which was designed and built in 1858 to complement Toledo's varied past. It is ornate and worth taking time to explore. The station sits a short distance from the historical center and it is a longer walk than most individuals would want to undertake.

Once you are in Toledo, you have several options for getting into the historical center: catching a cab, local bus, walking, or taking the Hop-On Bus.

Taxi: Taxis are generally available right outside of the station. This is a small station, so you don't have to look far to find them. Advance reservation of a taxi is not needed.

Given the nature of this historic community, vehicles are often limited to where they can go in town. If you do not have a specific destination in mind, consider asking to be taken to one of the

Coming with Luggage?

If you want to store luggage for the day while in Toledo, Luggage storage is available both in the train station and in town at Plaza de Zocodover.

If you need to take luggage to your hotel from the train station, consider taking one of several bus lines to Plaza de Zocodover. You can bring luggage onto the bus and, from the plaza, it is a short walk to many hotels in town.

two points listed below. Each of these make for great starting points to begin your explorations:

- Tourist Information Office: Plaza Merchán, or
- Plaza de Zocodover.

Walking: There are two different paths to consider, both provide great views of the majestic city as you cross the river from the station. Both routes will lead you to the base of the escalator at the bus parking area. This is a 15-20-minute walk which involves walking along some very busy roads. A plus to doing this is that the walks provide great photo opportunities of the city standing proudly on a hill before you.

Once you go up the escalator (Remonte Mecánico de Safont), you will arrive at a spot with a great overlook of the river below. From here, it is a short walk into the heart of the Old Town.

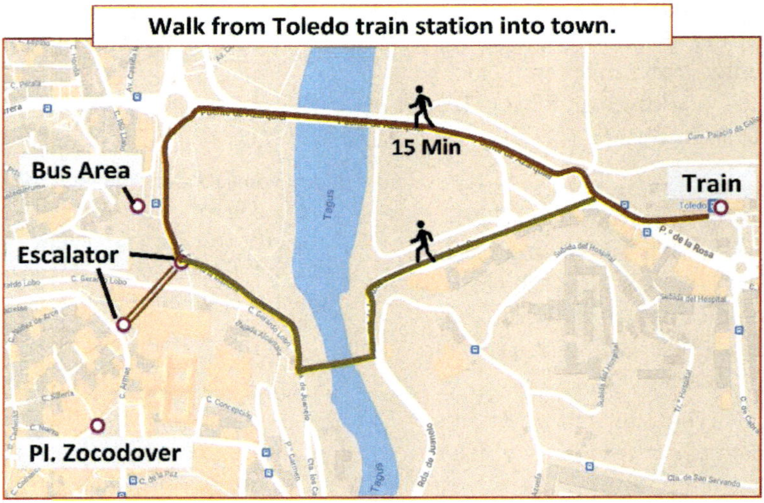

Hop-On/Hop-Off Bus: A fun and informative way to make your entrance into Toledo is to catch the Hop-On bus. The train station is one of the stops on this route and, if you have purchased a voucher in advance, you may board without further fees.

The bus stops here every thirty minutes during high season and circumnavigates Toledo. This gives visitors a great view of the city from several vantage points. Once you are on board, you can select the stop of your choice to determine where you will begin your explorations of Toledo's Old Town. This bus does not travel very far into the old city.

See chapter 5 for further details on this travel option.

Train station with taxis and Hop-On bus at the front entrance.
Photo Source: Google Maps

Bus from Madrid to Toledo:

Buses from Madrid take as little as one hour via the Alsa service, a regional bus company. While this is a slightly longer travel time than taking the train, this bus service does offer the distinct advantage of taking you directly to either the bus station at the base of the escalator, or to Plaza de Zocodover. The stop in Toledo varies depending on which bus you catch, but both end points in Toledo are convenient.

Some buses take 90 minutes and have multiple stops, so take care to ensure you are on the direct route which takes only one hour. Buses depart from Madrid every 60 minutes and most will depart from the Plaza Eliptica in central Madrid.

Check **www.Alsa.com** for current schedules. You may purchase tickets from this site.

Driving to Toledo from Madrid:

If you will be driving to Toledo from Madrid, this is roughly a 50-minute trip, depending on your starting point in Madrid. Several routes are available and most are along major highways. While direct and quick, the drive offers little in the way of scenery.

The fastest route is along the A-42 highway. This is a mostly flat stretch but has several opportunities for gas or toilets along the way should they be needed.

The A-42 highway from Madrid to Toledo
Photo Source: Google Maps

Once you arrive in Toledo, there are a limited number of open parking areas and garages to select from.

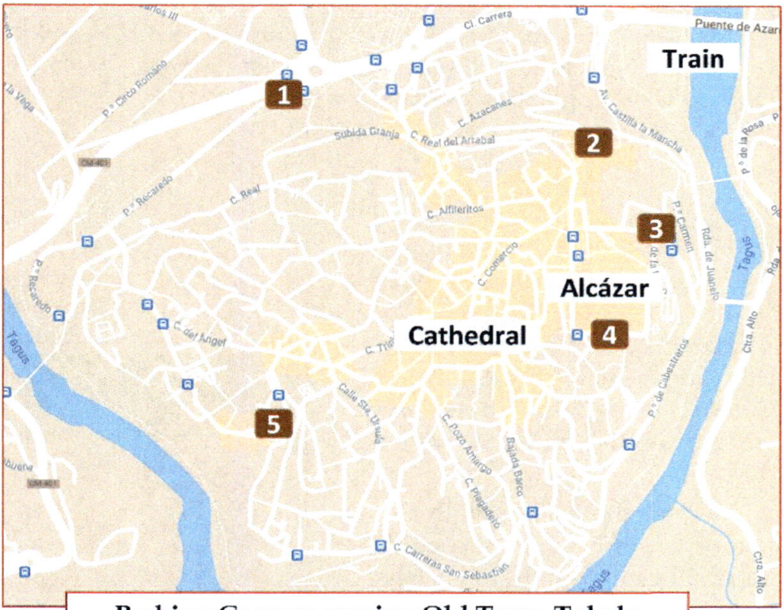

Parking Garages serving Old Town Toledo

1. **Parking Indigo Recardeo** – Large parking lot along the northern edge of the historic center, not far from the Tourist Information Office.
   - Plaza Recaredo, 22, 45004 Toledo
2. **Aparcamiento Mirado** – Very convenient to the escalator, Remonte de Safont, which leads up into town.
   - Calle Gerado Logo 45001, Toledo
3. **Aparcamiento – Garaje Anvonia V. Garcia** - a bit smaller and fills up quickly but very convenient to the Alcázar or Plaza de Zocodover.
   - Calle Miguel de Cervantes, 9, 45001 Toledo

4. **Garaje Alcázar** - this garage is next to the Alcázar. A great location if you have lodgings in the heart of town.
   - Cta. De los Capuchinos, 6, 45001 Toledo
5. **Garaje Tránsito.** Closest parking facility to the El Greco Museum. Not close to the heart of town, but a great spot if you have lodging in this sector of town.
   - Aldea Transito, 1, 45002 Toledo

Bus Tours from Madrid:

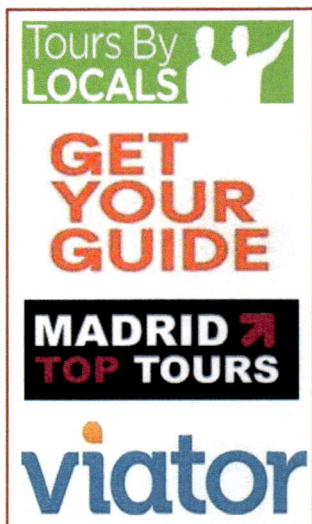

Many bus and van tours to Toledo are available from Madrid. Consider using one of these if you will only be visiting Toledo for one day.

Most of these tours will drop you off (with or without a guide, depending on the tour) at the large lot on the northeastern side of Old Town. From here, it is an easy ascent up the escalator into the heart of the historic area.

Most tours are for a full-day, and a few are half-day tours. This shorter option is not recommended as it gives you minimal time to explore the historical treasures in Toledo.

Several firms offer the tours, and they range from large-group bus tours to private car excursions. For details on available tours from Madrid, listed below are several of the leading providers. Many other tour providers are also available for these tours. In each case, you will need to then search within the site for tours to Toledo.

- Tours By Locals - **www.ToursByLocals.com**
- Get Your Guide - **www.GetYourGuide.com**
- Viator (a subsidiary of Trip Advisor) - **www.Viator.com**
- Madrid Top Tours - **www.MadridTopTours.com**

~ ~ ~ ~ ~ ~

4: Where to Stay in Toledo

Where you choose to stay when visiting a new city is essentially a personal choice. You may prefer hotels or rental apartments, or picking a place guided by your budget may be critical to you.

Regardless of the motives which drive your selection or the type of accommodation you prefer, the "Where in town should I stay?" question is critical to helping you have an enjoyable visit.

Budget and accommodation-type issues aside, the following criteria may be of importance to you:

- Convenience to historical sites, restaurants, shopping.
- Convenience to transportation.
- Noise levels around where you will stay.

This guide does not provide details on all the hotels in Toledo as there are too many to describe. There are many fine and dynamic online sources such as **Trip Advisor, Booking.com**, and others which provide far more detail than can be provided here. These sites will provide answers to every question you may have about a property and allow you to make reservations

Recommendation:
If you are arriving by train, stay in the Old Town area.
If you are driving - consider the area south of town.

once you have made your selection.

This is a popular destination and, as a result, quality lodging of all types can be found throughout the Toledo area. To help you in your selection, this guide outlines two sections of town to consider with a focus on hotels instead of rental apartments. Many other sectors of town have fine lodging such as near the train station, but do not fit the criteria of convenience to attractions, dining, and shopping.

The two suggested areas are (a) in the heart of Old Town, or (b) just across the Tagus River, south of town, on the bluff which looks back toward this beautiful spot. Both of these areas offer positives and negatives which are outlined further in this chapter.

Recommended Areas for Lodging in Toledo

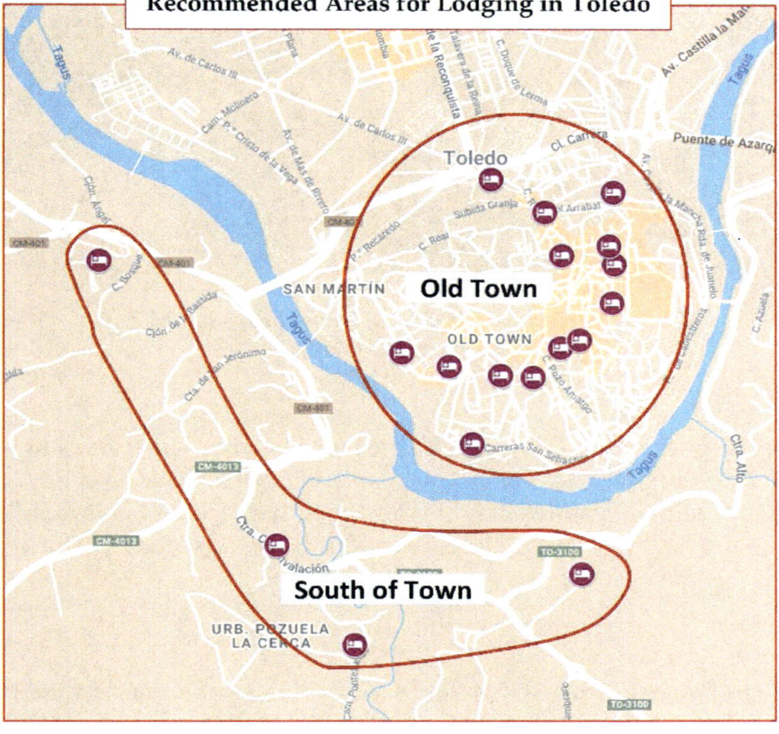

Old Town Area:[8]

This is a lively area with a regular stream of visitors from around the world. As a result of the popularity, there are many lodging opportunities here ranging from hostels to apartment rentals and luxury hotels.

The Eugenia de Montijo hotel in the heart of Old Town
A Marriott "Autograph Collection" property.

The positives to staying in the historic center are numerous including proximity to restaurants, bars and shops along with having a wealth of historic sites at your fingertips. Another enjoyable aspect of staying here is simply spending time in such an historic

[8] **Hotel Ratings:** All hotel ratings in this guide are a composite of ratings from the author's personal experiences, travel blogs, and several popular sites such as Trip Advisor, Booking.com, Hotels.com, and others.

area while having your hotel or inn situated along one of Toledo's narrow and historic streets.

There are some downsides to staying here. The biggest two are noise and parking. Lodging along narrow streets crowded with tourists can be very noisy. Luckily, the better properties have good sound insulation which reduces this, but it does mean that opening a window for fresh air might not provide a restful sleep. Parking is the other problem as it is limited here and can be problematic for many (not all) of the properties listed.

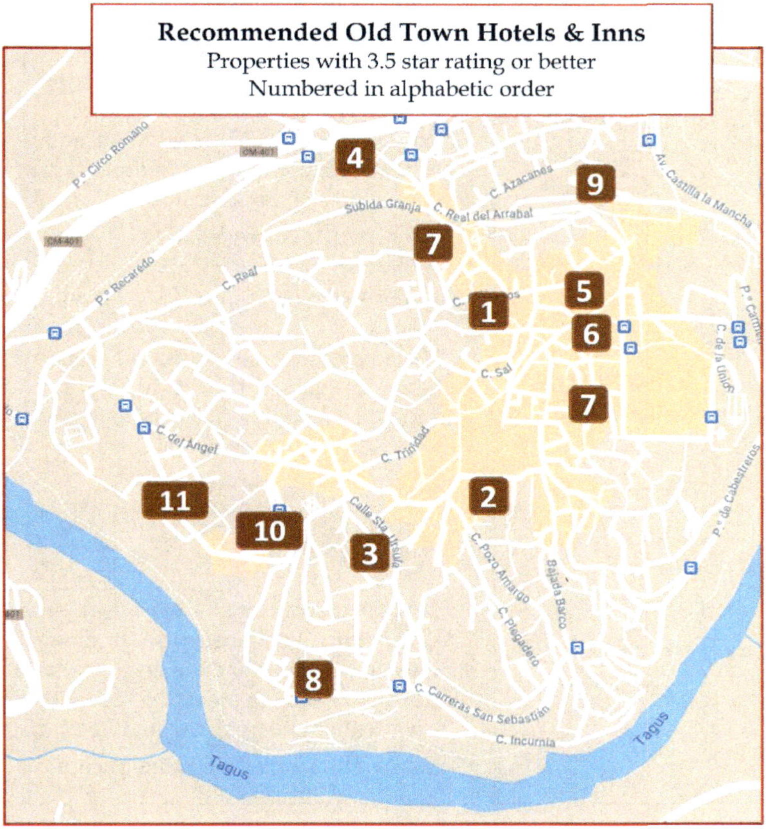

Suggested Lodging in Old Town (All selected lodging has 3.5 or better rating)			
	Hotel	**Address & Details**	**Rating**
1	**Casa de los Mozárabes**	Cjón Menores, 10 Very charming apartment hotel with an old world feel. Built around an open courtyard. This is not a full-service property, but you can cook in the apartment. **www.CasaDeLosMozarbes.com**	4 stars
2	**Casa Palacio Rincon de la Catedral**	Calle Bajade Del, C. Pozo Amargo, 2 Luxury hotel with old world Spain ambiance. Very close to the cathedral. Large rooms and open courtyard. **www.RinconDelaCatedral.es**	4.5 stars
3	**Eugenia de Montijo**	Plaza del Juego de Pelota, 7 A Marriott Autograph Collection property. Full-service, luxury. One of the largest hotels in Old Town. Large rooms and suites. Author recommendation. **www.Marriott.com**	5 stars
4	**Hacienda del Cardenal**	Plaza Recaredo, 24 Near the northern edge of Old Town. A relaxing setting with large patio for dining. Rooms are spacious and the property has a pool. A great way to enjoy the feel of Old Town without being in the middle of it. **www.HaciendaDelCardenal.com**	4 stars

Suggested Lodging in Old Town (All selected lodging has 3.5 or better rating)			
Hotel		Address & Details	Rating
5	**Hospedium Hotel Posadade de la Silleria**	Calle de la Silleria,10 Tucked away on a narrow lane a block from Plaza de Zocodover. Boutique hotel with rooms ranging from single to small suites. Recently renovated. **www.HotelPosadaSilleria.es**	3.5 stars
6	**Hotel Boutique Adolfo**	Plaza Zocodover, 14 Well located next to Plaza Zocodover. Full-service hotel with a good restaurant. Head upstairs to the patio to relax and enjoy the views. **www.HotelBoutiqueAdolfo.com**	4 stars
7	**Hotel Carlos V Toledo**	Plaza del Horno de la Magdelena, 4 Expansive rooftop bar with views of Old Town. Well located near the Alcazar and many shops and restaurants. Easy to miss as it is tucked back on a narrow lane. **www.CarlosSV.com**	4 stars
8	**Hotel Casona de la Reyna**	C. Carreras, San Sebastian, 26 This is the least central of the properties listed here. While this makes it a further walk into the heart of Old Town, this adds the advantages of being away from noise and parking is readily available. **www.CasaDeLaReyna.com**	3.5 stars

Suggested Lodging in Old Town (All selected lodging has 3.5 or better rating)			
Hotel		**Address & Details**	**Rating**
9	**Hotel Medina De Toledo**	Bajada Desamparados, 2 Located in the northeast sector of Old Town, this hotel offers great views of the valley below. It is a bit of an uphill walk into town and noise can be a factor here. **www.HotelMedina.com**	3.5 stars
10	**Hotel Pintor El Greco**	del Tránsito, Calle de los Alamillos A nice contemporary-Spanish flavor. Located in the southern portions of Old Town near the El Greco Museum. Relaxing boutique hotel with large rooms. **www.HotelPintorElGreco.com**	4 stars
11	**Hotel San Juan de los Reyes**	C. de los Reys Catolicos, 5 Beautiful building, large rooms, full service, and parking available. A little away from central Old Town, but this reduces noise and crowds. **www.HotelSanJuanDeLosReyes.com**	4 stars

~ ~ ~ ~ ~ ~

South of Old Town - Across the Tagus River:

This second suggested lodging area in Toledo offers an entirely different experience from staying in the heart of the historic district. Several of the city's more notable resorts sit across the Tagus River. These are generally more upscale hotels with parking, outdoor restaurants, pools, and other services.

If you are driving to Toledo and plan on exploring the area, such as day trips to the windmills of Consuegra or other stops on the Don Quixote Route, this group of resorts make excellent base-camps for this. (See chapter 8 for more details.)

The sights of Old Town Toledo from these hotels are superior and provide great views while dining. The biggest downside to lodging here is that it requires visitors to take a city bus or Hop On bus to get into town. It is walkable, but the trek can be up to 30-minutes over steep terrain each way.

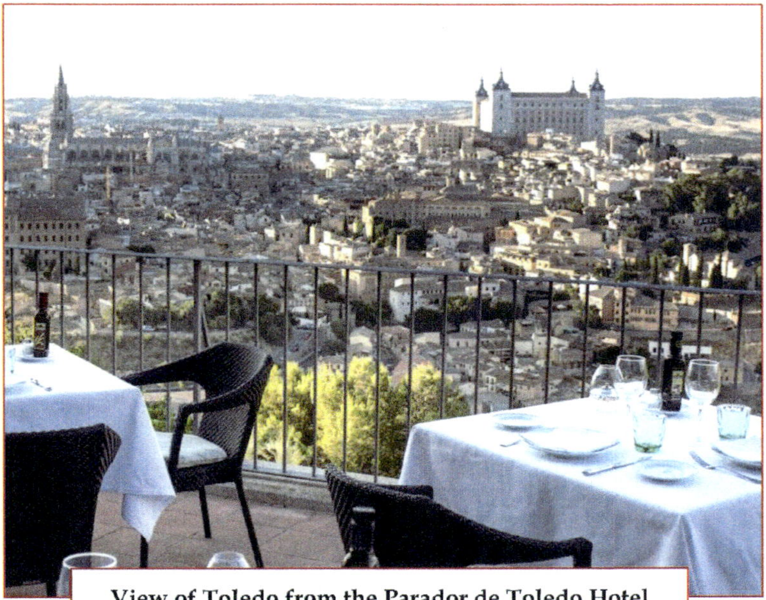

View of Toledo from the Parador de Toledo Hotel

Lodging Across the Tagus River from Old Town

Properties with 3.5 star rating or better

Numbered in alphabetic order

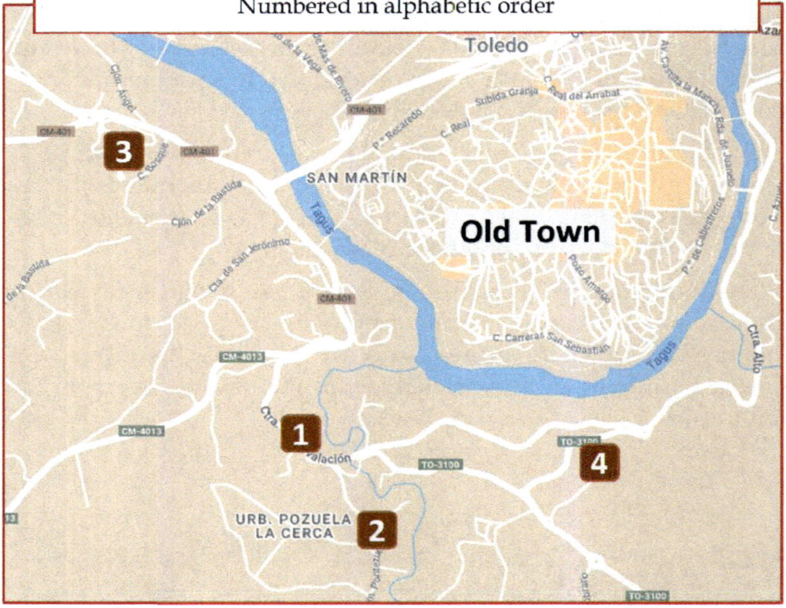

Suggested Lodging South of Old Town (All selected lodging has 3.5 or better rating)			
	Hotel	**Address & Details**	**Rating**
1	**AC Hotel by Marriott Cuidad de To-ledo**	Ctra De Circunvalación, 15 Large Marriott property with a quality restaurant plus fitness center and small casino. A top-quality experience with great views of Old Town. Free parking. **www.Marriott.com**	4.5 stars

Suggested Lodging South of Old Town (All selected lodging has 3.5 or better rating)			
Hotel		Address & Details	Rating
2	**Hotel Abaceria**	Cam. Pontezuelas, 8 A boutique hotel. Many rooms have balconies with views of Old Town. Large pool and outdoor eating area. **www.HotelAbaceria.com**	3.5 stars
3	**Hotel Cigarral El Bosque**	Ctra. Navalpino, 49 A luxury resort with expansive grounds and facilities. Large rooms, superb dining, and beautiful grounds. Reasonable walk to the historic Puente San Martin bridge. **www.HotelCigarraleBosque.com**	5 stars
4	**Parador de Toledo**	Cerro del Emperador A quality lodging experience with large rooms facing Old Town. Large pool and free parking. Warm and inviting ambiance with a Spanish flair. **www.Parador.es**	4.5 stars

~ ~ ~ ~ ~ ~

5: Toledo City & Area Tours[9]

Many companies provide tours of the city and the surrounding area. These tours include options such as city walking tours, food tastings, bike tours, and much more. There are numerous tour providers and resellers which, as a result, ensure there are tour opportunities to meet every preference.

Toledo is not a city to simply stroll around casually and perhaps visit a few leading attractions. There is simply too much history here and much of this past is not obvious. Many structures incorporate elements and history from multiple cultures and a good tour guide will be able to point this out and do so in

A Great Tour Resource:
Check out the "Tourismo Toledo" website for details on tours provided by local firms.
www.Turismo.Toledo.es

[9] **Tours for the independent-minded traveler & a personal note.** Like many individuals, the author has been disinclined to join in group tours, preferring to go it alone. This isn't always the best choice. After participating in some group tours with his family, he soon discovered how much could be gained from a well-informed guide. Now, with each new city, the author builds in at least one guided tour and, in every case, has found the experiences rewarding and educational.

a fun and informative way. By attempting to go it alone, most of us will miss the fascinating history and stories behind many of these buildings.

Toledo Tourist Train and Hop-On Bus Tours:

In addition to the numerous walking tours of Toledo, there are two notable riding options which enable visitors to see much of the city and do so without wear-and-tear on their feet.

These two tour options of the Toledo Train Vision (Tourist Train) and the Hop-On-Hop-Off tour bus have some overlap, so both are not needed. There are key differences in these offerings which are worth noting.

Toledo Train Vision: This is NOT a Hop-On tour. Once you board, you are required to stay on for most of the ride. The one exception to this is at the overlook of Mirador de Valle where the train stops

Toledo Train Vision
A relaxing, narrated tour of Old Town

to provide a photo opportunity. The ride is in a quaint open-air mini train which includes narration via headphones in multiple languages.

- Duration: 45 minutes.
- Frequency: Trains depart every 30 minutes and operate year-round. High season hours are from 10am to 10pm.
- Where does it go: The mini train winds its way through a mix of the narrow streets within Old Town and then across the Tagus River to view the historic bridges with a stop at Mirador de Valle.
- Tour departure point: Plaza de Zocodover.
- Website: **www.ToledoTrainVision.com**
- Handicapped: Wheelchairs may come on board.

Toledo Hop On/Hop Off Bus: This is a traditional Hop-On tour which allows riders to get on or exit at any of the 10 stops along the route. This tour primarily circumnavigates Toledo's Old Town and spends little time in town. The ride is in a double-decker bus with the top level open for enhanced viewing.

Tour options are available ranging from just the bus tour to packages which include admission to the Alcázar and Bullfighting Museum. Both are stops along this route. A walking tour of Old Town is also available. Advance reservations are not needed but having a pre-purchased mobile voucher can expedite entry. These vouchers are available from the website listed on the next page.

- Duration: The bus tour takes 50 minutes if you stay on and do not exit along the way. Once a ticket is purchased, it is good for unlimited travel for 24 hours.
- Frequency: Buses depart every 30 minutes and operate year-round.
- Where does it go: As cited above, this bus, due to its size, spends little time within the Old Town which may be a disappointment to some. The route includes several stops around

the edge of town which provide great views and takes visitors to out-of-the way stops such as the Bullfighting Museum and two historic bridges which cross over the Tagus River. This tour is a great way to travel to multiple sites which have great views and photo opportunities of the ancient town.

- Tour departure point: The route begins and ends at the Alcázar, but you may board at any of the stops. This is convenient for visitors who arrive in town via train as the train station is one of the stops.
- Website: **www.Hop-On-Hop-Off-Bus-Tours.com** (Then go to the page for Toledo)
- Handicapped: Wheelchairs may come on the bus.

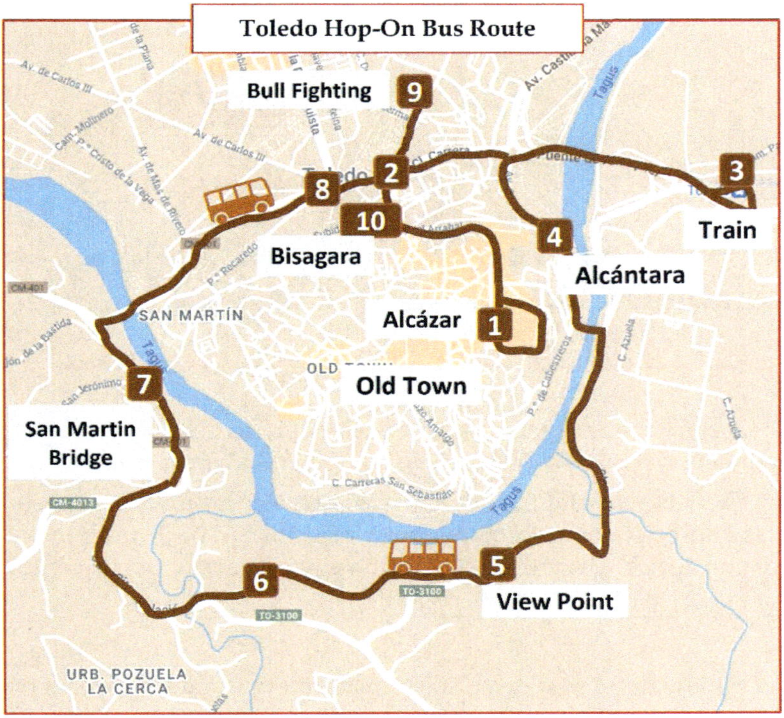

Toledo Tour Providers: [10]

With Toledo being such a popular destination, there are many agencies who provide tours here and the variety of tour options is impressive. In most cases, you can reserve and purchase a tour in advance from their website. This has a positive and negative aspect. On the positive side, you have the comfort of knowing you have locked in your tour and this component of your trip is set. On the negative side, if your plans change and you need to cancel, you may have difficulty in getting your money back.

Several of the larger firms, such as Viator, may provide refunds, reducing the issues which can go along with advance purchase.

There is a substantial overlap in tours sold through these agencies and prices tend to be the same or similar. The Tourist Information Office will provide details on a good variety of sites but if

[10] **Tour Providers Listed Here:** The tour companies described in this chapter are a representative sample of the many excellent local and international services which provide tours in Toledo. This is not a complete list of providers.

you wish to explore options before traveling to Toledo, below are some of the leading providers to check into. This is not a complete list of quality tour providers, but the tours they offer are comprehensive and there is something here for any preference.

Rutas de Toledo. www.RutasDeToledo.es This firm has some fun and unique offerings. Most tours are walking and focus on the Old Town. The tour duration typically is between one hour to ninety minutes.

Some of the tours provide unique experiences which go well beyond traditional tours which are limited to the major attractions.

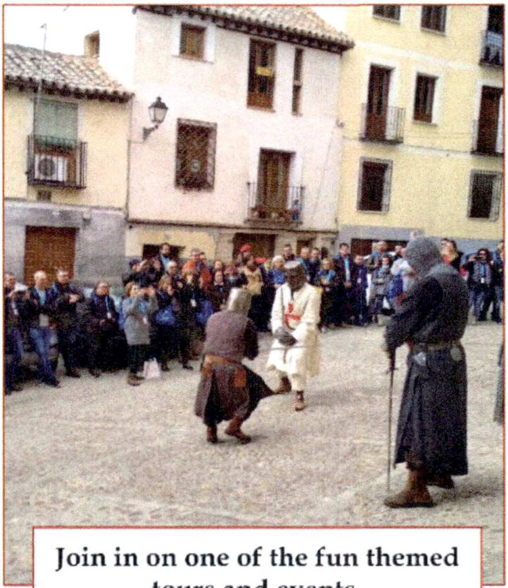

Join in on one of the fun themed tours and events.
Photo Source: Rutas de Toledo

This firm's unique tours include:

- Underground tour
- Magical Toledo
- Craft Beer Tour
- Templars in Toledo
- Tourist Bracelet Tour
- Many others

Several of the tours are at night, which can add to the fun. These are generally group walking tours and have different starting points, based on the nature of the tour.

Toledo Free Tour: www.ToledoFreeTour.com This group tour has no upfront fee, and their revenue comes solely from tips. It is a nearly two-hour walking tour into the heart of Old Town taking visitors to a dozen locales.

The tours are well rated and provide a great way to obtain a comprehensive understanding of Toledo before heading out on your own to explore further.

Not all tours require a tour company. Consider a Self-Guided Walking Tour
The Toledo Tourist Office will provide maps for several suggested walking tours.

The tours run twice each day. Once at noon and the later tour starts at 3:30PM. Tours start from Zocodover Square and are in English. This firm operates just this one tour option.

Advance booking, while not required, is highly recommended via their website.

Best Toledo Tours: www.BestToledoTours.com This local firm provides tours ranging from private and customized explorations to large group walking tours. Their guides are all professionals with degrees in tourism, history and/or art.

In addition to the custom tours, some of the tours[11] focus on specific aspects of Toledo's history such as a Jewish heritage tour/route, the Christian Heritage tour, or the El Greco tour.

All tours must be booked in advance, and it is best to do so via their website.

[11] **Tours and Routes:** Many tour companies in Spain use the term "Routes/Rutas" instead of tour.

Tours By Locals: www.ToursByLocals.com/Toledo-Tours This is an international firm which hires local guides to provide a wide array of tours in each city they operate in.

If you are considering visiting Toledo as a day trip from Madrid, several options are available ranging from private to small group tours. Several religious heritage tours are available which are an excellent way to better understand Toledo's diverse history.

One caution. These tours can be expensive. A 4-hour small group walking tour of Toledo will be roughly $260+ per person and a private tour from Madrid will be over $400 for a small group plus transportation cost.

Viator: [12] **www.Viator.com** or **www.TripAdvisor.com.** Viator is a leading example of a tour reseller. They do not provide their own proprietary tours and many of the listings cited here are likely to be found under other tour provider listings.

The tours and activities they sell range from walking tours of Toledo to hot air balloon rides. Many tours from Madrid are included among their listings.

Viator, a subsidiary of Trip Advisor, provides excellent customer service should you run into problems.

---

[12] **Other tour resellers like Viator**: Many other firms also resell these tours like this such as GetYourGuide.com, Booking.com, and others. If you have a preferred source for reserving hotels and tours, then in all probability, you can use them for many available tours in and around Toledo. The author has frequently used Viator and found them to be a reliable resource.

6: Points of Interest in Toledo

A positive aspect of visiting Toledo is that most attractions are either right in Old Town or adjacent to it. Unlike some cities which have their points of interest spread across several miles or even neighboring towns, here almost everything is within walking distance.

This chapter lists over twenty attractions with the goal of providing visitors with a good cross section of sights ranging from historic bridges, top museums and, of course, leading sights such as the cathedral and the Alcázar. [13]

Toledo Points of Interest

Attraction Type	Map #	Attraction
Bridges	1	Alcántara Bridge / Puente de Alcántara
	2	San Martin's Bridge
Castles	3	Alcázar de Toledo & Army Museum
	4	Castillo de San Servando

[13] **Attractions Organization:** The Points of Interest in this chapter are first grouped by type of attraction such as bridges or churches, then alphabetically within that grouping. This is not a "Top 10" type of list as the intent is to be comprehensive in outlining the available attractions.

Toledo Points of Interest		
Attraction Type	**Map #**	**Attraction**
City Gates	5	Puerta de Bisagara
	6	Puerta del Cambrón
	7	Puerta del Sol

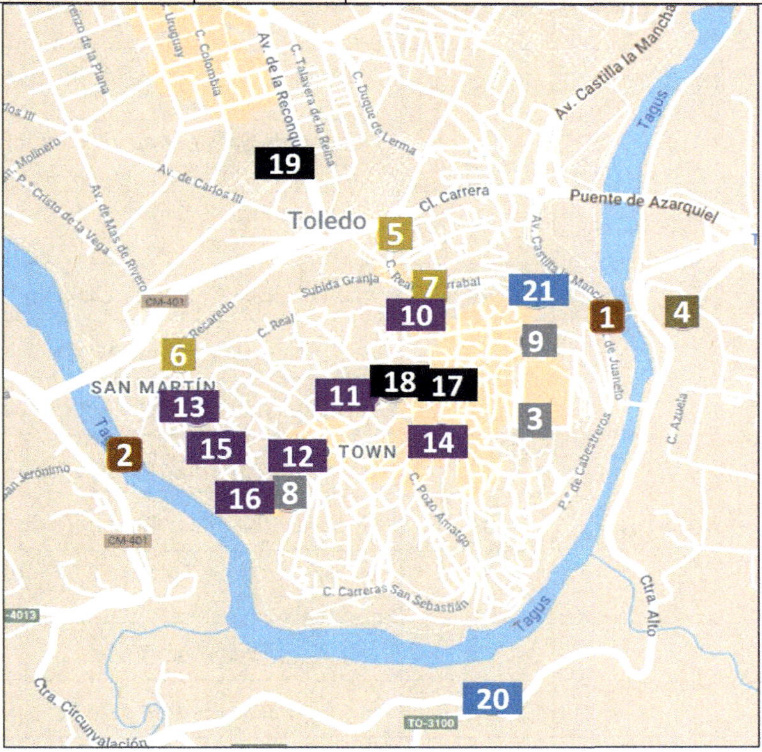

Museums	3	Army Museum / Museo del Ejército Part of Alcázar de Toledo

Toledo Points of Interest		
Attraction Type	**Map #**	**Attraction**
	8	El Greco Museum / Museo del Greco
	9	Santa Cruz Museum / Museo de Santa Cruz
Plaza	10	Zocodover Square / Plaza Zocodover
Religious Buildings	11	Iglesia de los Jesuitas / Catholic Church
	12	Iglesia de Santo Tomé / Catholic Church
	13	Monasterio de San Juan de los Reyes
	14	Santa Iglesia Catedral / Cathedral
	15	Sinagoga de Santa Maria
	16	Sinagoga del Tránsito / Synagogue
Roman Ruins	17	Caves of Hercules
	18	Termas Romanas / Roman Baths
	19	Roman Circus of Toledo / Circo Romano
Viewpoints	20	Mirador del Valle
	21	Paseo del Miradero

What if you only have a few hours?

There are many choices of attractions to visit within Toledo and over twenty are outlined here. This wealth of history and sights could cause visitors with limited time to be concerned about how best to spend their time. This is especially the case if you are coming in for a day trip without taking a formal tour or are just passing through with only a few hours to spend in Toledo.

Personal preferences will likely guide much of the decision making but the following are recommended by the author as something of "the best of the best" to help guide your selections.

1. **The Old Town area**: The main attraction in Toledo is simply Toledo. Consider spending time roaming the streets, especially around the areas of the Cathedral and Plaza Zocodover. Take time to explore the shops and have a relaxing lunch at one of numerous outdoor cafes.
2. **The Cathedral (Item #14 in this chapter):** The Cathedral Primada, built in the 13th century, is stunning. It is also, unfortunately, crowded during the high season. This Gothic church is huge and there is impressive art to find in every room.
3. **Alcázar de Toledo & Army Museum (Item #3 in this chapter):** This building is iconic for Toledo and can be seen for miles. There is a large Army Museum inside which is a central part of the exhibit. Visiting this complex gives visitors a great insight into the region's past, as far back as Roman times.
4. **El Greco Museum (Item #8 in this chapter):** El Greco, the noted 17th century artist, is another icon of Toledo. This museum displays some of his most notable works.
5. **Termas Romanas & Caves of Hercules (Items 17 & 18 in this chapter):** There are several intriguing underground attractions in Old Town Toledo and this set of Roman era ruins and baths are interesting to explore.

1-Alcántara Bridge / Puente de Alcántara:

Description: One of two scenic bridges over the Tagus River. This bridge, with a length of nearly 600 feet (182 meters) was built nearly two thousand years ago by the Romans in 104 AD. The bridge has six arches and five prominent pillars. The most prominent arch is known as the Arch of Triumph. The name comes from an Arabic term meaning "The Arch."

The Alcántara Bridge at the base of Toledo's Old Town
Photo Source: Wikimedia Commons

The bridge has had a rough past as it has been damaged by various warring factions over the centuries only to be rebuilt again. There is no fee to enter and cross the bridge.

Location: The bridge is at the base of the northeastern sector of Old Town. It sits well below the town, but is easy to reach via the escalator "Remonte de Safont" which takes riders to the bus plaza, a short stroll to the bridge.

2- San Martin's Bridge / Puente de San Martin:

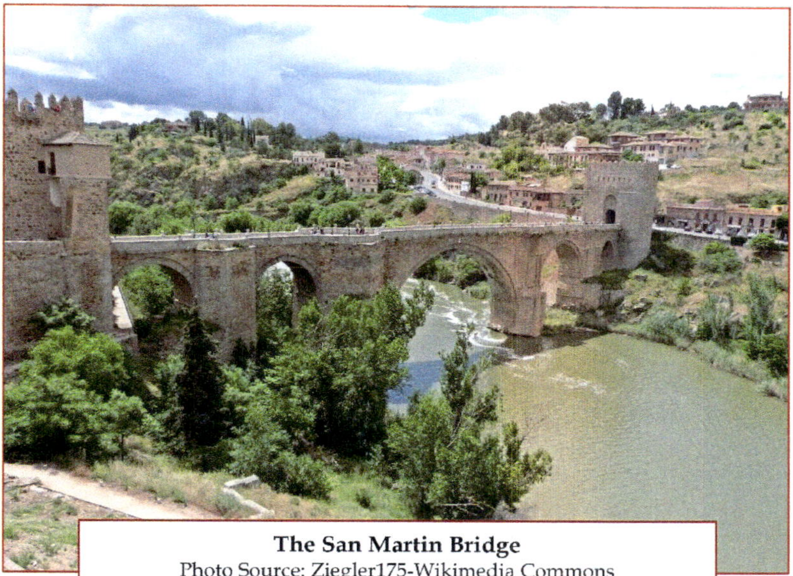

The San Martin Bridge
Photo Source: Ziegler175-Wikimedia Commons

Description: At the extreme opposite side of town from the Alcántara Bridge, at the western edge, is the notable San Martin's Bridge. It is a bit further afield from the center of Old Town, but worth the trip as the views along the river channel and up into the town are quite good.

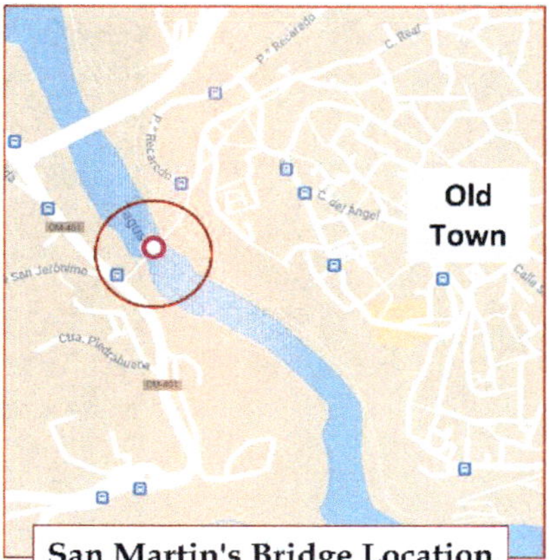

San Martin's Bridge Location

The bridge was built in Medieval times during the 14th century to provide easier access to central Toledo from the west. Like the Puente de Alcántara, it has fortified towers at each end. The bridge has five stone arches with a large center arch spanning 40 meters.

There is no fee to enter and cross the bridge.

Location: This bridge is a 15-20-minute downhill walk from the heart of Old Town. Much of the walk is attractive and portions are along ancient city walls. It is fairly close to the Monasterio de San Juan, and a combined visit is reasonable. Walking from the center of town requires navigating the delightful maze of Toledo's streets so having a map app available is highly recommended. NOTE: **This is a stop on the Hop-On/Hop Off bus route** which greatly adds to the ease of reaching it.

3- Alcázar de Toledo and Army Museum:

The Alcázar de Toledo
Photo Source: Carlos Delgado-Wikimedia Commons

Description: This is Toledo's most iconic structure which sits at the highest point in the historic area. It can be seen from a great distance as you approach the town If you visit only one of Toledo's attractions, this should be it.[14]

Courtyard in the Alcázar de Toledo
Photo Source: Heparina1985-Wikimedia Commons

A quick point of clarification regarding this structure's name may be helpful. The term "Alcázar" is a fairly generic term throughout Spain. The word comes from Arabic (dating back to

---

[14] **Possible Limited Access:** Due to extensive and ongoing renovations and damage resulting from a fire in June 2022, it is possible that your access may be limited. Check for updates at the front entrance when visiting.

Toledo's Moorish history) and essentially means castle or palace. In addition to the Alcázar de Toledo, several buildings with this title may be found throughout Spain such as the prominent ones found in Seville or Segovia.

The history of this prominent building goes back to Roman times. The first parts of the structure began in the third century when it was used as a palace. Much later, in the 16th century, the structure was fully restored by the current ruler of Spain, Charles I. The primary use continued to be a palace. Later still, during the Spanish Civil War which ran from 1936 to 1939, the building was utilized as a fortress and was successful in holding off the Spanish Republican forces. It was also a notorious prison at the time.

The Spanish Civil War was another period where this structure, and many others here, saw significant damage. It was eventually rebuilt to its current splendor and modified to house the Army Museum.

You must enter the Army Museum to explore most areas of the Alcázar de Toledo.

In size, it is the same distance in every direction including vertically. Each side measures 60 meters in length (197 feet) and each of the four towers are also 60 meters high.

The Army Museum / Museo del Ejécito: The most prominent attraction within the Alcázar is the expansive Army Museum. When visiting here, this is where most time will be spent. This museum's collection had been in Madrid until 2010 when it was moved to Toledo. The museum is in two parts, the permanent exhibits are within the Alcázar, and additional displays are in an adjoining building.

A visit to this museum is a must if you wish to explore the Alcázar's interior and upper levels. Inside the museum, there is a large collection of military-related items including uniforms, army miniatures, swords, flags, and more. A portion of the museum includes an impressive Roman dig and ruins.

There are a café and a gift shop inside the museum.

One caution, this is a very popular site to visit and long lines often occur during high summer season.

Hours and Fees: Open Tuesday to Sunday and closed on Monday and several holidays. Normal hours are from 10am to 5pm.

Entrance fee, as of early 2023, is €5 per adult. There is an additional fee for using the available audio guide.

Website: **www.Museu.Ejercito.es**

4 - Castle of San Servando / Castillo de San Servando:

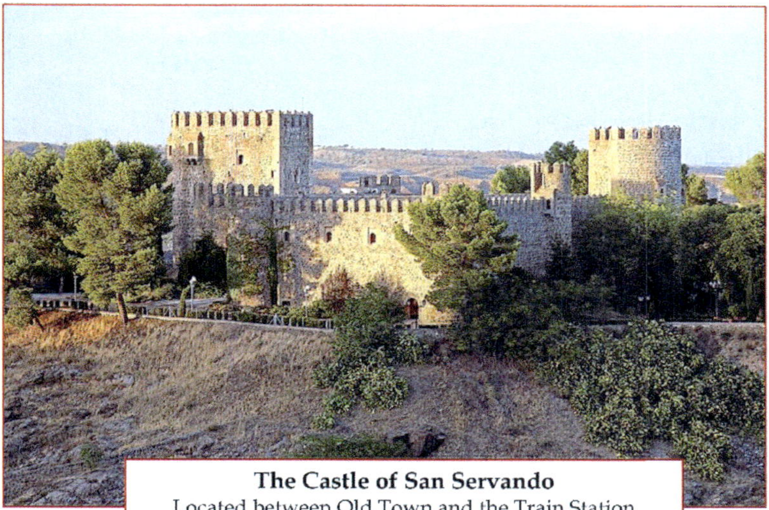

The Castle of San Servando
Located between Old Town and the Train Station
Photo Source: Rafesmar-Wikimedia Commons

Description: Newer and smaller than the Alcázar de Toledo is another castle. This structure started as a monastery in the 7th century. It was converted to a fortress by the Knights Templar in the

13th century to protect against Muslim attack of Toledo and kept this status until the 14th century.

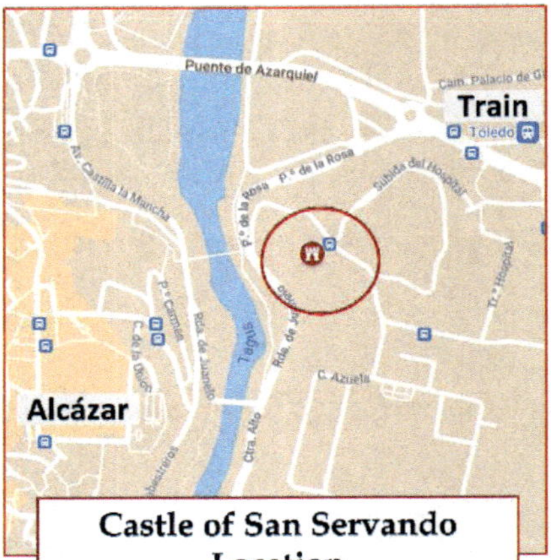

Castle of San Servando Location

Today, this historic structure **primarily serves as a hostel** and tours are very limited. The best way to appreciate this building is from the outside as it is photogenic and a visit can easily be combined with a stroll across the historic bridge Puente de Alcántara.

If you wish to learn more about the hostel for a possible stay, the website is **Juventud.Jccm.es.**

5, 6 & 7: City Gates:

Description: Toledo has several historic gates which form part of the ancient city walls. Three of these are listed here and, in each case, they make for a grand entrance into Toledo's Old Town. These city gates may be freely passed through, but the interior portions are not open. The upper portion of some of the gates, such as the Puerta del Sol, may be visited for some excellent views.

Puente de Bisagra / Bisagra Gate: This gate is an excellent example of a structure with mixed cultures It was initially Moorish, built in the 10th century and later in the 16th century, incorporating the Renaissance style.

This gate has the appearance of a castle with two tall towers and even an inner courtyard.

Puerta de Bisagra - One of several ancient city gates leading into Toledo's Old Town.

There is no public access to the upper level.

This structure is near the Toledo Tourist Office and, once you pass through, it is a short walk slightly uphill into the heart of Old Town.

Toledo's Historic City Gates

Puerta del Cambrón: This is the least central of the three gates outlined here. This castle-like structure was previously known as the "Gate of the Jews." It is built primarily in Renaissance style with two sets of towers and there is an interior courtyard. This gate was originally built by the Visigoths, but the original structure was replaced in the 16th century leaving very little of the original construction. This is the only ancient city gate open to vehicles.

Puerta del Sol: This gate entrance, built in the 13th and 14th centuries, received its name due to its orientation to the sun as one side points east to the rising sun.

The actual gate building and courtyard no longer exist, and this is the remaining entrance. It is built in the Moorish style.

Puerta del Sol
Photo Source: Selby May-Wikipedia

~ ~ ~ ~ ~ ~

8 - El Greco Museum / Museo del Greco:

Description: El Greco, the 16th & early 17thth century artist, is almost synonymous with the city of Toledo. Representations of the artist and his works may be found throughout the city.

Many of his notable paintings are on display in some of the world's leading museums, but this still leaves a large number of works to view

Gallery in the El Greco Museum
Photo Source: Tim Adams-Wikipedia

here. The exhibits are largely devoted to his art (other artists are also represented). This museum has been active since 1911 and is in a surprisingly low-key setting near the southwest sector of Toledo in the Jewish Quarter.

The museum is in two buildings. One is intended to recreate El Greco's home so visitors are treated not only to his art but will gain a good understanding of his life as well. One of the more impressive collections is a complete series of paintings of Christ.

Address: Plaza del Tránsito, 45002 Toledo

Hours: Closed Monday. Open Tuesday to Sunday from 9:30am to 4pm.

Entry Fee: €3 for adult (as of early 2023)

9- Santa Cruz Museum / Museo de Santa Cruz:

Description: If your schedule allows, consider exploring this comprehensive museum which is focused on Toledo and the region. Works and displays include art, including items by El Greco, archeology exhibits, and displays covering the area's culture and history.

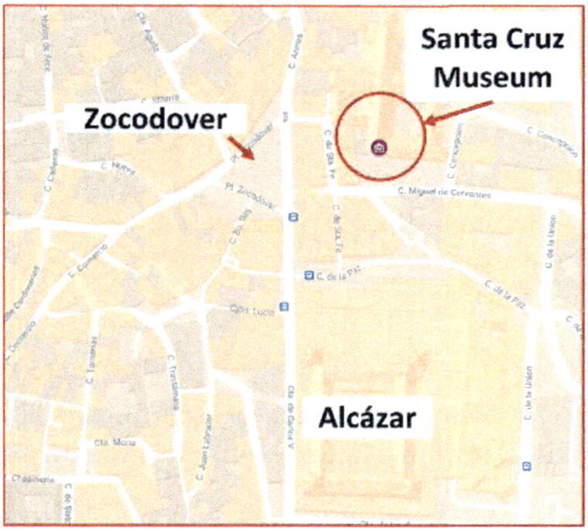

The museum gets its name from the building which it now occupies, the "Old Hospital de Santa Cruz."

Even if you do not wish to spend time exploring a museum, come here for the building as its halls and courtyard are a treat to visit. This is a large structure which was built in the 16th century." It has been a recognized and prominent museum in Spain since 1944.

Courtyard in the Santa Cruz Museum
Photo Source: Wikimedia Commons

Among the many exhibits are folk handicrafts dating back centuries. Displays also delve deeply into the region's Roman and Visigoth history. There are three floors of exhibits here.

Reaching this museum is easy as it is very close to the noted Plaza Zocodover and also near the Alcázar with its large Army Museum.

Address: Calle Miguel de Cervantes, 3, 45001 Toledo

Hours: Open every day except holidays. Monday to Saturday the hours are 10am to 6pm. Sunday, the museum closes at 3pm.

Entry Fee: €4 for adult (as of early 2023)

10 - Zocodover Square / Plaza de Zocodover:

Description: The main square in Old Town Toledo is the triangular shaped plaza of Plaza de Zocodover. This is near several major museums and in the shadow of the Alcázar fortress. This is an excellent place to start explorations of this city.

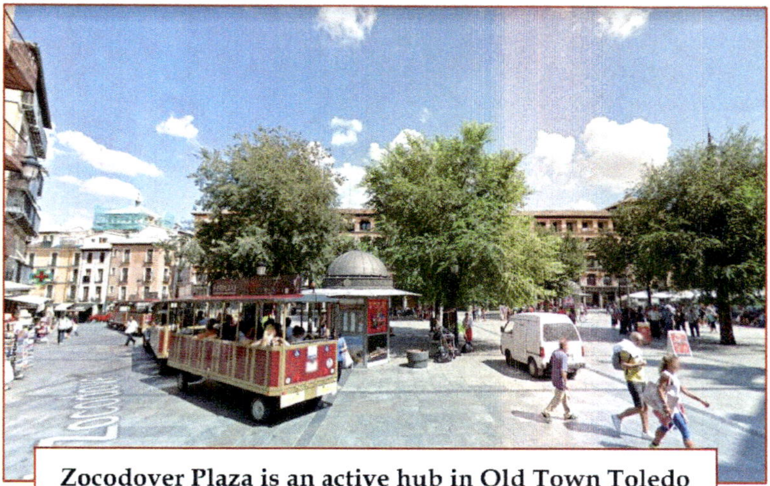

Zocodover Plaza is an active hub in Old Town Toledo
Photo Source: Google Maps

Compared to prominent squares in other Spanish cities, this one is small, but when you consider that this open space was created inside of a walled city where space was at a premium, it takes on a different perspective. The name of this plaza is derived from Arabic for a market of "burden beasts." This name held true for many years when the area was often used to buy and sell horses, donkeys, and other animals.

Today, this is an active center with many shops, restaurants, and bars. Several tours start out from here including the small tourist train. During Christmas, this is the focal point of celebrations with many stalls and exhibits.

11 - Church of San Ildefonso Jesuit Church:

Description: Toledo has a wealth of churches packed into a small area and this large Catholic church sits only a short distance from the city's main cathedral. Given the size and beauty of this 18th century church, it would be easy at first to think it was the cathedral if you did not know there were two magnificent structures so close to each other.

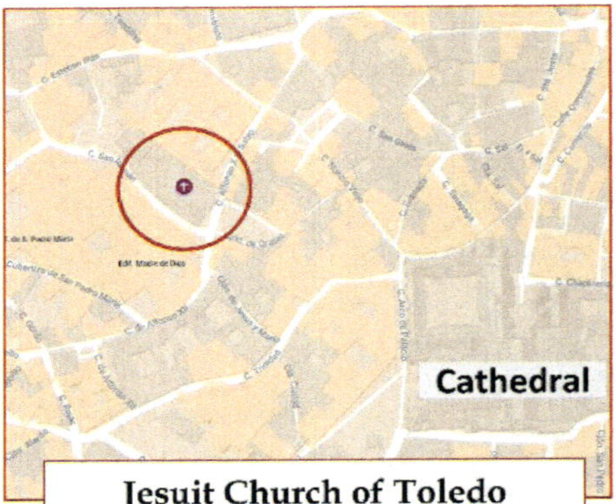

Jesuit Church of Toledo Location

Interior of San Ildefonso Jesuit Church of Toledo

For many visitors, this provides a better experience than visiting the cathedral as it is far less crowded. It can be difficult to locate as it requires finding your way through a series of narrow lanes.

This church goes by several names which can be confusing. Often, it is simply referred to as "The Church of the Jesuits Toledo," while a more formal name is "Iglesia de los Jesuitas" or "Church of San lldefonso."

Included in the Toledo Tourist Bracelet program.

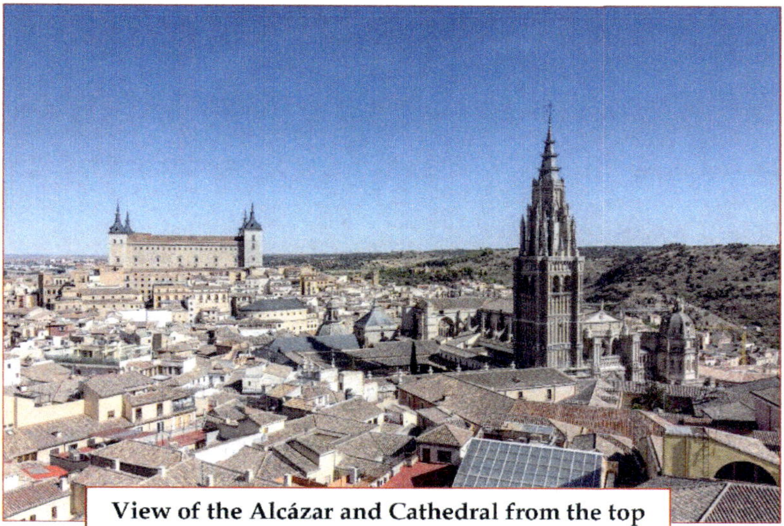

View of the Alcázar and Cathedral from the top of San Ildefonso Jesuit Church

Construction took over one hundred years, starting in 1629 and finishing in 1765. This is the largest baroque temple in Toledo and sits high above the town providing great views of the city from the towers. It was constructed in a position which has the front facing not only a small plaza, but the cathedral as well. The construction is a traditional cross for the nave which has a high dome over the center.

Visitors are allowed to go to the upper towers where there are tremendous views of the city. If you do not wish to take this arduous 50-meter hike up narrow steps, consider just going up one level where you have an excellent view of the interior.

Address: Plaza Padre Juan de Mariana, 1, Toledo

Hours: Open Monday to Sunday and closed on Saturday. Typical hours are from 10am to 6pm.

Fee: Included in the Toledo Tourist Bracelet program, otherwise there is a modest fee of roughly €3 to enter.

12 - Iglesia de Santo Tomé / Church of Santo Tomé:

Description: The mixture of cultures in Toledo is evident in this 12th century church which incorporates many elements from a previous 11th century mosque.

Later, in the 14th century, a major rebuilding occurred which added new features such as an ornate bell tower. This is a fairly small church when compared to the nearby cathedral, but is quite ornate and incorporates elements from Gothic, Baroque, and even Moorish periods.

The most popular draw here is a the noted El Greco work *The Burial of the Count of Orgaz.* This large painting, created near the end of the 16th century, is considered to be among his greatest and is prominently located near the rear of the church. El Greco, who frequented this church, painted himself and his son into the panel. The El Greco Museum is in the same neighborhood as this church.

***The Burial of the Count of Orgaz* by El Greco located in the Church of Santo Tomé**

Address: Plaza del Conde 4, 45002 Toledo

Hours: Monday to Sunday from 10am to 5:45pm.

Fees: There is a fee of €3 unless you have the Toledo Tourist Bracelet.

Website: **www.SantoTome.org**

13- Monastery of San Juan de los Reyes:

Description: Come to this monastery for the Gothic and Moorish architecture, and many photo opportunities.

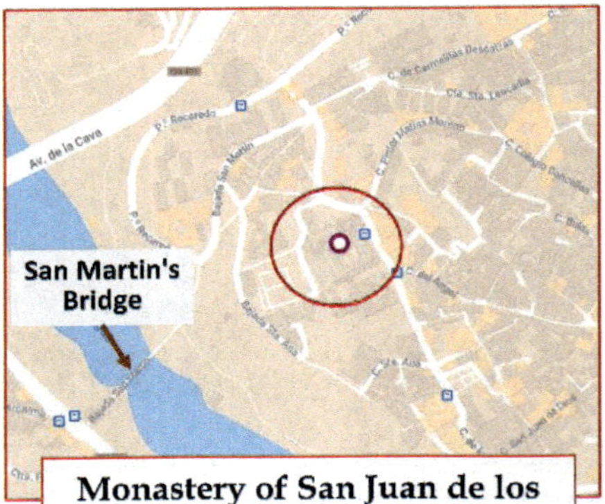

Monastery of San Juan de los Reyes Location

The highlights of this 15th century complex include the large chapel and the two-level cloister. This was originally built to be the burial site for Catholic monarchs and this held only until 1492 when this function was moved to Granada. Today, it is decorated with the coat of arms of Catholic leaders. The building and courtyard were structured with the goal of providing peace and a space for quiet reflection. Being away from the heart of the Old Town, this is a good area to visit to get away from the tourist crowds.

This monastery was abandoned in 1809 after being severely damaged by Napoleon's troops. It wasn't until 1967 that repair work was completed and the building was given over to the Franciscan order.

Located in the Jewish quarter this is one of the more remote sections of Toledo's Old Town. This area, about 15 minutes from the cathedral plaza, includes the El Greco Museum and historic synagogues.

Address: Calle de los Reyes Católicos 17, 45002 Toledo

Hours: Daily from 10am to 6:45pm.

Fees: There is a fee of €3 unless you have the Toledo Tourist Bracelet.

Website: www.SanJuanDeLosReyes.org

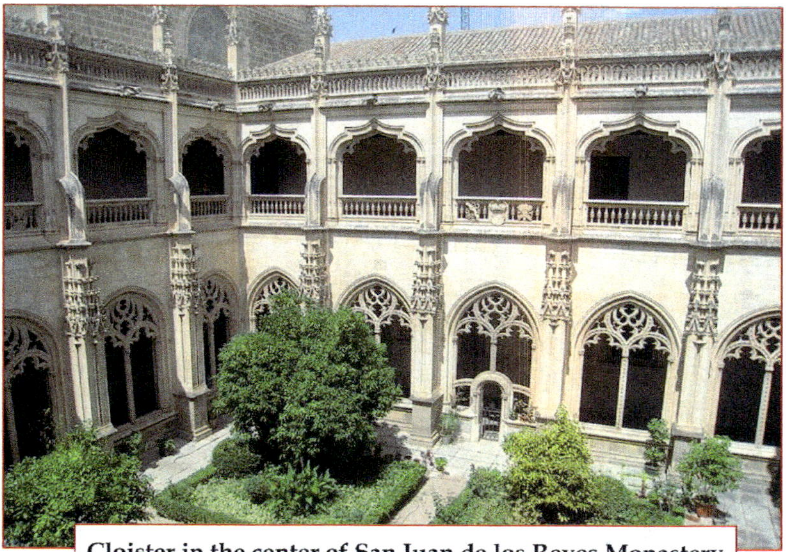

Cloister in the center of San Juan de los Reyes Monastery
Photo Source: Daderot - Wikipedia

~ ~ ~ ~ ~ ~

14-Toledo Cathedral / Santa Iglesia Catedral Primada de Toledo:

Description: This cathedral, often cited simply as the "Catedral Primada" or "the Toledo Cathedral" is Toledo's top spot to visit for many reasons. The building is magnificent inside and out. It is located in the center of Old Town so a visit to the cathedral is easy to combine with explorations of the town and nearby historical treasures.

Toledo Cathedral / Catedral Primada Toledo
Photo Source: Wikimedia Commons

There is a bit of a downside in that its popularity also means crowds but, unless you are severely time-constrained, it is well worth taking the time as this is not simply just another cathedral among many in Europe. It is one of the best examples of Spanish Gothic architecture in Spain and is rated as one of the most beautiful buildings in this country. Touring the massive chambers with their ornate design is awe inspiring.

The cathedral, which is on top of an old mosque, took over 250 years to build with construction beginning in 1226 and was not fully completed until 1493. Every dimension is notable, in height the cathedral towers above the city at 146 feet. (44.5 meters) and it is almost 200 feet wide (59 meters).

Toledo Cathedral Interior
Photo Source: Divot - Wikipedia

Inside the cathedral there are numerous works of art with one of the more notable being the ornate chapel and the raised altarpiece. The entrance fee includes use of an audio guide which, given the large number of rooms and art to view, can be very helpful. If you follow the full audio tour, it will take roughly one hour.

Substantial restoration work has been ongoing, primarily to the exterior. This work can cause occasional closings or a reduction in the areas which are open to view.

Address: Calle Cardenal Cisneros, 1 45002 Toledo

Hours: Monday to Saturday from 10am to 6pm and Sunday from 2pm to 6pm. Many religious holidays have restricted hours.

Fees: There is a fee of €10 (subject to change) which is NOT covered by the Toledo Tourist Bracelet. Tickets should be purchased from the cathedral store which is near the front entrance.

Website: www.CatedralPrimada.es

15-Sinagoga de Santa María la Blanca:

Description: Currently a museum, this former synagogue is considered to be one of the oldest synagogues in Europe.

Sinagoga de Santa Maria Location

This is another instance in Toledo of a structure which changed cultural and religious identities over the centuries. Built in the 12th century in Moorish style, it was first a Jewish synagogue. Later, in the 14th century, Christians took over and it became a catholic church, giving it the confusing name of

"Sinagoga de Santa Maria la Blanca," a name which is a mix of Jewish and Christian.

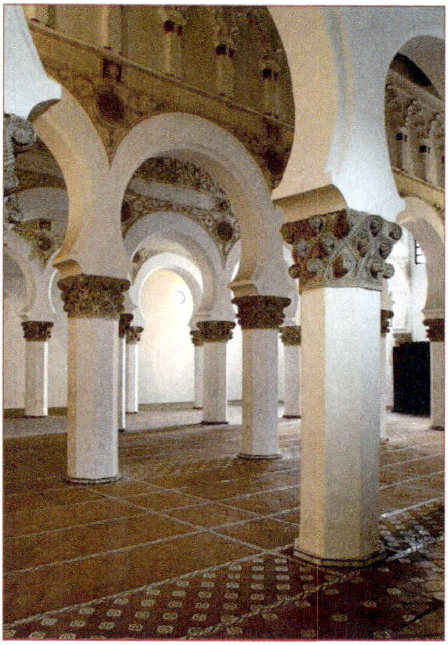

The primary style of the building, especially the interior, is Moorish. During the period it was built, it was common for the Moors to build structures for other religious groups such as the Jews.

Visitors will encounter a simple, but intriguing structure which is primarily one large room which had been used as the main prayer room. The Moorish style is very evident throughout. Less than 30 minutes is needed for most visitors.

Address: Calle de los Reyes Católicos, 4, 45002 Toledo (near the southwestern corner of Old Town)

Hours: Daily from 10am to 5:45pm.

Fees: There is a fee of €3, but there is no charge if you have a Toledo Tourist Bracelet.

~ ~ ~ ~ ~ ~

16-Sinagoga del Tránsito:

Description: Also known as the "Synagogue of El Tránsito" this historic 14th century building is an example of a religious structure which was caused to change its nature as powers ebbed and flowed over time.

Sinagoga del Tránsito Location

Originally built as a synagogue in 1357, it was an annex to an adjoining palace. Later, in 1492, it was converted to a Catholic church. During the Napoleonic Wars in the 19th century, it was a military barracks.

Today, this building is a combination museum and national monument and now carries the name of "National Museum for Hispanic-Hebraic Art." The building is another great representation of Toledo's nickname of "The city of 3 cultures" as elements of Jewish, Christian, and Moorish design are present.

Address: C. Samuel Levi, 45002 Toledo (near the El Greco Museum)

Hours: Closed Monday. Tuesday to Saturday 9:30am to 7pm. Sunday from 10am to 2:45pm.

Fees: There is a fee of €3 for adults.

Website: **www.SinagogaDelTransito.com**

17 & 18-Cave of Hercules & Roman Baths:

Description: Roman ruins and foundations are found throughout Toledo as evidenced by the large dig in the Army Museum. Two below ground small archeological sites provide great insights into early Roman life in Toledo. Both sites are close to the cathedral, have no entrance fee, and each takes only a short while to view.

The Cave of Hercules Roman Ruins under Toledo

Cave of Hercules / Cuevas de Hércules: This is a large underground space which is believed to have been used for water storage by the Romans. It was constructed in the 1st century and, until the mid-19th century, was under a church which has since been demolished.

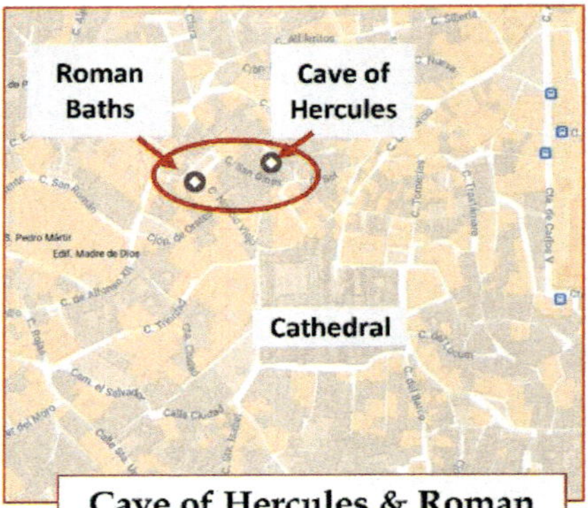

Cave of Hercules & Roman Bath Locations

Visitors need to traverse a tight set of winding stairs to reach the lower level.

Address: Cjón San Ginés, 3, 45001 Toledo

Roman Baths / Termas Romanas: Built in the 1st and 2nd century, this underground archeological site which was a combination of ancient baths and part of the town's water system was supplied by water via an aqueduct system. Guided tours are available. This is an easy site to visit but, like the Cave of Hercules, does require navigating some tight stairs which will reduce access to mobility impaired individuals.

Address: Pl. Amador de los Rios 3, 45001 Toledo

~ ~ ~ ~ ~ ~

19-Roman Circus of Toledo / Circo Romano:

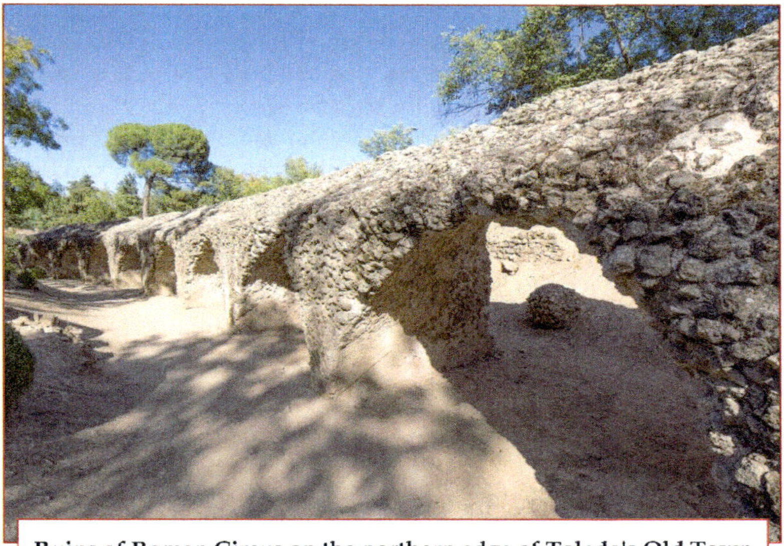

Ruins of Roman Circus on the northern edge of Toledo's Old Town

Description: Also referred to as the "Roman Circus at Toletum", the early Roman name for Toledo. This is a traditional Roman Circus which was built in the 1st century. It was built on the edge of the walled city and was used as a sports facility which was believed to have a capacity of somewhere between 15 to 30 thousand spectators.

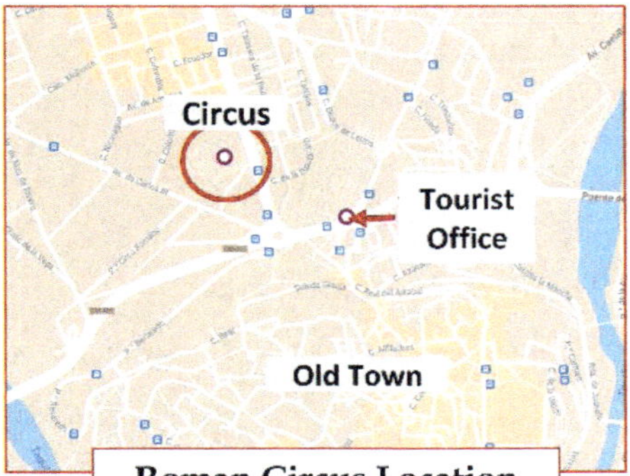

Roman Circus Location

Less than half of this large structure has been excavated. Over the centuries, it has largely been left to go to ruin and was even used as a cemetery by the Moors.

Today, this set of ruins is mostly open to explore freely and it functions as a city park. There are, unfortunately, few descriptive plaques to help you understand what you are viewing. If you tour Toledo by the Hop-On Bus system, this is one of the stops on the route. It is also within an easy walk of the Plaza de Toros and Bull fighting museum.

Address: Avenida de Carlos III, 9, 45004 Toledo (Near the Tourist Information Office)

Fees: There is no charge to enter and explore the ruins.

20-Mirador del Valle / Scenic Overlook:

Description: This location provides one of the best views of Toledo available. It sits just south of town, across the river and is not easily reached on foot but it is serviced by both the city's Hop-On Bus and Tourist Train. (Toledo Train Vision)

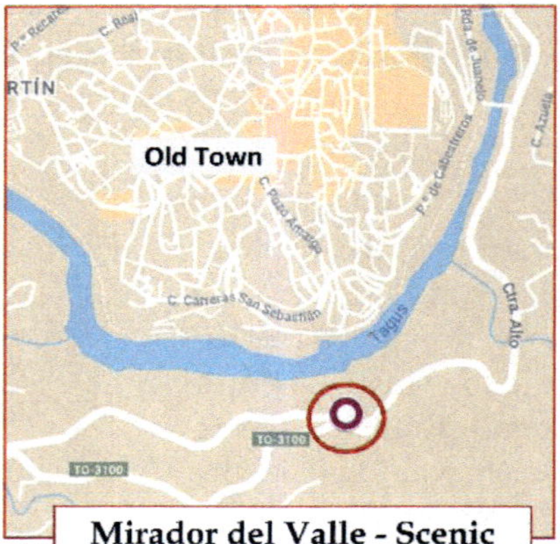

Mirador del Valle - Scenic Overlook Location

There is a small kiosk selling souvenirs here, but no restroom opportunity.

The city is beautiful from this vantage point both during the day and at night.

Address: Ctra. Circunvalación, 45004, Toledo

Mirador del Valle - Scenic Overlook
Photo Source: Google Maps

21-Paseo del Miradero / Scenic Overlook:

Description: While the above cited Mirador del Valley viewpoint looks toward Toledo; this large and modern overlook provides excellent views away from town and toward the river and valley below.

Paseo del Miradero - Scenic Overlook Location

This is a popular site and is easy to reach as escalators lead right to it. If you have arrived in town by train or bus, it is likely that you will enter the town via the escalators from the bus parking area. If so, consider spending some time here as the views are photo worthy. In addition to the views, there is a large restaurant and bar, the Terraza Miradero.

Address: Calle Gerado Lobo, 1, 45001, Toledo

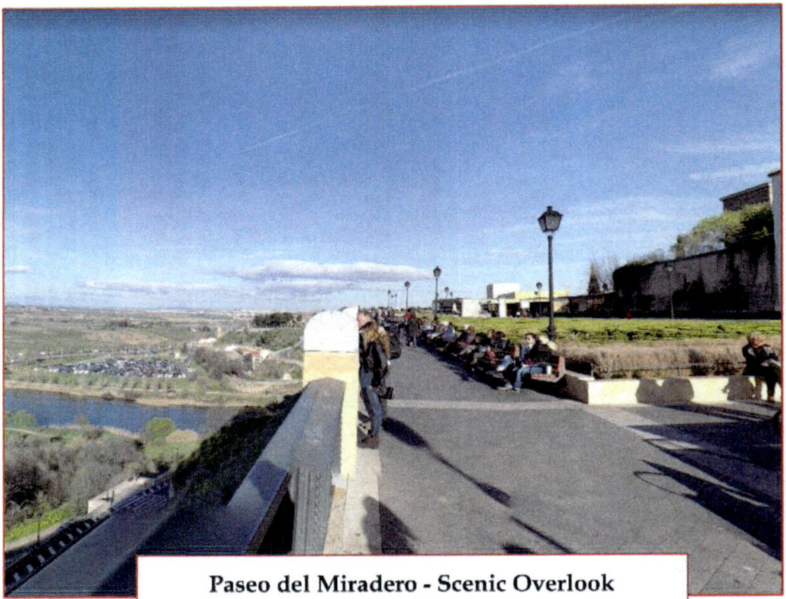

Paseo del Miradero - Scenic Overlook
Photo Source: Google Maps

~ ~ ~ ~ ~ ~

7: Shopping & Souvenirs in Toledo

Shopping in Old Town Toledo is generally characterized by the fun experience of browsing through numerous small boutiques. These little shops may be found almost anywhere in town and, of course, near the Cathedral and Alcázar.

Toledo Steel - some of the world's finest knives and swords are made here.

A popular area for shopping is the street "Calle Commercio" which spans the distance from Plaza de Zocodover to the cathedral. This quarter-mile long stretch is pretty much "shopping central" and includes not only numerous boutiques specializing in local goods, but shops for leading Spanish names such as Lladro. Some of the area's most high-end shops may be found here.[15]

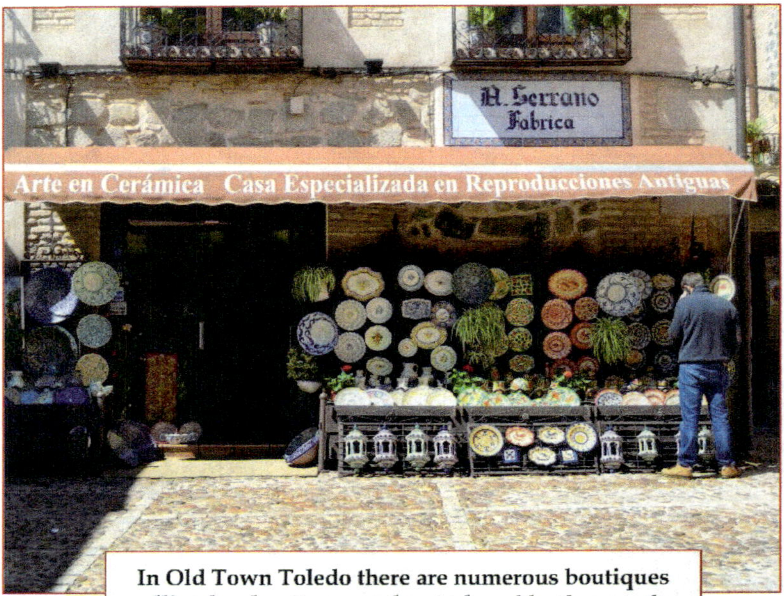

In Old Town Toledo there are numerous boutiques selling local pottery, candy, steel, and leather goods.

There are many categories of gifts and souvenirs to consider here with several specific to Toledo. At the top of the list for many visitors are "Toledo Steel" items, and these can range anywhere from simple letter openers to impressive swords. In addition to this, you will find an impressive array of local sweets such as the area's popular marzipan, pottery, leather goods, and Spanish wines.

---

[15] **Shopping Centers**: If you wish to visit a traditional shopping center, there are two small malls a short distance north from Old Town, the Buenavista Mall and the Mall Santa Teresa.

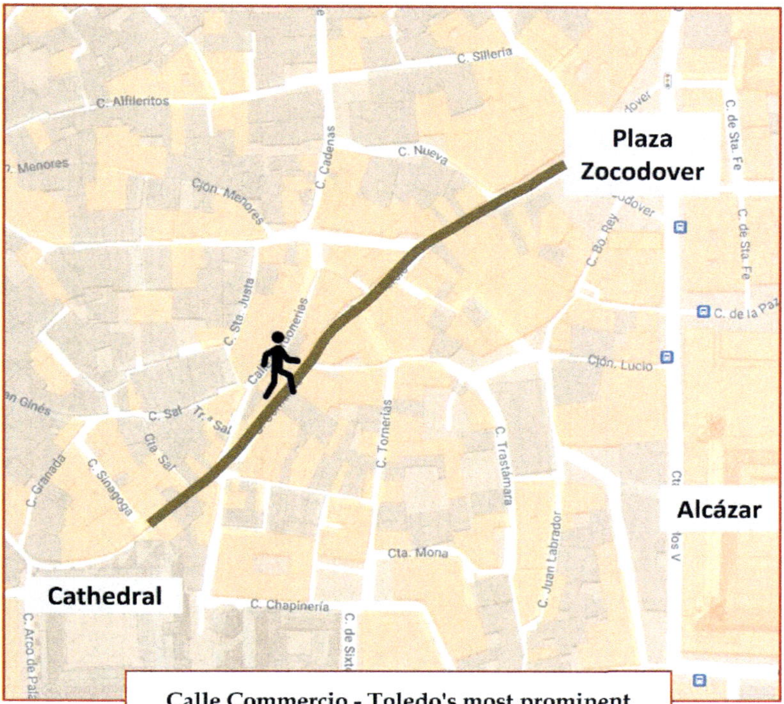

Calle Commercio - Toledo's most prominent shopping street.

Siesta is very much in practice here, so don't be surprised to find many shops shut down in the afternoon, generally between 2pm and 4:30pm. This even holds true during the busy season in the summer.

~ ~ ~ ~ ~ ~

Calle Commercio -A popular shopping street.
Photo Source: Ben Bender - Wikimedia Commons

Some Specialty Shops to Consider:

The following is a list of some of Old Town's more noted shops. These are well-rated stores which focus on local, artisan goods such as Toledo steel or leather. The great thing about this list is it isn't needed. Just strolling down **Calle Commercio** will bring you to many of these shops or others like them.

Ten stores are outlined in the table on the following pages and are cited alphabetically.

Some Leading Shops in Toledo to Consider		
Map #	**Name & Details**	
1	**Artesanía Burgueño**	
	Type of Goods:	Local handicrafts including jewelry and swords.
	Address:	Pl. Sta Isabel, 6, 45002 Toledo South of the cathedral
2	**Artesania Morales**	
	Type of Goods:	Focus is on Toledo Steel knives, souvenirs, and swords.
	Address:	Pl. del Conde, 3, 45002 Toledo Near El Greco Museum
	Website:	www.ArtesaniaMorales.com
3	**Artesanias Medina**	
	Type of Goods	Large store with broad range of local goods including ceramics and textiles.
	Address:	Calle Horno de los Bizcochos, 3, 45001, Toledo Near southwest corner of the Alcázar
	Website:	www.ArtesaniasMedina.com
4	**Cerámica J Serrano**	
	Type of Goods:	Ceramics and pottery
	Address:	Calle San Juan de Dios. 16. 45002 Toledo Near the El Greco Museum

Some Leading Shops in Toledo to Consider		
Map #	**Name & Details**	
	Website:	www.CeramicaJSerrano.com
5	**Cuartero House - Toledo**	
	Type of Goods:	Gourmet oils, food delicacies, and cheese items
	Address:	Calle Hombre de Palo 5, 45001 Toledo Along northern edge of the cathedral.
	Website:	www.CasaCuartero.com
6	**Cuerho House of Leather**	
	Type of Goods:	Leather goods, purses, wallets, and belts.
	Address:	Pl. Cuatro Calles, 5, 45001 Toledo Northeast from the cathedral, close to Calle Comercio
7	**La Catedral del Mazapan**	
	Type of Goods:	Marzapan – a favorite candy for the area
	Address:	Cta. Pajaritos, 6, 45001 Toledo In a small alleyway, just off Calle Comercio
8	**La Espada Artesana Moreno Fernández**	
	Type of Goods:	Focus is on Toledo steel items such as knives, swords, and decorative items.
	Address:	Calle Comercio, 31, 45001 Toledo Midway between the cathedral and Plaza Zocodover

Some Leading Shops in Toledo to Consider		
Map #	**Name & Details**	
	Website:	www.LaEsparadaArtesana.com
9	**Mariano Zamorano Swords Factory**	
	Type of Goods:	See swords and daggers being made in this workshop focusing on high quality, historically accurate items
	Address:	Cjón Santa Clara, 2, 45002 Toledo A little north of the Cave of Hercules.
	Website:	www.MarianoZamorano.com
10	**Toledo Swords & Knives / Artesania Alcázar**	
	Type of Goods:	A full range of swords and knives including a special line of "movie swords."
	Address:	Plaza el Salvador, 4, 45002 Toledo Near the El Greco Museum
	Website:	www.Artesania-Alcazar.com

~ ~ ~ ~ ~ ~

8: The Don Quixote Route

A Great Way to Explore the La Mancha Region

The names "La Mancha" and "Don Quixote" are almost synonymous and visiting the area described in the famous novel is a great way to explore the region for which Toledo is the capital.

Written by Miguel Cervantes in 1605, the epic novel under the original title of *The Ingenious Gentleman Don Quixote of La Mancha*[16] details the quest of a low ranked nobleman and his farmer-partner Sancho Panza who travel the region to complete quests and, in part, earn the affections of a peasant woman, Dulcinea.

[16] **Don Quixote Original Title**: the full name for this story in Spanish is *El ingenioso hidalgo don Quixote de la Mancha*. It was originally published in two volumes over a period of 10 years.

Today, many of the places cited in this historic novel may be visited as either easy day trips from Toledo or part of a driving trip to explore the region.

The locales listed here may be visited in any order.

This chapter lists several of the more popular destinations. All require travel either by car or with a structured tour and all of these locations are south of Toledo. It is not necessary to visit every site and it is also easy to combine several in a one-day journey from Toledo as most only take a short while to visit.

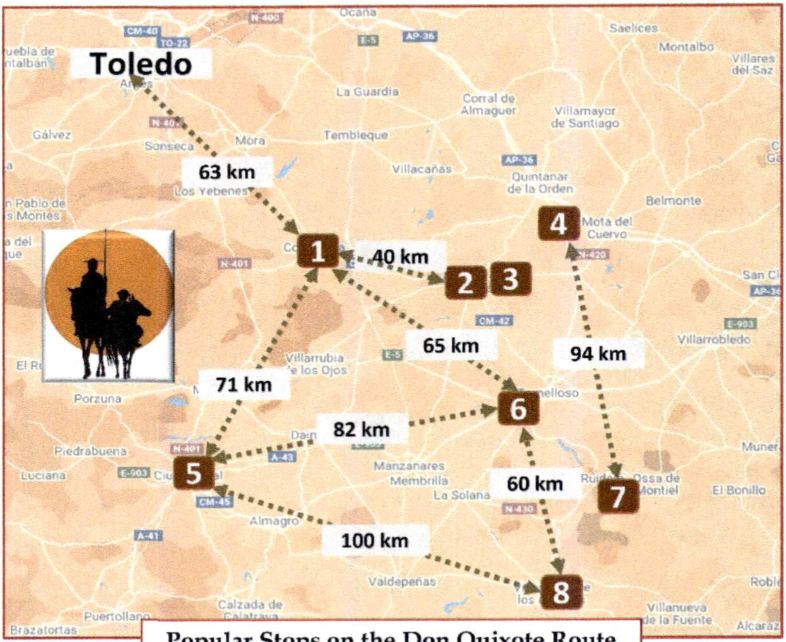

Popular Stops on the Don Quixote Route

Popular Stops on the Don Quixote Route		
Map #	**Name & Description**	**Driving Distance from Toledo [17]**
1	Consuegra - Windmills	39 mi / 63 km
2	Alcázar de San Juan - Small Town where Cervantes was baptized.	62 mi / 100 km
3	Campo de Criptana - Town & Windmills	69 mi / 111 km
4	El Toboso - Town where Dulcinea lived.	81 mi / 130 km
5	Cuidad Real - Large Town with Don Quixote Museum.	75 mi / 121 km
6	Argamasilla de Alba - Town where Cervantes was imprisoned.	79 mi / 128 km
7	Lagunas de Ruidera - Natural Park	109 mi / 176 km
8	Villaneuva de los Infantes - Attractive mid-size town.	105 mi / 169 km

[17] **Distance from Toledo:** Driving distances shown here are measured from the Tourist Information Office adjacent to Toledo's Old Town.

1-Consuegra:

Description: "Tilting[18] at windmills" is probably one of the most remembered aspects of Cervantes' novel. Consuegra is one of the best places along the Don Quixote route to view ancient windmills much as Don Quixote would have seen them as he attempted to slay these beasts.

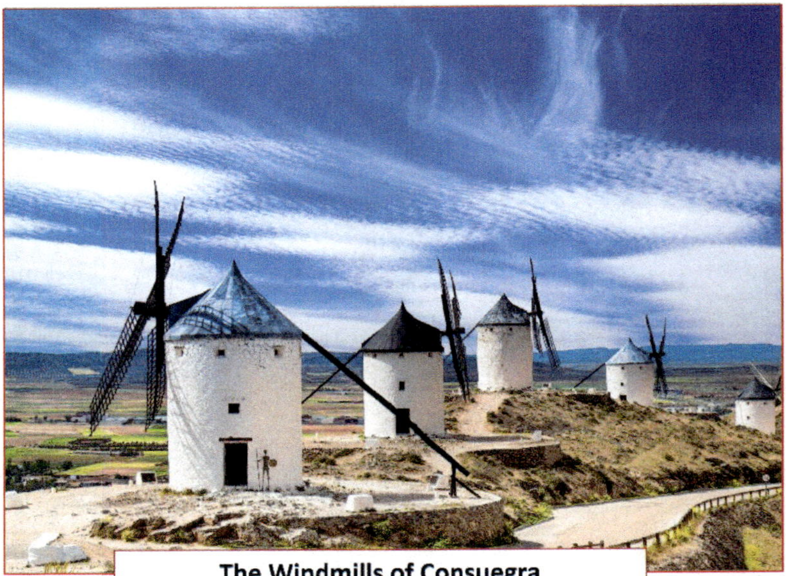

The Windmills of Consuegra
A popular stop along the Don Quixote Route

The dozen windmills are no longer active but had been used to grind wheat from the 16th century until the 1980s. Their official name is "Molinos de Viento de Consuegra." Each of the windmills

[18] **"Tilting" definition:** An ancient term for jousting where the horseman rides at full speed and inserts his lance into small metal rings.

has a nickname associated with Don Quixote and the one named "Sancho" still has all of the 16th century machinery in place.

This is close to Toledo and is often included in group tours due to its unique nature and proximity. It is definitely a place to bring your camera. Near the collection of windmills is the small Castle of La Muela and the attractive town of Consuegra, with nearly 11,000 people. It is a town with a history dating to pre-Roman times.

Windmills Address: Cerro Calderico, 45700 Consuegra

2-Alcázar de San Juan:

Description: This small city of over 30,000 with its set of windmills is easy to add on to a visit to Consuegra. According to legend,

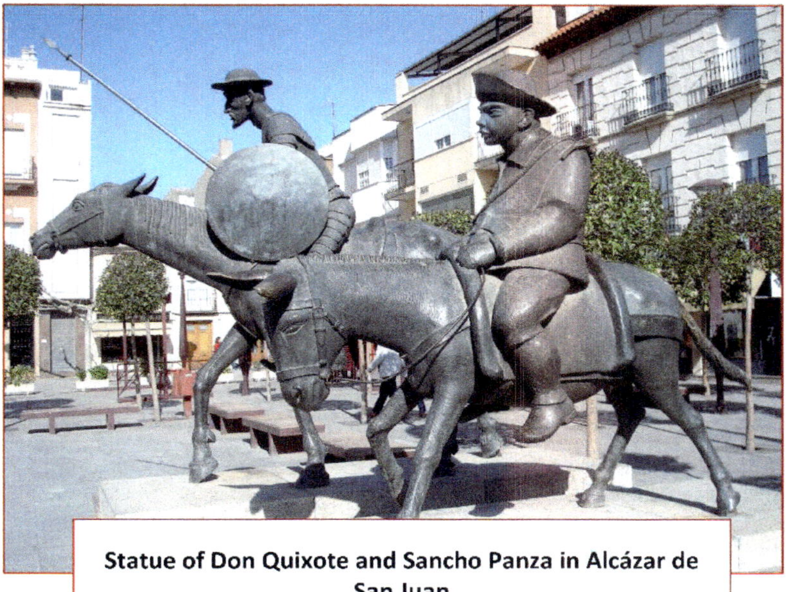

Statue of Don Quixote and Sancho Panza in Alcázar de San Juan

Photo Source: Luis Rogelio HM - Wikimedia Commons

Cervantes, the author of *Don Quixote*, was baptized here. In town, there is a notable museum, the Hidalgo House Museum (Museo Casa del Hidalgo), which is a large 16th century manor house. Several impressive statues, some associated with Cervantes, may be found throughout town.

3-Campo de Criptana:

Description: Don Quixote battled giants here… the ten windmills along the hillside lining this quaint town of Campo de Criptana. Three of these windmills are still fully functional and have the original mechanisms in place and are open to view. Presentations and tours are often available. The array of windmills has been declared as a cultural heritage site.

Campo de Criptana
10 Windmills sit on a low hill next to town and some are in town.

This town and its windmills are believed to have inspired Cervantes to write his famous novel and Don Quixote's adventures. A stroll through the quaint town is enjoyable. Many homes in the oldest section, known as the Albaicin, still have their original Arabic tiles which are painted in white and indigo.

The Photogenic Town of Campo de Criptana

It is 10-to-15-minute drive from Alcázar de San Juan and it is easy to visit both locales in one short trip which takes you through an attractive landscape lined with olive trees.

Windmills Formal Name & Address: Molinos de Viento de Campo de Criptana. Calle Senda Molinos, 13610, Camps de Criptana.

~ ~ ~ ~ ~ ~

4-El Toboso:

Description: El Toboso, the town where Dulcinea was from in the novel, is the northern most of the Don Quixote Trail locales outlined here. While over an hour drive from Toledo, the trip is relaxing and takes you through numerous groves of olive trees and vineyards and through the above cited locations of Campo de Criptana and Consuegra. [19]

Statue of Dulcinea & Don Quixote in El Toboso - the town where Dulcinea was from.

The main claim-to-fame for this town is it is the location in the story where Dulcinea, Don Quixote's imagined and made-up love

[19] **Wineries along the Don Quixote Route:** This is an area rich in local wine. When driving through here, watch for area wineries and take the opportunity to do some tasting and pick up some wines from vineyards which have been operating for hundreds of years.

interest, was born and lived. The attractive town of El Tobosa plays homage to this fiction and statues of her with Don Quixote may be found in the center of town.

According to legend, a woman from El Toboso, Ana Martinez Zarco de Morales, was the author's inspiration for the novel's love interest, "Dulcinea del Toboso." There is even a museum dedicated to her, the "Museo-Casa de Dulcinea del Toboso." This is a small town of two thousand and no major attractions, but it is a relaxing site to visit and stroll the tree-lined plaza. If you enjoy wine tasting, there are three wineries on the edge of town.

5-Cuidad Real:

Description: The four locations listed up to this point are all near one another along the northern sector of this route. The small city of Cuidad Real takes visitors in a different direction, leading more due south from Toledo.

Cuidad Real, a city of nearly 75,000, has several points of interest. The most notable attraction is the large museum dedicated to Don Quixote and the author Cervantes. The collection includes his library. The museum takes only a short while to tour and a video on Cervantes is included.

The other notable attraction in town is the cathedral, Iglesia Parroquial de San Pedro. Both the cathedral and Don Quixote Museum are in the center of town and near shops and restaurants.

On the edge of town, 8 km to the west, is the impressive "Alarcos Archaeological Park" which is an ancient settlement dating as far back as the Bronze age.

~ ~ ~ ~ ~ ~

6-Argamasilla de Alba:

Description: The town of Argamasilla de Alba sits roughly in the center of the eight destinations outlined here. According to legend, Cervantes was imprisoned in this town, and this is mentioned in the prologue of the novel. There are, however, few facts to back this up. The site known as the "Cave of Medrano" is where he is believed to have been imprisoned and had started writing *Don Quixote.*

Today, there is a rebuilt home, the "Casa de Medrano" which has the Cave of Medrano beneath it. This is an active museum in town which includes tours of the cave.

A short drive south of town is an interesting castle which is open for tours. Great views of the reservoir below are available from the castle's ramparts. It was built in the 12th century and is referred to in some literature as the "Fortress of the Guadiana River."

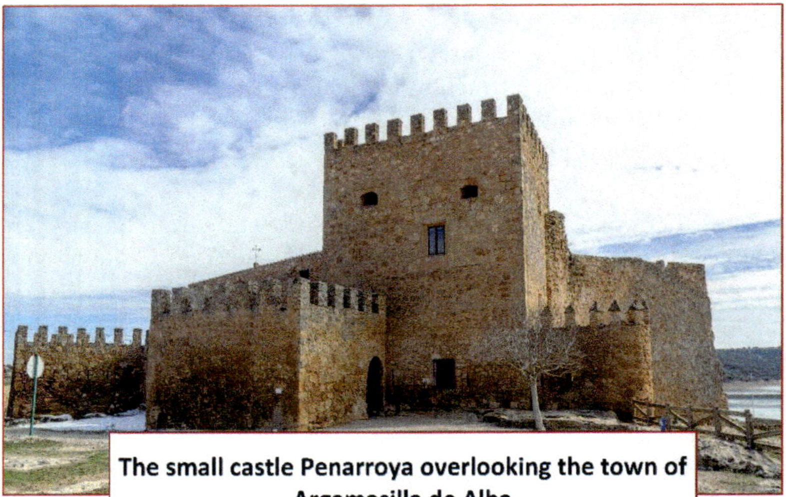

The small castle Penarroya overlooking the town of Argamasilla de Alba

7-Lagunas de Ruidera:

Description: As an enjoyable break from exploring villages and towns, consider spending some time in the natural park, "Lagunas de Ruidera," which was also cited in the novel *Don Quixote*. This set of 15 lakes was in the novel and is one of the sites which affected the protagonist's thoughts and imagination. There are several passages in the novel referring to this set of lakes and ponds.

This park includes an attractive series of low and scenic waterfalls. It is a great area to bring a picnic and do some hiking. Trails are well groomed and include walkways over marshy sections. It also carries the name of "The lagoons of La Mancha." Some areas are restricted to wildlife as this is an important conservation area.

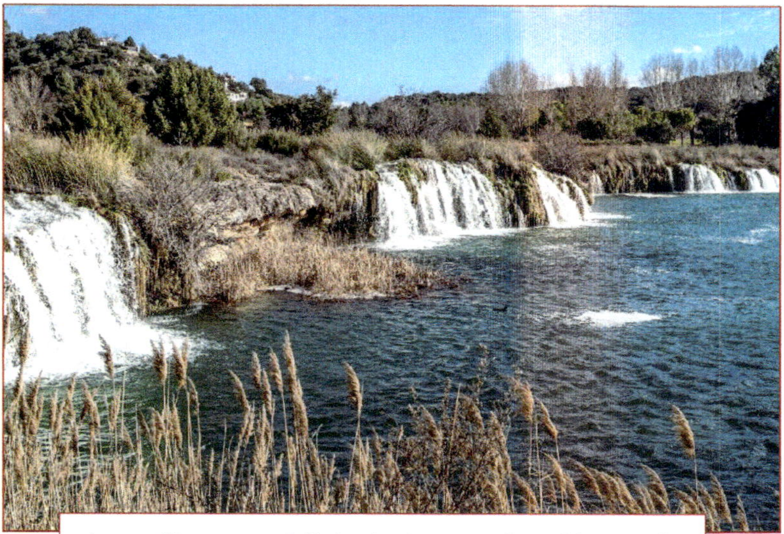

A set of low waterfalls in the Lagunas de Ruidera Park.

8-Villaneuva de los Infantes:

Description: This town of 5,700 is often cited as one of Spain's most beautiful towns It is cited in *Don Quixote* as "The place in La Mancha." A statue of Don Quixote, Sancho Panza, and their mule may be found in Plaza Major in the heart of town.

This is an attractive town to explore, especially the expansive cathedral, the parish church of San Andrés or "Iglesia de San Andres."

Wine vineyards and olive groves are abundant here and it is a great region to do some wine tasting. The town sits slightly more than 100 miles southeast of Toledo and is the furthest stop along this route.

Statue of Don Quixote and Sancho Panza near the cathedral in Villaneuva de los Infantes

~ ~ ~ ~ ~ ~

Appendix of Helpful Online References

To help you expand your knowledge of this area, several online reference sites are listed here. Toledo is a popular place to visit, so there is a wealth of material which can help in planning your trip.

Following is a list of online references about this city and area. The purpose of this list is to enhance your understanding of this area before embarking on your trip. Any online search will result in the websites outlined here plus many others. These are listed as they are professionally done and do not only try to sell you tours.

I. Toledo City and La Mancha Area Websites.	
Website Name	**Website address and description**
Regional Tourism Site	**www.TurismoCastillaLaMancha.es** Visitor site for entire the Castilla-La Mancha region of which Toledo is the capital.
Toledo Tourism Site	**www.Tourismo.Toledo.es OR** **www.ToledoSpain.click** City of Toledo tourist information websites.
All Pyrenees	**www.All-Andorra.com/Toledo** Website providing helpful descriptions of Toledo, the region, and top things to see and do.

I. Toledo City and La Mancha Area Websites	
Website Name	**Website address and description**
World Guides	**www.World-Guides.com/Europe/Spain** - then go to the area on Castile-la-Mancha Details on Toledo's and the area's history.
Spain Info	**www.Spain.info** Spain's official tourism website and an excellent site to find details on this city and region.

II. Transportation Information and Tickets	
Website Name	**Website Address & Description**
Renfe – Spain's Train System	**www.Renfe.com** Official website for Spain's train system. A great site to use for timetables and train ticket purchases.
Rome2Rio	**www.Rome2Rio.com** An excellent site and app to view travel options for train, flying, bus, and driving and to purchase tickets for most modes of travel.
Train Line	**www.TrainLine.com** One of several services which specialize in train travel including travel schedules and ticket purchase ability.
Alsa Bus Service	**www.Alsa.com** Bus services for all of Spain. Detailed schedules and ticket purchase abilities on the website and app.

III.	Tour and Hotel Booking Sites
Company	**Website address and description**
Toledo Train Vision	**www.ToledoTrainVision.com** Small "train" which takes visitors on a ride through central Toledo.
Toledo Hop-On Bus	**www.Hop-On-Hop-Off-Bus-Tours.com** Helpful bus service which takes riders around Toledo.
Toledo Tour Companies	Two companies based in Toledo which focus on tours of Old Town. Most tours are walking tours. **www.ToledoFreeTour.com** **www.BestToledoTours.com**
Hotel Sites	Numerous online sites enable you to review and book hotels online. Most of these sites also resell tours. - Booking.com - Hotels.com - Expedia.com - Travelocity.com - TripAdvisor.com
Tour Resellers	Many companies, such as the ones listed here, provide a full variety of tours to Toledo as well as day tours. - GetYourGuide.com - ToursByLocals.com - Viator.com - MadridTopTours.com

III. Tour and Hotel Booking Sites	
Company	**Website address and description**
Trip Advisor	**www.TripAdvisor.com** One of the most comprehensive sites on hotels and tours. Direct connection with Viator, a tour reseller.

Index of Sights in this Guide

~ ~ ~ ~ ~ ~

Starting-Point Guides

www.StartingPointGuides.com

This guidebook on Toledo, Spain is one of several current and planned ***Starting-Point Guides***. Each book in the series is developed with the concept of using one enjoyable city as your basecamp and then exploring from there.

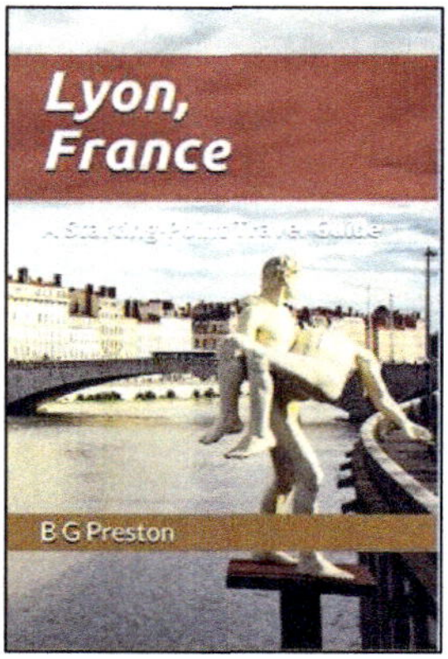

Current guidebooks are for:

- **Bordeaux, France** and the Gironde Region
- **Dijon, France** and the Burgundy Region.
- **Geneva, Switzerland** and the Lake Geneva area.
- **Gothenburg, Sweden** and the central coast of western Sweden.
- **Lille, France** and the Nord-Pas-de-Calais Area
- **Lucerne, Switzerland**, and the Lake Lucerne region.
- **Lyon, France** and the Saône and Rhône confluence area.
- **Nantes, France** and the western Loire Valley
- **Salzburg, Austria** and the Salzburg state.
- **Strasbourg, France** and the central Alsace area.
- **Stuttgart, Germany** and the Baden-Wurttemberg area.
- **Toulouse, France**, and the Haute-Garonne region.

Updates on these and other titles may be found on the author's Facebook page at:

www.Facebook.com/BGPreston.author

Feel free to use this Facebook page to provide feedback and suggestions to the author or email to: cincy3@gmail.com. Constructive feedback is always appreciated.

~ ~ ~ ~ ~ ~

Printed in Great Britain
by Amazon

19349761R00071